Atheists Who Kneel and Pray

TARRYN FISHER

PART ONE

THE E-MAIL

Dear Yara,

The band's in London November 12th. Want to catch up?

David

SO CASUAL. SO NONCHALANT. You'd think we were only acquaintances, that we'd once sipped a couple of beers together instead of tattooing love on our skin and reciting marriage vows. I read the e-mail again and analyze the shit out of it. How can I not? I count out the words: thirteen. The punctuation: four. His name, my name. They used to go together. A flippant, casual turn of the phrase: *catch up*. In the end, there's only so much psychoanalyzing you can do to a thirteen-word e-mail. I move on with my life, feeling rather pathetic. But not before I e-mail him back. And okay, sure, I don't move on with my life. I am stuck. What does moving on entail? Forgetting? Forgiving?

Being happy? Besides, I know what he wants to talk about. I know why he's coming.

> Hi David,
>
> Yeah, sounds good. Let me know when and where.
>
> Yara

My e-mail is a word shorter.

I'm that petty.

1

THE SPLINTER

THE FIRST TIME I saw him I had a splinter in my finger. I was wiping down the bar and there was a nick in the wood. My thumb happened to be in the wrong place at the wrong time. I yelped and held my finger up to my face to assess the damage. A sizable sliver of dark brown was buried in the pad of my thumb. You could see it from the outside and feel it from the inside.

"Let me see it," he said, sliding into a bar stool and holding out his hand. It was something a family member would do, or perhaps even a friend.

"See what?" I asked, looking around. I knew exactly what he was asking to see, but I wasn't about to let a strange man touch me. Where had he come from? I didn't even know we were open yet.

It was the morning after Thanksgiving and it was eerily quiet in the city, everyone gone for the long weekend. Perhaps he was someone's friend—the manager or one of the cooks. He wiggled his fingers impatiently at me and I stepped forward to place my hand in his. I don't know why I did it. But, it was early and I had a hangover. I was lulled by the day off and feeling less hostile than usual. He held my hand up to the light and nodded. It reminded me of a surgeon looking at an x-ray.

"Hand me that duct tape," he said.

I looked around. What duct tape? This was a restaurant, not a hardware store. But there it was; a roll of duct tape behind me, wedged in a wine locker. I hadn't noticed it before. I glanced back at him, my eyebrows raised.

"Do you want the splinter out or not?" he asked, tilting his head to the side. I grabbed the tape and handed it to him, more curious than in need of help. He used a pocketknife to slice a strip of it off the roll, one of those red Swiss Army things, then he applied the strip right over the splinter and put pressure on it until I flinched.

"What are you doing?" I asked.

"Sh." He had full lips, puckered to shush me. He looked up suddenly; his eyes were a soft, green. A warm flip in my belly let me know I was interested. *No. Nope.* I pushed the feeling away.

"Courage," he said, with a small grin.

The tape was yanked off and I made an embarrassing noise despite the fact that it didn't hurt. As soon as he let go of my hand, I lifted it to my face. The splinter was gone, the little sliver of it stuck to the tape. Pure genius.

"Hey there, MacGyver," I said, studying my finger. "Can I buy you a beer?" I asked. "For saving my life." It was a generous offer. If you bought men a beer, they thought you wanted to fuck them.

But, the guy—splinter guy—was already on his feet and picking up his jacket to go. He had a look I'd come to familiarize with Seattle: honest eyes, a beanie, plaid. Personally, I liked a little more structure around men, maybe in the form of a business suit. But, the more you looked at the guy, the more attractive he became. I stopped looking.

"I have somewhere to be," he said, glancing at his watch. "Maybe another time."

I stared after him, confused. Why come into a bar if you had somewhere else to be? He'd taken the duct tape and my splinter with him. The doors opened once more and a couple walked in just as he walked out. I didn't have time to think on it anymore, the lunch shift was starting.

2

CITIES

I AM IN LOVE with cities. All of them. Each one had their own thing going on, a unique spice they add to the world, but they all had one thing in common: energy. The frantic movement of cars, and buses, and people as they avoid collisions. The street food, greasy and paper wrapped— sold from trucks, and rusted carts, and metal fryers that hiss and steam in the middle of the sidewalk. Everyone had somewhere to be, and it all happened in a speed walk. Peacoats, rain boots, cell phones, the spray of water as it tussled with a tire. It was beautiful in all of its distracted, impatient ire. People came to cities to thrive. They hooked themselves up to the blood flow and tried to live their best lives. Sometimes it worked out and sometimes it didn't. For me, it had always worked out, but my expectations were low.

My current city: Seattle. I crossed 4th in a pack, all of us moving together like fish in a current. Some of us had our headphones in, some were looking down at phones, or shoes, or regrets. I was focused, eyes ahead, teeth grinding. I had to be at work early again. I still wore the remnants of last night's eyeliner, a battered black line that used to have wings. I looked down at my finger. You couldn't tell there'd ever been a splinter underneath my skin. How many minutes had our exchange been? Five…ten? Yet this was the fourth time I'd thought about him since he'd come into the bar yesterday.

It was just all so strange, I told myself. That's why I was thinking about it. And who wouldn't be thinking about a stranger who showed up out of nowhere and used duct tape to pull a splinter out of their finger? I was so distracted that I stepped out into the street in front of a car. The driver slammed on his brakes and I lifted a hand in apology.

Unlike New York, in Seattle, there was an absence of car horns. Reserved and polite liberals maneuvered their cars politely through the traffic, their Starbucks sitting in cup holders beside them. The driver—a man in his mid-thirties nodded in a way that said *we all makes mistakes*—and waited for me to clear the road.

The air smelled wet and mossy. I bought a bag of Cheetos and a newspaper from the corner store, my morning ritual. I paid with a ten and the clerk dropped three dollars and thirty in my hand. On my way out I handed my change to the homeless woman who sat outside the store. Six days a week my three dollars and thirty cents was put into her hands, a consistency I felt we both needed. She lifted her eyes and nodded at me and my heart swelled. I was the only one she looked at, and this simple gesture made me inexplicably happy. For everyone else her eyes were downcast, glued to the sidewalk. I unfolded the paper as I walked, the headlines glum. People at work made fun of me for my newspaper obsession. *Just look on your phone like the rest of us*—they'd say. But, I liked the smell of the paper and the black smudges the ink left on my fingers. For someone who moved around every six months, there was something rewarding about doing the same thing every day. Creating your own ritual. Besides, technology couldn't replace class. I opened the door to The Jane and everything felt normal and right. The spot on my finger where the splinter had pierced my skin throbbed lightly.

3

BAR LIFE

I OPENED MY CHEETOS and swapped it out with yesterday's bag, which was also open and propped next to the beer taps. I got in trouble all the time for leaving open bags of Cheetos around the restaurant.

"Roaches," the managers said.

But, they needed to be aired out just the right amount to get stale—which is the only way I'd eat them. Besides, it was winter. There were no roaches. I popped one in my mouth.

"Stale enough?" one of the servers asked as they walked into the bar and saw the bag. I shrugged. They weren't. A good bag of Cheetos needed to sit open for a week before they were just the right amount of stale, but I made do.

After my Cheetos breakfast, I readied the bar. For the last week, I'd been making the transition from the dinner shift to the lunch shift and everything felt wrong. My job every night was to close down the bar so it was ready for Dean the daytime bartender, but Dean had accepted a management position at The Jane—*a salary and insurance*—he told me proudly, and I was now needed a few mornings a week until they trained someone new. Dean's promotion had disrupted my daytime sleep patterns and forced me to go to bed at a regular time like a regular person. I didn't like the way that made me feel—being regular. I was resentful and over-rested.

I unwrapped containers of sectioned lemons and limes and filled the ice bins. It felt as if I was doing everything in reverse (at night I wrapped containers and emptied the ice bins). Every few minutes Dean texted me a reminder of something I needed to do. I turned my phone off to make it stop. The morning manager, Nate, fancied me. He was always hanging around, asking questions about my life outside of the bar. He watched me dump ice into the metal bin, his elbow resting on the far end of the bar, making comments about the soccer game playing on the television like I cared. He had a bald spot and smelled of cheap cologne and onions. I didn't blame him for the onions, smelling like grease and onions was the downfall of a restaurant job. I blamed him for being a sleazebag and always looking at my tits.

I ignored him until the first customers arrived, and then I had to ask him for a swipe. He watched my lips as he slid his card through the reader.

"You liking your new role, Yara?"

"As morning bartender?" I asked. "Feels exactly the same as night bartender, except the guests are happy and talkative. I like them better when they've been working all day and are miserable and quiet."

"Sure, sure," he said. "It'll just take some getting used to s'all." Nate pronounced *is all* as *saul*.

"You have a little bit of orange on your face," he said, gesturing to my cheek. I dusted it off without thanking him.

The Jane was well known for her breakfast cocktails so there was no avoiding early customers. A couple wandered in a few minutes after we opened, middle-aged and glassy-eyed. Their faces were puffy like they'd been drinking hard the night before. They ordered eggs, toast, and two spicy Bloody Marys, and then they told me about the son they dropped off at the University of Washington. A handsome boy, so smart, a future president, they assured me. His major—political science. When the woman told me he was captain of his high school debate team I wanted to gouge out my eyeballs with a toothpick. I once fucked a debate team captain, his name was a cheese—Colby...or Jack...or...Rodoric! That was it! I didn't tell her that though. What was a pretty girl like me doing working in a bar? —they wanted to know. This was the hard part, blowing off their question like it didn't bother me when it really did. Did I want a good tip, no customer complaints e-mailed to corporate? No, I just wanted to make it through this day, this month, this year. *You should model*, she said. Her husband nodded in agreement. I smiled dumbly and excused myself to get their food from the kitchen. I was not a face. I was tired of being called pretty. I was tired of people seeing my potential. I could be whoever I wanted to be, and for now, that was a bartender. Beauty was deceiving in the same way credit cards were. It felt like it was free, but there was high interest with little return. I breathed a sigh of relief when they left, but soon a different couple took their seats. Then another, and another, until it all blurred together. The morning crowd was hopeful and hungry for talk, their days not descended to shit yet.

4

THE JANE

THE JANE REMINDED ME of home. The tables and chairs were a glossy white set on top of grey concrete floors. Each one held a tiny succulent in a grey pot, which the headwaiter, Lora, lovingly took care of. A guest once tried to walk out with one of them and Lora had chased them down the street yelling in Bulgarian until they sheepishly handed it back to her. No one messed with Lora's succulents. The bar was modern and impressive. A neon pink sign that said *Are you the creator or the created?* —lit up one expansive white wall. "*Very European,*" I heard the guests say as they examined the space. *Europe: pink and white and neon!* I would think, smiling to myself.

It was defiant of the typical restaurant/bar scene in Seattle, which veered toward a chic grunge look. I took it that Kurt Cobain still had his fingers in everything, even from the grave. My home was London, an unparalleled city in every way. But, I was still searching, whoring around America till I burned off my emotional baggage. I wasn't ready to go back yet.

I was carrying in a tray of glasses, which I had poached from the dishwasher, when I saw him. He was scooted in at the far end of the bar, the place we call no man's land. His elbows rested right next to the container of maraschino cherries and olives I used to spruce up the drinks. I sighed because he looked like a talker. And then I recognized him. *Splinter guy!* I felt self-conscious and wished I'd put on fresh eyeliner this morning. Drew on new wings.

"Splinter guy!" I said.

"Oh, ouch. I've had better nicknames." He grinned at me. He looked sleepy, like he'd either just rolled out of bed or he hadn't seen one in a while.

"You ran off pretty quickly the other day," I said. "I barely had time to thank you."

"I had a…thing."

"A thing?" I repeated, a half smile on my lips. It was funny when men described their philandering as *a thing*.

I moved a tray of freshly filled salt shakers to a different spot on the bar to make room for the rack of glasses, and gave him a sideways stare.

"You're nosy," he said.

I shrugged like I wasn't and started setting the shakers on the tables.

"Okay," he said, defensively. "There was a thing with this girl. But, I'm not seeing her anymore. It's over." He said *"over"* with a large amount of relief. I finished setting out the salt shakers and dusted my hands, watching his face.

"Why is it over? What did she do that wasn't to your liking?"

He didn't hesitate to answer, which surprised me since he'd just called me nosy.

"She thought we were more serious than we were. I told her in the beginning that I wasn't looking for a relationship."

"Right," I said. "How many months ago was the beginning?"

"Six." He shrugged.

"So you're seeing this girl for half a year, fucking her I assume—"

He nodded.

"And she finally asks what's going on with the two of you?"

"Yes," he nods, "but that was already established from day one. We were just having fun."

I sighed. "First of all, you're a dick," I said.

He opened his mouth to argue, but I held up my hand to shush him.

"It's perfectly normal after seeing someone consistently for six months to wonder where the relationship is going."

"But, in the beginning—"

"No," I said. "That was the beginning. She's not a robot. She's a human being with feelings."

"Okay, okay." He held up his hands. "I'm a dick. I shouldn't have let it go on that long without having a discussion."

I nodded, both hands perched on my hips.

"God, I need a drink after that. What do you have for whiskey?"

He rubbed a hand across his face and I listed off our selection.

"I guess it's a little early for whiskey," he said. "What about beer?"

I pointed to the row of beer behind the bar. He chewed his lip while he studied them.

"Can you say each of their names?" he asked.

"What? Why?"

"I like to listen to you speak." He grinned. "I'm just trying to keep you talking."

"There are numbers you can call for that sort of fetish," I told him.

17

"One nine hundred girls, girls, girls," he said. We both laughed. Obviously, we'd both seen too many late night commercials.

"Your best IPA then," he said. His voice was deep and his lips puckered around the letter 'p' like it tasted good.

"You're not a morning person," he said, thoughtfully. "That may be a problem." So many 'p's—I was staring.

"A problem?" I asked.

"Yeah," he said. "I am a morning person. So how will that work?"

I set down the glass I was holding and dried my hands. He wasn't smirking, I checked twice.

"I'm not following." My smile was forced—we both knew that. I moved toward the tap, flipped it forward. Beer foamed then turned deep amber. I slid his beer across the counter until it nudged his hand. A gentle reminder to shut the fuck up.

"Our relationship," he said. "Our marriage. You're not a morning person. Who will make my breakfast?"

I glanced around to see if anyone else was around to hear this, but it was just the two of us. Again. The guy was a loon. I'd let a loon duct-tape my splinter. He was completely serious too.

I rested my elbows on the bar, adjusting my face so that I looked more amused than raged and leaned forward.

"Are you drunk?" I asked. I hoped he was because then I could forgive him.

He widened his eyes and shook his head like I was the one saying something absurd.

"Are you on meds?"

This time he pursed his lips. "For what?"

"Being insane."

"No," he said firmly. "I'm sound." He reached up and tapped his temple. He was wearing fingerless gloves.

I nodded. "Okay," I said, slowly. "You're just the type of guy who wants a woman around to make his breakfast. But only for six months, and it can't get too serious."

I moved away, lifting my elbows from the bar and turning my back on him to survey the bottles of liquor that needed restocking. Enough with this guy, enough with all guys. You could order a dildo right to your mailbox. Men needed to learn how dire that situation was for them.

"My asshole days are over," he said. "I've only been in love for a few minutes, I'm not sure how to handle it. Besides, I broke up with Elizabeth for you."

I spun around to look at him.

"Dude," I said—and I'd practiced saying it just like the Americans—"You're deeply in love with yourself. You're also drinking beer at eleven o' clock in the morning." I pushed a menu into his hands, during which time he never took his eyes off of my face. "I won't make you breakfast. Not ever. But, Jerry our cook will. He's a little on the angry side, but his eggs are the shit."

"I like angry," he said. "I like you. I'll take three of Jerry's angry scrambled eggs and a side of toast."

I rolled my eyes.

"You like me," he said. "Just a little." He held his fingers up and pinched the air to show me how little. I shook my head and he made his pinch smaller. I shrugged.

"I'll take it. I'm a man in love and I'm grasping at straws." He had an excellent poker face. I was almost convinced. I felt a little sad for the girls who'd fallen for the joker—especially Elizabeth: the sincere eyes and the emotional lips. How many hearts had he fucked beyond repair?

I busied myself at the computer, putting in his order. I could feel his eyes on my back, the sexual heat of someone wondering what your skin tastes like.

"Hey," he said when I brought him his breakfast and got him another beer. "Is that your newspaper?" He jutted his chin to where the paper sat behind me. "Do you mind?"

"You could just look on your phone," I said, with a small smile.

"Nah," he said. "Phones are bullshit, give me a newspaper any day."

I handed him my newspaper without looking at him. I didn't want him to know that I actually did like him.

"The Cheetos too," he said.

I didn't say anything as I dropped my half-stale bag of chips in front of him. He winked at me and I rolled my eyes.

"Cheesy," I said.

His mouth was already full. "Me or the Cheetos?"

"Both."

And then we got lunch-shift busy. I only saw him once more to drop off his check. He didn't leave his number like I expected he would, and I never learned his name. He was the guy in the beanie who wanted to marry me.

5
THIRD TIME'S A CHARM

HE CAME BACK A few days later. I was working the dinner shift, and my hair had seen better days. He was carrying a guitar case, which he propped against the wall before taking a seat at the bar. As I walked toward him, he smiled, and I knew the guitar case was planned. Carrying a guitar around was almost as sexy as carrying a baby. He was wearing a leather jacket over a pink T-shirt, his jeans ripped at the knees. No beanie this time. I eyed his hair and tried not to smile. A hard side-part in light chestnut brown.

"Who are you today?" I asked him. "You look like one of those punks from California."

"Hey now!" he said, shrugging off the jacket. "I'm wearing Docs, not Vans." He lifted a foot to show me. "I've never surfed," he told me. "And LA sucks."

I couldn't agree more. I'd lasted in LA for a month before moving on to Miami.

"I went on a date with a professional surfer once," I told him. "He said that the only way to really feel alive was on the waves."

"People make me feel alive," he said. "Licking the salt off of a woman's body at the beach. That's the way to tell if you're really living." He had a mint in his mouth, he'd held it still until now, and while his eyes narrowed, he moved it around the front of his mouth, which made his lips move in the most sensual way. I pulled my eyes away from his mouth and stared at the beer taps.

"IPA?" I asked him.

I had four other tables. I glanced around the room to see if they all looked happy. A table of women in their early twenties was laughing near the window, their pink fur and metallic coats draped across the backs of their seats, sweet fruit drinks at their elbows. For the moment they'd forgotten to be gluten-free and I didn't hate them.

"No," he said. "That's what I drink for breakfast. Jack and Coke."

His hair was still damp from a shower, and he smelled of cologne. I'd discovered in my first month of living in America that all of the men here wore one of three colognes: Acqua Di Gio, Armani Code, and Light Blue. He was wearing none of these. He smelled woodsy like pine and fresh dirt.

"Oh, look at you," I said. "Getting cooler by the minute."

He smiled and stole a cherry from the tray. I watched him put it in his mouth, pulling the stem from the fruit and setting it on the bar.

"What's your name?" he asked.

"You were planning our life together last time you came in and you didn't even know my name?"

He was a very still person, his movements paced. I'd noticed it the first time but now even more. Only one part of him moved at a time; right now it was his mouth as one corner turned up in a grin.

"I like to do things slowly," he said. "And out of order."

I slid his drink over. I was trying not to overthink that. He was playing a game with me.

"I like your attention-seeking haircut," I said. "What is that called? The jackass?"

He laughed. "This is already the most abusive relationship I've ever been in and it's all done with an accent, which somehow makes me enjoy it."

"I'm just getting started." I walked away before he could say anything else, the table of sequined girls beckoning me over.

For the next two hours, I made a point of ignoring him, only stopping by once to take his food order and refill his drink. I was a reactive person; it took a certain chemistry to lure me out of my shell. I didn't like that he was doing it. I was here to take a break from all that. A break from men—especially artists. Mostly artists. I ignored him, but he didn't ignore me. Every time I turned around, he was watching me, an almost thoughtful expression on his face. His eyes, a mossy green, were used as weapons. They were honest eyes, and so you trusted him, all the while he undressed you with them.

"Yara," I said. I was hoping to distract him, make him stop looking at me like that.

"What time do you get off, Yara?" he asked.

I was stacking plates on a tray so I could carry them to the kitchen. I licked my lips, not wanting to answer the question.

"Where are you from?" I asked.

He shrugged with his lips. "Here and there. I've been living in the city for about a year. How long have you been here?"

"Couple months," I said.

"Did you come straight from the UK?"

I shook my head and a whole section of my hair sprang out of the clip holding it together. It tumbled over my shoulder and his eyes widened.

"No. I've been traveling around. Chicago, LA, Miami, New Orleans, New York, and now Seattle."

"Trying to find a place you like?" He took a sip of his drink. He looked distracted.

Wouldn't that be something? Finding one place I liked.

I shook my head. "No. I'm just experiencing. I already have a place I like. What's your name?" That was a boundary crossed, asking a man his name. Then you had it to use, to think about.

"David," he said.

"David," I repeated. "That's a nice, solid name. And your surname?"

"My surname," he mimicked. His smile came late, a few seconds after his words. It was slow spreading and warm. "It's Lisey."

"David Lisey," I said, nodding. "Are you a musician?" I nodded over to his guitar case.

"I am. How did you guess?" he teased.

"I don't know," I said. "Maybe it's your asshole haircut."

"I'm not an asshole," he said. "I'm a heartless romantic."

"What's the difference?"

He thought about it. "I believe. But without the proof."

I rolled my eyes. It made me feel juvenile to roll my eyes, but there it was. Men always brought out the best in me.

"You fuck girls without getting to know them and hope to fall in love."

"Yes," he said. "Is that the wrong way to do it?"

"I don't know, let's ask Elizabeth."

"Ouch," he said.

I pursed my lips, rearranging my hair back into my clip. Did he look disappointed?

"Are you in a band?" I asked.

I wiped the counter as I spoke: circle, circle, circle. He had long fingers with calluses on the tips. You couldn't see them, but when he'd reached for his drink our fingers had brushed. I imagined they'd feel scratchy if they ran along your skin.

"Yes. I sing. I play too, but mostly I sing."

"Sing me something now," I said.

He didn't even hesitate. His mouth opened and right there in the bar, surrounded by a dozen or so people he sang the chorus to "When a Man Loves a Woman." His voice was husky and deep; an intimate voice. The girls with the fur jackets turned around in their seats to watch him. I felt his voice. It moved something in me. But, I wasn't going to do that again. I was done.

I didn't have time to respond. The doors to the restaurant opened and a group pushed into the bar in a loud clatter of voices. Regretfully I walked to greet them, leaving David Lisey on his bar stool staring after me, a slow molasses grin spreading across his face.

Nope. No more artists.

We got another late rush after that and for a while, I forgot about David Lisey who stayed rooted to his bar stool nursing the Jack and Cokes I poured for him. He watched me, and sometimes he watched the television, which was showing highlights of a Seahawks game. And even while he watched, I knew he wasn't entirely in the bar, he was somewhere in his own head. Occasionally I saw him pull out his phone to send a text, and that's when I watched him. One of the servers, a girl named Nya, stepped over to talk to him. They knew each other, not well, but there was familiarity. From the corner of my eye, I watched as her hand strayed to his arm, over and over. She was laughing in that whorish, flirty way girls do when they want to fuck you. The hostess came to get her. Her tables were looking for her. I made my way back over to check on David Lisey. Maybe I also wanted to know what Nya was saying.

"My band's playing at The Crocodile tomorrow, Yara. You should come."

"Is Nya going too?" The moment the words were out of my mouth I regretted them. Now he knew I'd been watching.

David's eyebrows crept together as he tilted his head to the side in mock exaggeration. "I didn't take you for the jealous type, but I like it."

"Ha!" I said—then another—"Ha." Then I took my tray of dirty dishes to the kitchen where I let my face burn red from embarrassment.

"Hey Yara, wait up," Nya called to me. She was waiting at the line for a cook to hand something over. A plate slid through the window and she turned and yelled, "Pick up." I lingered in-between the doorway to the kitchen and the rest of the restaurant waiting to hear what she had to say.

"That guy at the bar—David Lisey."

"Yeah?" I said too quickly.

"Are you into him?"

"No. Why?"

She switched the tray of food from one shoulder to another. "Because I am," she said, before walking away.

Nice of her to check. When I got back to the bar, David was sitting backward on his stool watching a couple make out at a table near the window.

"Creepy," I said.

"Shh," he shushed me. "I'm writing a song."

I made him another drink and watched the back of his head. And then he suddenly turned around and said: "So what do you say? Will you come?"

"I thought you were writing a song."

"You think you're good at changing the subject, but you're not," he said. He took a sip of his drink. "You made this stronger."

"You think you're good at pretending to be about me, but you're about you," I told him.

He shrugged. "Aren't we all?"

"Maybe next time."

I busied myself covering the garnishes with Saran Wrap and setting them in the fridge. The bar had emptied out in the last hour, spitting the last of my customers into the freezing rain where they dashed off down the sidewalk. I had the urge to run with them, disappear into the mist. David was the last one left. I glanced at him as I counted down my drawer. He was less drunk than I expected him to be, smiling at me and tossing back the last of his drink, his eyes bright and alert under the bar lights. I tried to talk myself out of liking him. Maybe I was lonely. *Am I lonely?* I considered myself a loner, perfectly content to drift through life as an observer rather than a partaker. I had a friend here, just one. Her name was Ann and she lived in the apartment below mine.

I wondered if he was going to make things awkward, hang around until we locked up, but he stood suddenly and slipped his arms through his jacket sleeves.

"Tomorrow," he said. "We'll be on at ten o'clock. I'll sing to you some more."

"How many girls have you said that to?" I called after him. But he was gone, and my manager was standing in the doorway looking at me funny.

6

RELENTLESS

RELENTLESS. THERE'S SOMETHING ABOUT a relentless man. You couldn't ignore them. If they asked long enough, eventually they wore you down. Women looked for that, persistent interest. An investor. We were, in ourselves, an entire universe. We felt too much, talked too much, wanted too much—the anti-simple.

"You didn't come to my show, Yara." —David, at the bar again.

I watched him as I poured a beer. He was disheveled today, his hard side-part not so hard, and he had dark half moons beneath his eyes. He came twice a week now, sometimes in the morning, sometimes late at night. Whatever time of day he came, his eyes never left me.

"No," I said, simply.

"Why not?"

I looked around the bar. Did I have time to answer that? I had four tables.

"Why do you want me to come?" I asked. I watched him think about it for a minute as he rolled his glass between his palms.

"So I can impress you."

"Why do you want to impress me?"

A man at a table nearby was looking around, searching for his server. I pegged him for a ketchup guy. He wanted a side.

"I'm obsessed with you. I'm fascinated by the fact that I'm obsessed with you. This has never happened to me before."

I smiled. I didn't believe him, of course, but it was fun to hear.

"Yara, can you explain this?" He sounded distressed.

"I can," I said. "Sort of. But I have to get ketchup for that guy over there." I motioned with my head and he turned to look.

"Okay," he said. "Hurry."

I did. I hurried. I went to the kitchen and retrieved a steel ramekin of ketchup from the fridge, I set it on the table, and I smiled—not at him, at David—who wanted to know why I made him feel the way I did. David waited at the bar behind me, and I felt him waiting. Why was I playing this game? I said I wasn't going to anymore. When I got back, he looked at me expectantly.

"What?" I asked him. "Why are you looking at me like that?"

"Tell me," he said. I sighed.

"Look, I've never called myself this so don't laugh," I warned him. "But I've dated a lot of artists. Probably exclusively artists," I admitted, somewhat embarrassed. "They seem to need me for a while…to spark something. I really don't know. But I've been called a muse." My face was hot, a fever of embarrassment. I didn't know why I was telling him any of this, I would agonize over it later. "It's simple for me and complex for them."

"What do you mean?" he asked me.

I looked around the bar at my tables. No one needed me, so I continued. "They're…different when I leave and I'm the same."

He considered that for a moment and then nodded.

"I can see that. I really can. And I'm not just saying that because I'm drunk." He lifted his glass in cheers and took a sip.

"I need a muse."

I laughed.

"I'm not kidding. I can't write anymore. I feel stale. And then by chance, I was walking by and I saw you through the window." He spun around on his stool and pointed to a spot on the sidewalk. "I was composing my speech, the one I was going to give Elizabeth. It was blah, blah, blah—I'm not the commitment sort of guy, and then I saw you and I wanted to marry you on the spot."

"You're full of it," I told him.

David reached up and crossed his heart.

"Pulled one splinter and everything changed. I started to write. I'm on the verge of something and I need your help."

"A coincidence," I said.

"No."

"Yes."

"Be my muse."

"You'd have to fall in love with me. Have you ever been in love?"

He almost answered. Almost. His mouth was poised around the words. But then a couple walked through the doors and sat down at the far end of the bar. I looked at him regretfully and walked away.

"Go home," I called back to him. "You're drunk."

By the time I was done taking their order, David Lisey's bar stool was empty. I smiled as I cleared what was left of his dinner dishes, stacking them on my arm. He'd left a scrap of paper under his plate, his number scribbled on it. *For Yara*, it said. *My muse.*

I threw it away. *No. Nope.* Not happening, Lisey. Asshole haircut or not. Cut arms or not. Magical singing voice or not. The men I'd been with had been cloying in their need for me. They wanted and expected and it drained me until there was nothing to do but leave. It was entirely one-sided, but none of them ever thought that. That was the thing about artists, they didn't often think of you. Their energy had a narrow focus, a spotlight on their art...their insecurities...the unfairness of the world. I'd tried dating a banker, an engineer, a botanist, but they'd been addicted to their careers in a different way, and I found them lacking the unbridled passion I was used to.

He didn't come back for two weeks. I thought I was in the clear. I'd come to Seattle to focus on myself, to embrace aloneness, and I had done just that. It was almost time to go home.

"Yara."

His voice startled me. The beer I was pouring flowed over my hand, pooling in the drain. I glanced over my shoulder and there he was, a beanie on his head, scruffy face, soft eyes—staring, staring.

"You again," I said.

He laughed. Placing a hand over his heart, he said, "I hope you say that to me every morning."

I hated that I smiled. That he could turn my jabs into something endearing.

"What time do you get off?"

"In ten minutes," I said. "But I'm not coming to your show and we're not getting a drink."

"Okay," he sighed. "I'll just have a drink here then." He slid into his usual bar stool and folded his hands on the counter, all proper like. It looked like he was preparing for a meeting.

"You're so ridiculous," I said.

"In love," he corrected with a grin.

"Sure," I shrugged. "It's late afternoon so I'm not sure if I'm supposed to get you a beer or Jack and Coke."

"Beer. Yara…let's talk." He tapped his palm on the bar top like he'd just thought of the best idea.

"Can't. I'm working."

He looked around the bar. "It's empty." It was true—he'd come in that in-between time, the witching hour between lunch and dinner.

"What do you want?"

He straightened up, cleared his throat. I almost laughed, but I was too weary.

"A muse."

"You want a new fuck buddy, not a muse."

A shit-eating grin spread across his pretty fucking face. *Caught*.

"What about both?"

I shook my head. "Doesn't work that way."

"Why not?"

"Because it doesn't."

"But what would you have to lose?"

I set down the rum bottle I was holding and stood in front of him, hands on my hips.

"Nothing. You'd lose. But, I'm not a cruel person, David. I don't want to hurt people."

"You're not going to hurt me, Yara." He said my name in the same way I'd said his: annoyed…condescending. I frowned at him. He had no idea what he was doing. Testosterone, lack of caution—the bull charging of men.

"So let me get this straight," I said, looking around. "You want me to make you fall in love with me, and you're giving me permission to leave and break your heart?"

He nodded.

"But you don't think I'd actually leave, Lisey. You think you can change me, but that's not how it works."

He shrugged. "Let's see how it plays out. Just come to our show. See what you think. Maybe you can help me, maybe you can't. I don't know how you decide these things."

"I don't," I said. "My relationships with the men I've been with happened organically. I don't go around putting ads on craigslist, for God's sake. What you're asking me to do is stage a relationship so you can feel inspired."

"I already feel something for you so it wouldn't be staged."

"What about me?" I said, raising my eyebrows. "I'm just supposed to force feelings?"

He laughed through his nose, his lips puckering into a know-it-all grin. "Yara, we have chemistry. You can try to deny it all you want, but man is it there. I can practically feel you undressing me every time I'm in here."

He wasn't too far off base so I didn't tell him to go fuck himself, but I did give him a dirty look before I went to hide in the kitchen.

"Fuck you, David Lisey," I said under my breath.

7
THE CROCODILE

I CURSED AS I stepped into the street from my building. It was cold as fuck. My Uber was waiting by the curb, the driver looking around anxiously. I matched the license plate on my phone to the white Prius and walked over. It was raining, the ground slick with patches of ice. It wasn't usually this cold here; they said it was the coldest winter in twenty years. *It was possibly my fault*, Ann said. I was the Ice Queen.

I stepped around the slick spots and pulled cold air into my lungs. I was annoyed with myself for doing this, but not enough to send me home. Once I'd set my mind to something I stuck with it. A determined loyalist even when it hurt my pride.

"The Crocodile," I told the driver, sliding into the backseat. He already knew because, hello, he wasn't a fucking cab driver, he was Uber and they knew shit. I just needed to say it out loud. *You're doing something outside of the norm, Yara. Chasing a boy. No. Meeting a boy who asked very nicely.*

"Oh, yeah?" the driver said. "Nice place." He laughed, and I nodded.

There was a shooting there just a few weeks ago. It got a little rough sometimes, but mostly it was a fun place. Going to a grungy venue to listen to live music wasn't unusual for me. Going because some guy asked me to was.

"Be safe," he told me as we pulled up.

I nodded solemnly. He didn't really care…it was just something to say.

I was wrapped in a worn leather jacket and I shivered as I left the warmth of the Prius. I walked toward the door, dodging a girl already vomiting on the sidewalk. It was only ten o'clock. Her friends waited against the building, frowning.

"You'll feel better after you yak," one of them called out.

"Atta girl," another said.

I wanted to tell them to put some food in her stomach and to never use the word yak again. She went too hard, too fast, but I walked on. It was none of my business. They'd learn eventually.

Why are you here? I asked myself again. I didn't even like the song he sang, especially when Michael Bolton covered it. It was because I liked David. He had that spark I looked for in people. And because he asked me to come. He took risks, flirted with volatile women, sang to them. He wasn't just some guy—there was something more. Humans liked to investigate things, and that was what I was doing.

Ann had been the one to tell me to go. And when I'd asked her to come with me she'd laughed and said, "No, nope. It would take more than the Crocodile to get me out of this apartment."

So I did my grungy shit alone, abandoned by my one and only friend who had shit taste in music anyway. Her idea of a good time was a *Housewives of New Jersey* marathon in her flannel pajamas.

I showed the bouncer my ID and stepped inside. Everyone knew that a good bar, a well-loved bar, smelled like despair. But, The Crocodile was a different kind of bar. Nirvana, Pearl Jam, Cheap Trick, and R.E.M. had all played there in their heyday. To me, The Crocodile smelled like a really good time, pure talent on the rise. I moved out of the main walkway and toward the bar where I ordered a shitty whiskey and soda. There was already a band on stage, the loud chords of an electric guitar ripped through the speakers. I sipped and sipped, and bobbed my head to the terrible music.

When a drunk girl speared my foot with her stiletto, I limped to a spot near the wall. Drunken women in heels were dangerous weapons of foot destruction. This was life, stinking of smoke, hangovers, occasional drugs, and reckless sex. I didn't want it to always be this way, but this was the way it was right now.

"Do you know which band is up next?" I asked the girl next to me. Her mascara was smudged and there was a sheen of sweat covering her face as she bounced up and down.

"David Lisey's band," she said. "They're awesome."

"What are they called?" I shouted over the music.

She leaned close to me and yelled, "Lazarus Come Forth," then pointed to a poster on the wall. I hadn't noticed it before: David and two other guys all wearing black.

I nodded knowingly. "Of course, yeah," I said, though she didn't hear me.

I was flustered by the fact that she knew who he was. I'd mentally taken ownership of him. He was the guy who duct-taped a splinter out of my finger and sang me a song. He also had really long eyelashes. He was my guy and I didn't like that she knew who he was. On the flip side, their band name made me roll my eyes. A bizarre Biblical reference about coming back from the dead. Who were these guys? They had the suburbs written all over them.

Back from the dead my ass. I imagined they liked the sound of it; musicians were in love with being doomed. I renamed them The Suburbs and went to the bar for another drink. When I got back, someone had stolen my spot on the wall and I had to move closer to the stage. More's the pity. I stayed there holding my cup, rattling the ice compulsively. A few moments later David walked on stage, followed by two other guys. He was wearing all black; nothing fancy—just a black long sleeve and tight, black jeans. Just like the posters. *The Suburbs,* I thought. His legs were long and I realized he was quite a bit taller than I remembered. Maybe 6'2" or 6'3". I pictured his pink T-shirt and leather jacket, the clothes he wore in real life. He glanced around the audience like he was looking for someone. *Me*, I thought.

I stared at his jacket so I wouldn't have to look at his face. I moved closer, just enough so that he could see me.

The girl with the smudged mascara jumped up and down waving her free hand in the air. She'd crawled up close like me. She was taking pictures of David, though she was moving too much to have any of them be clear. I shrugged and turned my attention back to the stage where David was messing around with his guitar.

A *ONE...TWO...THREE...*

They started with something fast. I strained to catch some of the lyrics, but the bass was turned up too loud. David's smoky voice was drowned out. I was disappointed and also a little tipsy. *Lightweight,* I told myself, disgusted. I wanted to move closer to the stage, but I didn't want him to think I was into him, even though I was.

He was a little stiff, if I were to be honest. He'd flirted with ease, a professional, but on the stage, he was a carbon copy of himself. Unsure. I tilted my head as I watched him, half fascinated and half disappointed. I loved the arts, all of them. But there was a common denominator in all messy, good art: an uninhibited wildness. I'd seen the disease on some. It overtook their inhibitions. David Lisey was not uninhibited, but I didn't think he knew that. He didn't quite believe what he was singing. They played a slow song. It was about a girl who had and didn't have at the same time. Husky voice, shirtsleeves pushed up to his elbows, David sang with both his hands clutching the mic stand and looked directly at me. It was the first time that night that I felt he was being honest.

When their set ended David hopped down from the stage and walked over to where I was standing. I tried not to notice the way he walked—the center of gravity in his shoulders. They were squared back, graceful. The rest of him moved, but it was all governed by what the shoulders decided.

"You came," he said.

"Clearly."

"Can I buy you a drink?"

I shook my head. I'd already had four. One more and I'd be taking him home. On second thought…

"I should be heading out," I said. "I have to open again tomorrow." It was a lie.

"Stay," he said. It wasn't so much a request as it was a command.

I looked at his lips, his nose, his mouth—so nicely put together—and I shrugged like it didn't matter. "Sure. Just for a few minutes."

What could it hurt?

"I don't want you to leave," David said, even though I'd already agreed to stay. "I'm drawn to you. I want to be near you."

I was in the middle of an existential crisis and he was making me his person. How could he afford to be that honest? I was cheap. I fell for it because most of us just really want to be wanted.

"Okay," I said. "But, not a minute after."

"Hey," he said. "You don't scare me. We're not the same. I recognize that. But you don't scare me."

8

THE CAR

I DIDN'T STAY FOR a few more minutes. I stayed. David walked me over to the bar and ordered me a Hendrick's and tonic, which I took gratefully. The cheap whiskey had left a stale taste in my mouth. Top shelf liquor for the band! Gin sort of made me crazy, but crazy was better than boring, and I was feeling wild around the edges.

I stayed to watch the last half of the show, still buzzing from my interaction with David. There had been a moment when I thought about refusing, pulling my arm out of his grip and marching straight for the door in an act of female defiance. But then we caught eyes and neither of us looked away, we just stood there and stared at each other until someone said—"Hey David, you're up, dude." He'd checked over me once more like he wasn't sure if I'd be here when he came back and disappeared into the crowd. I was rendered non-thinking, a teenage boy. I wanted to know what he looked like out of his clothes, how much tongue he used when he kissed. The parts of me that he touched felt bruised, tender. Yet he had been so gentle.

"Pretty good, huh?" the bartender said, jutting his chin toward the stage.

I shrugged. His forearms were as thick as my thighs and his eyes said he hadn't given a fuck for about ten years. *Me too, buddy, me too.* I considered the small hoop earring in his saggy left earlobe and sighed.

"They're okay," I said. "They need more heart."

But, he hadn't heard me, he'd moved off to someone else, probably to repeat the same line. *Just a cheap trick bartender,* I thought. I turned back to the band. The second half of the show was decidedly better. Or maybe I was more drunk. I wished I weren't like this, ripping everything apart. Looking for the flaws. In any case, when it was over, David found me edging toward the door. I wondered if he rushed down from the stage knowing I'd try to slip away. He was wearing his leather jacket over his black ensemble now. He took my hand and I let him lead me out of The Crocodile, and when we stepped into the wet night, the air burned through my lungs.

"Where are we going?" I asked.

He lifted his hand to say goodbye to someone over my shoulder.

"Does it matter?"

No, I suppose it didn't. Unless that was the gin talking. If he turned out to be a creep I had a switchblade in my bag.

"If you're going to murder me, don't fuck with my face," I said. "I want an open coffin at my funeral."

"No deal," he said. "I want your dimples as my trophy."

I laughed, and he looked at me warmly and said, "There they are."

We headed north, navigating the puddles, him slightly in the lead. A group of girls stopped us and asked for a picture with David. Their boyfriends stood off to the side looking indifferent.

I didn't tell him no when he held his car door open for me, and I realized it was twice in one night that I'd been unable to say it. An alarm went off in my head, but I silenced it. *Hush, cynicism.* As I climbed into the front seat of his beat-up Honda Accord I told myself that I was due some yeses. I was due. And maybe this would be different, this thing with David and me.

David played Mark Lanegan as we drove. Heat blasted from the vents until the interior of the car felt hot and crackly like a toaster. I pulled off my scarf and David cracked his window.

"It's hot," he said, but he didn't turn the heat down.

I could see the beads of sweat dot above his lip. At the next light, he shrugged off his coat. At the junction between 4th and Union, I slid off my boots and socks. We didn't speak, we undressed. The soundtrack played as we tossed our fabric in the backseat, damp from the heat of our bodies. I took off my leather jacket next, and his long sleeve black shirt followed. He was shirtless. Just his black jeans and boots remained. The car smelled of sweat and cigarettes. "Cold Molly" started to play and I tore off my sweater. It was so hot I felt like I was going to throw up. But, we were playing a game of dare.

Outside, a group of people burst from the doors of a nightclub, their breath snaked from their mouths in hazy, white clouds. I wondered briefly who they were, where they lived, and who'd sleep with whom at the end of the night. Inside the car, David's head moved up and down with the music. I closed my eyes and leaned my head back against the seat. I was sitting in my bra now, my bare feet propped on the dash, toes wiggling. We were in Florida, Hawaii, Bali. We were not in Seattle in the dead of the coldest winter in twenty years. David pulled off one boot, and then the other, a cigarette balanced between his lips. His boots went flying past my head into the backseat. They were heavy with yellow stitching: Doc Martens. I laughed, but the music swallowed it, a vortex of beat and vocals. And then suddenly we were racing to take off our pants. The light was red as we struggled: lifting hips, yanking the thick wavy denim, chins bumping into the dash. When the car moved forward, our skin stuck to the leather. It was a sauna. A cleansing. I could barely stand it, but I didn't want it to end. I didn't know where he was driving us, and I didn't care. For once. He pulled into a spot on the street. *We're in Fremont,* I thought. I stared at the two of us: stripped naked to our underwear, sweating in an old Honda Accord, our pale skin illuminated by the neon lights of the storefronts. David was still wearing his socks, his thighs lean muscle and soft hair. His briefs were pink. As soon as he put the car in park, I was on him. An awkward business, crossing over from seat to lap. I straddled him and felt the stickiness of our bodies, the suction of sweat and skin. Outside of the car, people walked by: pink fur, North Face, scarves that covered their chins, hands deep in pockets. They were in Seattle, cold and frigid, but in this car, we were hot and sweaty—wet in all the right places. David's fingers were inside of me, working my body into a white-hot explosion. His car windows were not tinted. We were a spectacle. A woman in a pink lace bra squirming on top of a man whose face was buried in her neck. I reached for him and took him in my hand. He felt good. I wanted to feel more of him, but there was a sharp rapping on the window—knuckles against glass. We looked up and two guys were staring, laughing. They waved and gave us a thumbs up, their goofy, drunk smiles rearranging their boring faces. David wrapped his arms around me and laughed into my neck. The spell was broken, and I was no longer hot.

"It's cold in here," I said.

He ran a hand up the goose bumps on my arms.

"Let's go somewhere to get warm then," he suggested.

I crossed over, back to my own seat. We had to fish our clothes from the backseat one item at a time. He handed me my jeans, I handed him his shirt. It went like that until we were dressed. And then the Honda was back on the road driving quickly toward another unknown destination. *What a strange way to get naked with someone,* I thought.

9

RUINED DATE

I SLEPT TERRIBLY THE week after I saw David's show at
The Crocodile. My apartment was too warm, and most
nights I woke up covered in sweat. When I cracked a
window, it would get unbearably cold and leave me
shivering under the covers wishing for another body to
warm me. Too cold to sleep, too hot to sleep. I was
unsettled. It was David. He crossed my mind even when I
didn't want him to—like when I walked to work the next
day slouched over with heavy bags underneath my eyes,
him being the reason. And when I clocked in at the
computer and forgot my server number because I was
wondering if he'd show up later that day. He didn't. In
fact, I didn't see him until two weeks after Christmas. I'd
almost forgotten to care when one day there he was, sitting
at the bar with a shit-eating grin on his face. How often do
we lie to ourselves and say we don't care about something
when we do?

"Hey, Yara?" he said. "Want to get tacos when your
shift is done?"

Who said no to tacos? Not me.

"No," I said. "I'm busy tonight."

"Okay, good. I'll just wait here until you're done then."

"I have a date," I told him. And it was true, one of the regulars, an accountant, was taking me out for a drink after my shift.

"He's picking me up from here. Ah, here he is…" I pretended to be more excited than I was.

David swiveled around on his stool to watch as Brian walked through the door and waved to me.

"Hey you." I glanced sideways at David, who didn't seem perturbed at all. He was studying Brian with mild interest. "I thought I was meeting you after work."

Brian was on the shorter side, stocky. He wore his hair spiked up in the front and gelled flat in the back. It reminded me of how the boys in high school used to wear their hair.

"I thought I'd come in for a drink and walk over with you," he said.

"A gentleman," David mouthed to me, nodding in approval. I ignored him and smiled at Brian.

"Great. What can I get for you?"

"A beer and that appetizer you told me to get last time."

"Sure," I said, watching David warily. I put in Brian's order and ran back to the kitchen to grab a rack of clean glasses. When I came back, Brian had moved stools to sit next to David and they were engaged in a lively conversation.

"Yara," David said, "Brian and I went to the same high school. Three years apart. Isn't that crazy?"

"So crazy," I said between my teeth.

I tried to ignore them for the next thirty minutes, and they ignored me, laughing and clapping each other on the back like they were best friends.

It made my stomach roll to watch them.

When my shift was over, and I'd closed down the bar, David and Brian were standing outside talking while Brian smoked.

"Ready?" Brian asked when he saw me. He tossed his cigarette into the gutter and kicked back from the wall he was leaning against to come stand next to me.

"Yeah," I said, eyeing David who looked smug.

Brian glanced back at him. "Oh, I hope you don't mind. I asked David to come with us. Since you're already friends…" I waved his comment away and smiled sweetly. Brian took a phone call and walked a step ahead of us.

"Not at all. Lovely of you to join us, David." And when he was close enough I whispered, "Psycho motherfucker," under my breath.

"I've never fucked a mother!" David said, cheerfully. "Though I've always wanted to."

"What are you even getting at?" I hissed. "This is stalkery."

"Yara, I'm disappointed. Brian's a nice guy but, man, I had that haircut in tenth grade. And an accountant? What's a girl like you doing having drinks with an accountant?"

"Shut up," I hissed. Brian had just hung up the phone and was turning back to us.

"Sorry, guys," Brian said. "Work, work, work—right?"

David gave him a thumbs up.

"So how do you two know each other?" he asked, looking from me to David. *Too many questions, Brian. What are you, a fucking shrink?*

"Well," David said before I could answer. "I'm in love with Yara, have been for a while now, but she won't date me."

"He's joking," I said to Brian. "He's bloody mental." I didn't know why I cared—I didn't even like him. A car drove by and someone yelled something out the window.

David shrugged while Brian laughed awkwardly. The guys bounced back into conversation while I walked beside them silently fuming. But why was I mad? I glared at David and it was like he could feel me doing it. He turned and winked at me. Winked!

Fuck you, David Lisey.

The bar we were headed to was on Capitol Hill. I'd been once before and had gotten too drunk to walk home. The bartender recognized me as soon as I walked in.

"The drunk British girl!" he said, slamming his fist on the bar. "Best kisser!"

I pressed my lips together trying not to smile. According to my work colleagues who I'd come here with, I'd leaned across the bar and kissed him on the mouth when he made the best Old Fashioned I'd ever tasted.

David looked at me in surprise.

"What? Shut up," I snapped. "I'm not always uptight."

He narrowed his eyes and nodded real slow, a small smile touching his lips.

"Hey, British girl," the bartender called. "You wearing your boots?"

I lifted a foot and waved it in the air.

"That's right," he said. "Those boots were made for dancing."

David's mouth made a little "o" like he was getting ready to ask me a question.

"Where is Brian?" I asked before he could get the words out. "Are we not supposed to be on a date?"

"He's over there, I think," David said. "Talking to some girl." I peered past his shoulder and sure enough, my date was picking up some half naked blonde near the door.

"This is your fault," I said, jabbing a finger at David.

He held up his hands in mock surrender. "I don't know what you're talking about."

"Lying sack of shit!" I said. "You made my date fall in love with *you* and then told him you're in love with me! He backed down for you!"

"Oh come on, Yara. Maybe he wasn't that into you."

He was standing sideways to face me, his forearm resting on the bar.

"He's been coming in three times a week for two months. He asks me out every single time."

David made a face and then shook his head sadly. "Sounds kind of stalkerish, if you ask me."

"Yeah? Takes one to know one."

"What are you drinking, British girl?" the bartender asked.

"Your most expensive bourbon on the rocks, because this douchebag is paying," I said.

David nodded seriously and pulled out his credit card. "Same for me. And dude, stop hitting on my girl. The boots are mine."

The bartender eyed David with a frown. "You with this guy, British girl? Or is he hassling you?"

I glanced at David and sighed. "Unfortunately he's my date for the night, but I'll let you know if I need another kiss." He winked at me and moved away to make our drinks.

We stood at the bar like that for two hours, right up until they closed. At one point Brian came over to tell us he was leaving (with the half naked girl) but we blew him off, too engrossed in our conversation.

"Have you ever had your heart broken?" I asked. "Like really just mauled and destroyed in the worst possible way." I leaned my elbows on the bar and turned my head to look at him. I'd been waiting for an answer to this question since our last conversation.

He looked perplexed. "By a woman?"

"Yes, by a woman," I laughed. "Or hey, by a man. Whatever."

He shook his head. "No, I guess not. I'm usually the one to do the breaking up. When it stops feeling right, you know? I don't want to lead her on." He swiveled his chair from side to side, his tone light.

"That's your problem," I told him. "Take Bukowski, for example. He didn't only write about his poor broken heart, but he was a bit of a mad man always on the verge of suicide and madness. He lived enough to get hurt and then he channeled it into his art."

"Are you saying my songs lack madness?" David smiled.

"That's exactly what I'm saying." I shrugged.

His smile didn't falter; in fact, he looked like he was really considering what I said.

"Is that what you do?" he asked. "Bring the madness?"

I shrugged.

"It's not an easy thing to get your heart broken. You have to really love someone," he said.

That was true—if it wasn't in their possession, they couldn't break it.

"Have you ever really been in love then?" I asked.

"Puppy love." He nodded. "The wound is shallow but present."

I liked that so much I repeated it to myself: *shallow but present.*

I'd dated a handful of artists—not by choice—it just happened that way. Some of their hearts broke when I chose to move on and leave the state; others were as indifferent as I was. But the ones who did love me were always confused when I told them I was leaving.

"What about me?" they'd say. *"Us?"*

And then I'd have to explain that we'd always been temporary. I was a gypsy. It wasn't about them, not my arrival to a place or my leaving of it, but they didn't understand that. I'd warned them all beforehand, before their feelings got involved, that the minute I landed in one place I was already on my way out. I think they all thought they could make me fall in love with them and stay in one place.

"Don't you want American citizenship?" a painter from Chicago had asked me. *"If you marry me you can stay forever."*

That sent me running sooner rather than later. I didn't want to stay anywhere forever. The said painter had gone on to paint a series of portraits called *Leaving*, which were displayed in various galleries across the US. All of them were of a blonde woman's back as she walked away from cities across the US. I heard that he received six figures for each of them and eventually opened his own gallery. I never contacted him, I thought it would be tacky, but I was happy for his success.

"So what do you say, Yara? A real date, not some shitty bar."

"And then what?" I asked.

"Another date, if it goes well. Maybe some hot sex on the beach."

"There is no beach here."

"Aha! You're interested though; otherwise, you would have shut me down."

The painter had been an older man with a teenage daughter. On weekends we'd pick her up from her mother's house and take her to the mall where she'd choose expensive sneakers and backpacks, and her father would pay for them, a look of guilt on his face. It's the same thing I would have done to my father had I known him and had he been willing. When I left, I had just been one of his heartbreaks, not his first. The first was powerful; it changed you. My own had been so devastating, altering the way I looked at men and love. And it wasn't something that just wore off with time, returning you to your previous state of belief. Once you lost your faith, it was gone.

David walked me home when the bar closed. He didn't ask to come up and I made no move to invite him.

"I'll see you, Yara," he said.

I nodded because I didn't know what to say. I'd actually enjoyed myself, but wasn't ready to admit it.

DAVID CAME TO THE JANE a few days later, scruff on his face, a baseball cap covering his hair. He was distracted, glancing at his phone every few minutes. I watched him stare out the window and stare at the TV all in the same minute, not committed to either of them. He smiled at me once, while I was carrying a tray of food to a table. The tray rested on my shoulder, the plates clinking softly together with my steps. But I was used to David's smiles and this one didn't reach his eyes. I served the dishes, casting a worried glance over my shoulder at him. There was something wrong. I didn't have time to talk to him during the lunch rush, and when I finally made my way over to where he'd been sitting, he was gone, a twenty dollar bill on the bar and a note written on the back of the check I had given him. He'd written down his number and asked me to go to the art museum with him.

Meet me there tomorrow, it said. *I know you have the day off, I asked your manager. 10:00. Let the heart breaking commence.*

An art museum, he knew the way to my heart. I crumpled up the receipt and threw it in the trash, but later I fished it out and stuck it in my purse. It seemed significant somehow that this boy was pursuing my company in such a relentless way. *I know you have the day off, I asked your manager.*

I sighed. I would go. I could try to tell myself that I wouldn't and that I didn't care a thing about David Lisey's attention, but it just wasn't true. I had daddy issues just like everyone else, and the pursuit of the heart was something that appealed to me. When the people who were supposed to like you didn't—it made male attention a requirement.

Sometimes I searched for my mother on the internet. I didn't even know my father's name to look for him, but my mother had a Facebook page and some of her albums were open to the public. I wouldn't dare friend request her. I didn't want her to know I cared. Her profile was set to private, but every so often she changed her profile picture, and I would study it for hours, saving it to my phone and then deleting it. Saving it again. Was it me or her? Why had she decided not to mother me? Did she love me? I'd never know because I'd never ask. That was the thing about pride, it shortsighted our hearts. Her profile pictures were of her alone, smiling—standing in front of some pub or a national landmark. Sometimes she posed with a brown mottled cat that only had one eye. I'd zoom in on that cat and its disfigured eye—wonder what it had that I hadn't. My mother hated animals—I'd once seen her kick a dog.

"Anything that's not a human is a rodent," she'd told me once. *"And some humans are rodents too,"* she'd added.

At the time I'd wondered if she was talking about me. She often referred to children as parasites. Seeing her embracing an animal, look at it with sincere fondness—I told myself the cat belonged to a neighbor or a friend— that she was only posting it for appearances' sake—like those people who wore fur and pretended to like animals. But I wasn't sure. Maybe she'd changed. That hurt worse than her just being the way she was. That she'd become the type of person who hugged cats close to her chest but had never hugged her daughter. I pushed it all away—I was so good at that. Compartmentalizing was the key to success.

I changed my outfit three times the next morning. First, it was a pair of black jeans and a pink sweater, then grey sweatpants and a thermal top. Then I changed again for obvious reasons, back into the pink sweater. Finally, I settled on all black. I was emo, I was goth, I was an assassin of hearts and I didn't give a fuck about David fucking Lisey. I pulled my hair into a tight severe bun and slashed eyeliner across my lids. My lipstick...there was none, because girls who didn't wear lipstick didn't care. That's what my mum used to say. I put Chapstick on instead of lipstick in case he tried to kiss me.

SAM. Seattle's art museum. He was waiting for me outside. I spotted him before he spotted me. I stopped in the middle of the street when I saw him, just as the light changed to red. A car honked at me. I didn't know why I stopped; maybe it was that I saw him and then I couldn't move. I made it to the other side just as he saw me. His hands were in his pockets, he didn't take them out as he watched me walk toward him. There was this look on his face.

"You don't even seem surprised that I came," I said.

"I'm not." He shrugged.

"Why not?"

"When there's chemistry you can't stop the reaction."

"Isn't that clever, Bill Nye," I said.

"How do you know about the science guy, English?"

"We have the internet too over on my side of the pond."

He took my hand as we walked toward the doors, and I let him. He'd given me a nickname and I hadn't even kissed him yet.

"I like your boots," he said.

I looked down at my boots. The same ones the bartender had commented on a few nights earlier.

"Why?" I asked him. "What do you like about them?"

"They look like you've had them for a dozen years. Like they're well loved. If you can love boots like that, how much more could you love me?"

I was speechless. Dumb. I felt so stupid for liking what he said, so vulnerable.

"They're just boots," I told him. "You're making a thing out of boots."

"You're not even from here, Yara," he said as he held the door open for me. "Everything you have means something."

He was right. So right.

"I'll tell you about the boots if you tell me what was wrong with you yesterday."

He looked at me in surprise, his fingers squeezing mine for the briefest of moments.

"How do you know something was wrong?" he asked me.

"I could just tell."

He looked away then back at me. "My dad," he said. "He had a stroke. He's all right," he said quickly. "But, we were scared. Seeing your hero lie on a hospital bed—pale and helpless—really puts things in perspective, you know?"

I didn't know. I had no heroes. No idols.

"I don't know," I said. "But, I don't like it when you hurt." I imagined that we both looked surprised. I certainly was.

"Forget I said that," I said.

"Said what?"

I smiled.

"I like it when you care about me and then pretend that you don't," David said. "It's almost like I'm the only one who has that privilege."

"Do I come across that cold?"

"Yes."

I sighed. "You have to. When you've been hurt and you're trying to be okay. You can't let people know they have power over you."

He didn't chastise me or try to prove me wrong. I appreciated the lack of clichés—sympathy. We stopped in front of a painting of a boy on a skateboard. No one was watching him, but he was performing for himself.

"It's better that you're cautious," he said. "If there's no one to protect you, you have to protect yourself."

"Wow," I said. "That almost made me like you."

"What would seal the deal, Yara? I give great head." And just like that, we were back to normal—flirty, witty…

I shook my head and he smiled and we looked at a sculpture of a face between a lotus flower. Perfect.

Yeah, I was going to date him. I knew that then. Serious one minute, making jokes the next. He made my truth light and funny without diminishing the importance of it. The perfect man. Perfect for me.

11

THE FIRST TIME

THE FIRST TIME WE HAD sex it wasn't like it was in books and movies. Nothing choreographed, nothing seamless. We'd gone back to my apartment after spending the afternoon at the museum and a quick dinner of sushi and wine. He couldn't open my bra strap and I had to reach back myself and unhook it while his lips kissed a line across my collarbone, and he moaned like he was already inside of me. He didn't shove his dick in my mouth and tell me to take it while I gagged and pretended to like choking on a cock. He touched my body reverently, like it was made of something breakable—glass. It was like he'd never seen breasts as beautiful as mine, a stomach as beautiful as mine. My legs were one of the Seven Wonders of the World to David Lisey. I watched him experience me and I was both fascinated and wary. His face a mixture of pain and anger that I didn't understand until 1 asked him about it later.

"I was angry that other men had touched you before me. I was trying not to lose my shit."

Was I angry that he'd been touched by other women? No. I wasn't the type to care about the past. I knew that most women were jealous of ex-lovers and past relationships, but that wasn't me. My friend Ann, upon hearing my life story, told me I'd never been in love. But she was wrong. I'd been in love more times than I could count. At the time, I'd argued that I'd fallen hard for all the men I'd been with, I was just the type of woman who knew when it was time to move on.

"That's the thing, Yara," she'd said to me. *"There is no moving on when you're truly in love. You try and you keep trying, but that love is a stain on your life. It's just not that easy."*

Sex with David had been different. There was a sincerity in the way he touched me, an honesty and openness. Many men had taken me, proven their expertise, left bruises on my body and tingling in my limbs. It had been a big show each time, the way they wanted to impress rather than being impressed. No one had kissed my nipples with such reverence. No one had slipped a finger inside of me and moaned in pleasure. This was what it was like to be worshiped.

After, we lay separately staring up at the ceiling. One of his hands was under the sheet on my upper thigh, hot and weighted. I liked the feeling and detested it at the same time. You shouldn't grow to like the feel of a man's hand on your body because it would soon be gone, and then what would you do? Cry yourself to sleep every night like my mother? Both of my hands clutched the sheet to my chest as my eyes moved rapidly over the ceiling. I looked over at David and he was staring at me.

"Why are you looking at me like that?" I asked. Was I blushing? That would be embarrassing.

"Tell me about your boots," he said. "The ones you always wear."

I pursed my lips and crossed my eyes. "Everything isn't a story, David," I said. "They're just boots."

"Maybe you don't think the simple story of your boots is important, but it's the simple things that tell the most about our complexities."

His interest in me felt like a burden. If he dug too deep, he'd come up empty-handed.

"Humor me." He reached out and touched a piece of my hair, lifting it between his fingers and tugging.

I sighed, but I was already in compliance with his request, pulling from my memory the story of the boots.

"When I left England and came here to America, I started out in New York. Everyone's dream, right? To see the great city of New York." I laughed at myself remembering, but he only nodded. "The only pair of shoes I brought with me was a pair of sandals. It was summer and I figured I'd buy what I needed when I got settled. Anyway, I got a job in a restaurant in Manhattan and of course, I had to buy a pair of those terrible non-slip shoes that restaurants often require. So then it was just the sandals and the ugly restaurant shoes. I got really depressed that fall. It was a combination of missing home and not being able to find my place in New York yet. One day I was walking to work with my head down, thinking about what an awful failure I was, when I looked up and saw these boots in a shop window. They were badass, tough—you know…" I glanced at David and he nodded like he knew exactly.

"So, I marched into the store and bought them. Except they were four hundred dollars and took every penny in my bank account. But, I didn't care. I was convinced the boots would make me tough. And I've been wearing them for a year now and they show no signs of wear. Best four hundred dollars I ever spent, even if I had to eat every meal from the free salad bar at work for the next month."

David rolled onto his back and now it was his turn to stare at the ceiling.

"And you didn't want to tell me that story," he said, shaking his head.

"Are you going to write a song about it?" I teased. It was a joke, only a joke, but he nodded seriously.

"Yes, probably."

I rolled my shoulders and stretched, suddenly embarrassed and wanting to change the subject.

"Did all that great sex put a kink in your neck?" He was leaning up on his elbow all of a sudden, his eyes mischievous.

I laughed and put a hand over his face to push him away. He kissed my palm and then fell onto his back. We were playful together. It didn't feel like work to be with him.

"I've not been worshiped that way before," I told him, half joking and half serious.

I rolled on top of him to distract him from my outlandish statement, pressing my nose to his.

"That seems wrong," he said, his voice husky. "Something as powerful as you." He reached up to knead my behind and I closed my eyes and buried my face in the crook of his neck.

"Again," I said. "Let's go to church again…"

He grabbed my thighs and moved them apart so that I was straddling him.

"Open then," he said. "Let me in."

12 COFFEE

OPEN THEN, LET ME IN.

I put the coffee on and then slipped into the bathroom to brush my teeth and get my hair in order. I could hear him snoring softly from the bedroom, a gentle sound, yet it gave me anxiety. I didn't normally let them spend the night, but he wasn't like the others, was he? No, around the others I'd always felt too dressed, armored. They'd pried and pulled a little, but my armor was custom-made, strong. With David, I felt naked, the softest parts of my flesh exposed and vulnerable. That's why I was in the bathroom straightening myself up when it normally wouldn't matter. Like I could cover one thing up with another, you know?

I reached for the mugs and set them on the counter, my hands shaking. He was a good boy, but he was a boy. Not at all like the men I usually sleep with: hard...detached...sleazy. I heard him stir in the other room and then the rustle of sheets as he got out of bed. I prepared my face, arranged it so that I looked bored. *No big deal, men are whatevs.* It was awful to be this person, so jammed up with bad experiences you couldn't let anyone see your real face. He came up behind me and wrapped his arms up and under my T-shirt so we were skin to skin. I liked it, though under no circumstances would I ever have admitted that. I felt like one of those babies in the preemie ward who needed kangaroo care to bond.

"Hello," I said. "I've made the coffee."

I turned away, busied myself with the sugar and cream. So white. One was smooth and rich, the other was grainy and hard. I liked the way they looked sitting next to each other: the pot of cream and the bowl of sugar.

"I can see that."

He spun me around, the tops of his fingers already skimming the right places on my underwear. I let him back me up until I was pressed against the counter, the coffee pot hissed softly behind me. I decided right then that the sound of coffee brewing was the best soundtrack for sex. His hair was disheveled, his eyes filled with me as he stared on steadfastly. *Be careful, David,* I wanted to say. He was trying to see into me and that was never a good idea. Both of his thumbs looped through the sides of my panties as he worked at tugging them off. They slid down my legs and I closed my eyes against the feeling: soft cotton became so erotic paired with desire. The hissing of the coffee, the finger that found me and pressed in. My knees buckled, just a little and I sucked air through my teeth until I made my own hissing.

"Oh yeah?" he said, looking interested. "Tell me more." He had such full lips, such earnest eyes.

I bit my bottom lip, determined not to make another sound. I wouldn't tell him a damn thing.

"Tell me, Yara," he urged.

I tilted my head up, trying not to pant, calling to the white expanse of the ceiling for help.

"You don't want to give me your voice, but your eyes speak too," he said. I closed them. "Ah. Well, that takes care of that." He switched up his movements: one thumb on the outside, two fingers inside. Everything was moving in a circle.

Rhythm, I thought. *He's a musician.* I felt his free hand move to my chest. Not my breast, but to the general area where my heart was beating out a fast song.

"What about this?" he said. "Can you slow your heart rate too...your breathing?" I did. I took a couple of deep breaths, relaxed. I was climbing, even so, it was uphill, a bit strained.

"All right," he said. Our cheeks were pressed together and I could feel his breath on my ear.

"You forgot about one thing though, Yara." He added speed and pressure to the movement his fingers were making. I wasn't sure if I was supposed to ask him what it was I forgot, and I was afraid of what my voice would sound like if I did.

"You're very, very wet," he said. "Your body will always betray you. It's a tattletale." And then I came so hard there really was no way to keep the sounds inside of my body. I cried out and when I was finished, I slid down to the floor exhausted. David whistled while he poured the coffee. He glanced down once to ask how many sugars I took and I held up two fingers without looking at him. Then he handed me my mug and sat down next to me on the floor.

"This is nice," he said. He sipped his coffee and stared at the wall with me, one leg up, his forearm resting casually across his knee.

"We're just staring at a wall," I said.

"We are," he assured me. "We're staring at a wall, and my fingers smell like you, and just a few hours ago I came really fucking hard inside the most beautiful woman I've ever seen. And now we're doing my favorite thing—

drinking coffee and being reflective…while staring at a wall."

I nodded with a new appreciation for my wall. "It's a nice wall," I said. "Very white."

"Very white," he agreed. "And smooth."

"It wouldn't be as white if I had kids. People with kids always have dingy walls." I don't know what possessed me to say it. Why in that moment I was even thinking of kids, especially since I DID NOT WANT THEM. David seized the moment.

"Whoa, whoa, whoa, I know I'm good in bed, but damn, girl. Already planning out our life together." I stared at him, mortified and he laughed. "Relax, English," he said. "I'll ask you to marry me first. Stages."

I sighed. "You were pretty good," I said. "Pity you were only good for about four minutes before…"

A nightmare: he began to tickle me. Long fingers wiggling between my ribs, crawling up my sides. I fell over onto the wood laughing so hard I couldn't breathe. David straddled me, laying kisses all over my face while his hands continued to find my weak spots. By sheer miracle, neither coffee mug was turned over, and when he was done with me he stood up and pulled me to my feet.

"If we practice every day—twice a day, actually—I think I can add a minute to my time each time." He was joking, but he sounded so hopeful, like fucking me for an extended length of time would bring him true happiness.

He pulled me toward my bedroom then suddenly stopped halfway through the doorway.

"Do you want kids?" he asked.

I shook my head no.

"Hmm." He pondered my face thoughtfully, like he didn't quite believe me. "Why not?"

"I don't want to fuck anyone else up," I told him. It was the truth. Those of us who'd been fucked up thought of those things. Not everyone was an optimist.

"Do you think you'll change your mind?" he asked, and I wondered if this was about to be a deal breaker. Usually men ran when you told them you wanted to have their babies, David was disappointed that I didn't want to have his babies, or anyone else's.

"Don't look at me like that," I said. "I'm not broken because I don't want the same thing as everyone else. And, no, you're not invited to fix me, or soften my heart, or make me want things I never knew I wanted."

He looked at me for a long time, and then he said: "It's human nature to want to fix things. That was my first thought, actually, but you're right. Someone should take you as you are, not have an agenda for how they want to change you."

I breathed.

I liked him a little more. More than I did five minutes ago when we were staring at a wall and drinking our coffee. If this kept up I was going to be in love by nightfall.

"Okay," he said. "What about adoption? That way you're not bringing more souls into the world, you're just helping the ones already here."

I'd thought about adoption before. But, I was only twenty-five. It still seemed like a remote idea.

"An older child," I said. "Maybe eight or nine."

"Wonderful," he said. "I like that. I like that a lot."

"Cool. Now, can we get down to business, or do you want to plan out our retirement next?"

"You're catching on, English." He smiled. "Seeing us as a long-term deal."

I didn't know if I was smiling because he was calling me English, which was utterly ridiculous, or if I was amused by the fact he was planning our life together.

We were on our way to the bed when he looked at me and said, "You're not the same as everyone else. You think I sound crazy, but as soon as I looked at you, I wanted to write a song. That means something."

"It means I'm attractive," I told him. "And you have a dick. You're not the first man to use his dick to store inspiration."

"Shut up," he said. "You talk too much."

WHEN I WAS OUT of the city and in the country, I felt choked, cut off from the vine. There weren't enough heartbeats in the country; you had to be patient, have an ear for the voice of nature. I found that sort of silence too loud, so I squashed my life, compressed it into a dozen tiny studio apartments. I did that over and over, sampling the cities of America, learning their beats and then moving on. New York, and New Orleans, Chicago, and Miami. I wore bikinis and tanned to golden brown, and then I faded to a milky white and covered myself in down coats and scarves—my nose perpetually dressed in a cold. I found reasons not to go home to the city that I loved most. It was almost time, though. I was on my last stop.

Except…David. He was making it difficult to think of leaving. I told myself that I was just having fun, so of course, I didn't want to leave yet. But like all of my relationships, the desire to be with him would soon fade out and then I'd be ready to go home.

David had this grin. His lips would compress in a pucker between two deep smile lines and he'd look at you like he could already see you naked. Sometimes when he was singing, he'd grin like that and girls would lose their shit, holding their hands up to the stage and screaming. I could imagine him in a larger setting, grinning like that to an audience of thousands. It made me feel sick to think about. But, when he smiled at me like that, I imagined having his babies. I never told him that, but I did. Me imagining babies. His grin thwarted my mission. I was a muse, not a wife, not a mother. More than anything I was scared. Perhaps Ann had been right.

I learned that the best time to ask him questions about himself was post-sex while still tangled together and recovering. He'd taught me that trick the first time we'd been together, asking about my boots. Sometimes we took turns asking each other things; sometimes there was just one talker and one listener.

"Why are you a singer? Why do you have a band?" We were camped out in my bed, the clean white sheets tucked around us. Outside the rain fell. As soon as I said those words, he rolled onto his back and started laughing. Then he repeated everything I said in the worst attempt at a British accent I'd ever heard.

"Jackass," I said. "So much for being interested in your life."

"Come on, English." He rubbed his socked feet against mine and stared up at the ceiling. "I'm a singer because I'm a narcissist. Isn't that the way? And I have a band because I can't play all the instruments myself." His eyes were all lit up. He got off on teasing me. I got off on it too.

"No one is that basic," I said. "We all have our shit."

He rubbed a hand across his face and stared up at the ceiling.

"Why do I feel like I just hit a nerve?" I asked. I was suddenly excited. David was hesitant to talk about himself, he preferred to listen. To me, that was the mark of a true artist—someone who gathered instead of took. I propped my head on my hand and ran my fingers up his chest. If I could get him a little bit hard he'd tell me anything I wanted to know.

"What is it? Tell me," I urged.

"I'm average," he said. "Middle child all the way." I wanted to laugh, but I didn't. "—So I had to find something to be good at. To set me apart from my cocksucker older brother and my needy baby sister." I laughed at his description of his siblings. Whenever people spoke about their siblings, there was both love and resentment present.

"So, you…"

"Started playing on my older brother's guitar. Turns out I had a pretty good voice too. But I didn't know that until a girl told me."

"What did she say? Who was she?"

"She was my neighbor. She'd hear me singing in the backyard and one day she told me that I sounded like Mark Lanegan. I didn't know who he was so I looked him up. The biggest compliment came when she asked me to sing at her birthday party. She was three years older than me. Paid me a hundred bucks too. First paid gig."

I imagined long legs, tan, dark brown hair—and I was jealous of her because she heard him sing before I did, recognized Lanegan in his voice.

"Do you think you sound like him?"

"I don't know. I don't think about it."

"But that's what narcissists do," I said. "They think about themselves…"

He laughed, lifting my fingers to his lips and kissing them. He turned to look at me. "Do you think I'm good?"

The vulnerability in his eyes warned me to be careful: soft eyes and thick lashes. He cared about my opinion. How had I become that to him in such a short time? And he was good…but he could be better. Maybe that was cruel of me.

"I think there's always room to be better," I told him.

"What does that mean?"

I rolled away, aware that I'd committed a sin. I needed to learn to keep my mouth shut. The truth wasn't necessary in every situation. *Tact, Yara.*

"You're good. No one can refute that. But, it's almost like you're faking it."

TACT, YARA!

David got out of bed and walked out of the room. I couldn't see his face so I didn't know what he was thinking.

"You don't have to be a bloody baby about it," I called after him.

I got up too, pulled on my clothes in a huff. I heard the stitching rip in my shirt as I yanked it over my head. I was angry he'd taken offense, angry I'd said what I had. What was wrong with me? I blew things up in less than a month. I needed to take a walk, clear my head. I was halfway to the door still trying to wedge the heel of my foot into my shoe when he grabbed me around the waist. He lifted me easily and I didn't struggle when he carried me back to the bed and tossed me down onto my back. It was one of those moments when I realized I could be mature and talk this out instead of leaving town and starting a new life. I had already decided on Santa Fe.

"Just because you hurt my damn feelings doesn't mean I want you to go," he said. "My feelings are my problem, not yours."

I propped a leg on my knee and stared up at the ceiling, not convinced. I could smell him on the sheets.

"How mature," I managed. It was true, but it came out sounding sarcastic. Not many people could do what he'd just done.

"Sometimes I feel like I'm faking too," he said. "It was a hard thing to hear. Like you're in my brain fucking around with my insecurities."

I sat up right away. "Is your family supportive of what you do?"

"Are you kidding? No way. They want me to do something respectable with my life. This has all become as much about proving them wrong as it is about the passion."

"Well, there's your problem then," I said, sighing. "When you try to prove your art you're going to fail every time."

"Yeah?"

"Yeah."

"How do you know that?" he asked.

He wasn't being snarky. It was a genuine question from a genuine man. A naked man. He never seemed to notice that he was naked, not even now as he leaned against the doorframe, half erect.

"I'm not an artist, but I've been with artists." I glanced down at his dick and cleared my throat. "The real ones and the fakes. I've seen them succeed and fail, and the ones who fail always had something to prove. It became about the proof rather than the art. The purity was lost."

He stared at me for a long time. "I get the impression that you think I'm deeper than I actually am. I'm sorry if I gave you that impression."

I laughed. Maybe he was right. The last man I'd slept with read books on philosophy as wide as my face, and took trips to places like India and the Congo to discover himself. He'd bored me to death with his self-exploration, never taking a moment to step outside of his own head and explore what was inside of everyone else's. David was his opposite.

"I'll tone it down," I said. "I'm just so hungry for information."

"Don't change," he said softly. "I sort of like it. I know myself better with you around. I also get more headaches…"

"Because I'm too much all the time?"

"Because you're so beautiful you make my eyes hurt."

That was enough to woo an already lovesick girl. I pulled off my pants, took off my shirt, and climbed back into bed.

"Are we together, Yara?" he asked. "Are we in something?"

"No," I said. "I don't want a relationship. You know that."

"Okay." He nodded.

"Now come here," I said, patting the bed. "You're naked."

14

CREPES

I WOKE UP ONE morning with one of David's songs stuck in my head. It was a song called "Five Dollars," and it made no sense even when he'd tried to explain it to me. After he left my apartment for rehearsal, I made myself coffee and played the song, listening carefully to the message he insisted was there. It was catchy and I couldn't shake it even when I put on a Cat Stevens record and tried to listen to something else. And if his song was in my head it meant that he was in my head.

I got dressed in my sweats, deciding to take a walk down to Pike for breakfast. The fresh air, and crepes, and the hustle of the Market would cleanse my mind of David Lisey. My favorite crepe place was buried under the Market. The locals knew where it was, but the tourists had to stumble across it, and then it was hard to find the next time they tried to go back. My hair was pulled up in a greasy ponytail and the only thing I was wearing on my face was a little Chapstick. Pike Place Market was my favorite thing about Seattle. Its off-kilter shops and weird shop owners reminded me of Camden Town back home. Not in an obvious way—if you held the two together they'd look and smell nothing alike. There was a subversive quality to it, an overthrow of pretentiousness. I passed Rachel the golden pig everyone loved to pose with and turned left. Someone was straddling her back, lifting their arms in the air for a photo. I turned my head at the last minute and pulled a tongue to photobomb them. I was having deep thoughts about tourists when I rounded the corner and spotted David. He was standing right in front of me, the donut shop behind him. At first, I smiled because just a few hours ago he was inside of me. But, then I saw that he wasn't alone and my emotions deflated like a balloon. There was no ducking away, no hiding.

"Oh hi," I said, flustered.

I tried not to look at the girl he was with but there was the fact that I knew her. Nya was clinging to his arm holding a plastic bag in her free hand. *They could have just run into each other,* I thought. *Wait to react.*

"What are you guys doing here?"

The drummer and the bass player from his band were also with them. They all came to an abrupt stop when they saw me.

"We just had breakfast," Nya informed me. "And now we're going for a walk."

"Oh," I said. I couldn't look at him. I looked over his shoulder at the colorful pepper displays hanging from a market stall.

"You remember Ferdinand and Brick," he said, motioning to the two guys flanking them. "They're in the band."

Everything about Ferdinand was large. I had to tilt my neck back to look into his face. He nodded at me, amused. Brick, the most solidly built of the three, had sleepy eyes and dreadlocks wound into a hive on his head. He looked bored despite the building drama.

"Where are you off to?" David said it so softly I almost didn't hear him.

"Breakfast," I said. "Crepe De France."

"That's where we came from," Nya said, matter-of-factly. Was it just me or was her voice aggressive?

You're not allowed to feel anything about this, I told myself. And it was true. No emotional contracts had been drafted. I'd rejected his request for a relationship at least a dozen times. We weren't officially anything, but we liked each other and we liked to fuck. Still, you'd think he'd wait a couple hours before going on his next date. I wondered how long he'd been seeing Nya. And then I felt it, oh yuck…jealousy.

Suddenly I didn't feel like eating.

"So how many girls do you fuck in a day?" I asked. It was casual. I could have been asking about the weather. What's the point in making yourself look like you're not hurt, you know? We spend so much time pretending nothing can touch us that men have actually started to believe it. Both Ferdinand and Brick looked suddenly alert, eyes wide, while David looked steadily at me. I had to give it to him—nothing fazed this fucking wanker. I didn't look at Nya, not even once. She was a terrible server and I was going to fuck up all of her drink orders from now on.

"We aren't sleeping together, Yara," he said gently, fighting back a smile. "But, I can see how it looks that way. We ran into each other and Nya suggested we grab something to eat."

"Oh she did, did she?"

Nya dropped his arm. I wanted to find something to still be mad at, but I was sort of embarrassed.

"Well," I said. "If you intend to fuck someone else you should let me know. Sexual courtesy and all."

His mouth twitched, but he kept a straight face.

"Absolutely," he said. "Though I don't plan on…er…fucking anyone else in the foreseeable future. I like fucking you. You have a really fantastic pussy."

Brick clapped once and then crossed his arms over his chest. My move. I scratched my head.

"Yes, but you know how women are. Always offering and when something is right there, men usually take it."

"Usually?" David placed a hand over his heart. "I am a member of one church. I've not been church shopping. I don't know what type of men you're used to…"

Ferdinand, the bassist, reached out a hand and squeezed David's shoulder while looking at me, his lips pressed together trying to suppress his own laughter.

I cleared my throat, my face burning. Nya had taken a step away from David and was looking around for an escape, her plan to steal my guy thwarted.

"I also…quite as well…enjoy it," I managed to choke out. "The music is decent and—"

"Decent?" Ferdinand said. I ignored him. He wasn't part of this congregation.

"Well, good then." David nodded. "So we're going steady and our relationship seems to be solely based on sex." He sounded quite cheerful about it.

"No," I rushed. "I didn't say that."

"Which part?" he asked. He looked at Ferdinand. "I'm confused, Ferdinand. Are you confused?"

"Yeah, man. You two are perfect for each other. I don't know what the fuck you're talking about. Church and shit."

"I don't even know what we're talking about anymore either," I said to David. And then I added, "I'm not looking for trouble."

"Oh, English. You've found trouble," he said. "I'm glad you're my girlfriend."

English.

"Fine. All right. But you have to take me out to dinner tonight to celebrate. Somewhere fancy and expensive."

"Fine," he mimicked. "But, as my girlfriend, you have to give me a blow job in the car before we go into the restaurant."

"I don't swallow," I said.

"No one's perfect."

I pushed past them, my face stony and determined. What the ever-loving fuck just happened? Also, suddenly I was hungry again.

15
DINNER DATE

DAVID MADE GOOD ON DINNER. And having dinner with David was like having dinner with any other guy. That was a lie. Having dinner with David wasn't at all like anything I'd experienced before. He was…fun—unpretentious. The dip underneath his neck and above his collarbone was smooth and tan. I wanted to touch that spot, lick it. He didn't seem to care if I was having a good time either, because he was having a good time, and he assumed I was lively enough to join him. He broke out into song at random times too, singing things instead of saying them. It could have been annoying but it wasn't. The way his lips moved when he sang was sexy. He wore a plaid sport coat and grey pants that were rolled above his ankles. He opened doors and ordered the calamari. The conversation lagged while we ate and every few minutes he would glance up at me when I wasn't looking. Was he studying my face? Wondering why he came? Perhaps I wasn't what he thought. No. I pushed those feelings away. I was acting like this was the first time we were hanging out. We'd been spending time together for weeks, just not as a couple. I flinched at my own thoughts and David tilted his head to the side.

"What are you thinking about, English? Are you having a freak-out moment?"

"Yes," I said. "Why are you grinning like that?"

"I like that I have the power to cause these freak-out moments."

"Oh, shut up," I said. "You're ridiculous."

But I was grinning too.

"When you play with your wineglass stem like that, Yara, it makes me kind of hard," he said, between bites.

I blushed and pulled back my hand. My London best friend, Posey, used to say I had a habit of running my fingers along phallic looking objects. *"It's like you have a stroking obsession, Yara,"* she'd say, shaking her head.

"I didn't want you to stop," he said. "I just felt like you should know."

I laughed.

"Look," he said after the server came around to fill our water glasses. "This place is boring the fuck out of me. We're too young for this shit. Let's eat fast and get out of here." He leaned forward like he was going to tell me a secret. "And then, tacos later."

"Yes," I nodded. I pushed my halibut around on my plate, thinking about tacos.

We declined dessert and drained the last of our cocktails. When it was time to pay the bill, David was five dollars short and I loaned him the rest. He didn't seem at all embarrassed by it, which made me like him more.

"I'll buy you a restaurant one day to make up for this," he said as we were leaving.

"I'd love that. I've always wanted to own a restaurant."

"Oh, yeah? What kind?" He took my hand and immediately his thumb began running circles across my skin. I was silently thrilled. It felt so good to hold his hand.

"Something soft," I told him.

He tilted his head to the side and made a face. I shrugged.

"Soft?" he repeated. "What does that even mean?"

"Soft lighting, food that melts on your tongue, brick walls, and muted colors. Some place that makes you feel good, you know?"

"Mmmm," he said. "Sounds like you're describing your vagina."

I punched him in the arm and he pulled me close so that he could kiss me on the temple.

"We'll get you that restaurant," he said. "What will we name it?"

"IOU," I joked.

"Oh my God, that's perfect. What vision! What excellent marketing we can do for IOU." He was being loud and enthusiastic, and I found myself getting caught up in it.

We launched into discussions of an ad campaign. By the time we reached my studio, David had composed a jingle for the commercial and we'd decided on some of the top menu items.

"Sing it again," I asked him as I opened the door to my building.

He humored me, and the people lulling around the lobby of my building turned to look at us as we walked toward the elevators.

"They're so hungry right now," I told him. "Look at their faces."

"They won't be after they eat at IOU!" He said this loud enough for them to hear, and I flinched and laughed at the same time. We were good together on a few drinks, our inhibitions set aside. I was stiff the first time he spoke to me, it was a wonder he came back.

"What did you see the first time you came to the bar and saw me?"

"In you?" he asked.

"Yes, in me."

"Well, you're beautiful, Yara. You could be covered in shit, walking down the street mooing like a cow, and people would still think you're beautiful."

"But, they'd also think I'm a nutter."

"That's beside the point. You said nut," he said. "There was just something. I looked and I knew. That's not happened to me before, so I decided to explore it."

By the time we reached my apartment, I felt better about my new boyfriend. Thank God I stopped for that bikini wax after the Market this morning.

David undressed me as soon as we walked through the door of my apartment. We didn't even make it to the bed. We consummated our new relationship with ten wonderful minutes, during which he looked strained. He told me later that he tried to last longer but my body just pulled everything out of him.

"You're like sexual magic," he said.

"It's always like that in the beginning," I told him. "But then something changes."

He was lying on the floor where we'd landed when we fell over naked and kissing. He propped his head up on his elbow and looked at me intently.

"What do you mean?"

I suddenly wished I could take back my words. I slumped down, turning my face to the front door and away from David. I sounded too cynical sometimes, that's what Ann told me, what Posey my London best friend used to tell me.

"Come on," he urged. "I want your thoughts, English."

"All right." I leaned up on my elbows and he reached out to caress my breast. So familiar.

"In the beginning of relationships, things are exciting. The sex is new, and the touches are new. You're addicted to everything about the other person because it's all fresh and untainted. Then monotony kicks in, the fighting about stupid things and the very same thing you found exciting becomes…irritating. Boring."

"I call bullshit," he said. "When you love someone nothing gets old."

I wanted to laugh, but the sincerity in his eyes choked off my humor. Who was I to take this boy's belief? Someone else would take it eventually, and then he'd know, but until then he had to learn the hard way. I lay back down on the hard floor and stared at the ceiling. It was one of those popcorn ceilings that looked like a skin disease. I'd never lain on my back in bed because I didn't want the popcorn skin disease ceiling to be the last thing I saw before I fell asleep.

"Why do you like being a bartender?" he asked.

I blew air out through my pursed lips. How did I explain something like that? I had a degree in hospitality management, and yet I had no desire to leave the bar for a more prestigious role in the restaurant business. I'd been offered all sorts of positions and had turned each one down.

"I like the way the bar sounds," I said. "The tinkling of ice in a glass, the smell of the liquor, the foam the soda gun leaves on top of a drink. It's all soothing. You can come to work and there's a formula for what people need. Not to mention the people. I like to watch them, listen to their lives without being involved in their lives. They're like friends but without the hassle."

David was laughing. He held his naked belly he laughed so hard.

"You have the personality of an artist, you know that?"

"No way," I said, shaking my head. "I don't have an artistic bone in my body."

"Sure you do. You just haven't found it yet." He said it with so much conviction I started to consider all the hidden talents I might have.

"One day you'll wake up and want to make something. Mark my words. Maybe it'll be a painting, or maybe it'll be a baby with me." He shrugged. I punched his arm and he rolled on top of me, my shoulder blades digging into the wood floor. "I know what we could make right now," he said, kissing my chin. I lifted my head so he had access to my neck.

"We could make—"

I shoved a hand over his mouth so he couldn't say the words. "Don't," I warned him. "We are not a cheesy eighties movie."

He started to sing "I'll Make Love to You" by Boyz II Men while I cringed and tried to roll out from underneath him, but in the end, he kissed me so well I lost the will to escape.

16

TYPES

DAVID LIVED IN A one-bedroom condo called Hillclimb Court, so close to Pike Place Market you could feel its pulse through the walls. It was the type of building architects in the eighties thought was cutting edge. It reminded me of an office space or a parking garage; all steel and concrete with a private courtyard to shield residents from the tourists that perused the street outside. To add some much needed creative flair, they threw in a wall of glass tile. *Ooh la la!* The residents made an effort to warm the place up with plants and that went a long way. It had a parking garage/greenhouse vibe. David's unit faced the Puget Sound where you could see the Olympic Mountains spread out in front of you like nature's buffet.

I was expecting something small and dingy, perhaps a place where he had roommates and a stained brown sofa with cigarette burns. But, it was none of that. It was industrial. I imagined the light was beautiful when it came in through the large west-facing windows. Brick walls, concrete floors, Edison lights that hung above the kitchen glowing yellow. He had copper pots and pans, and he drank water out of mason jars, which I wasn't surprised about. There was art hung tastefully on the walls, oil paintings of female nudes. And his one piece of furniture was an oily looking leather sectional that faced the television. I was especially impressed when I searched for a video game console and found none. David flicked a switch and a fire jumped to life below the television. He made us espresso while I looked around and we sat near the fire to drink it.

"You're wondering why I drive such a shit car and have such a nice place," he said.

"Yeah, I suppose I am." I set my espresso cup on the floor next to me.

"It's my aunt's place. She rents it to me."

"Oh," I said. "Where does she live?"

"Out on Bainbridge. She bought this twenty years ago when she worked in the city. She's attached, I guess, doesn't want to sell it, so she lets me stay."

"Lucky you," I said.

A slow lazy smile spread across his face, and he pulled me toward him. I liked the way he smelled, and I liked that he was wearing pink boxer briefs under his black clothes. And I liked the way he'd looked at me tonight while he was onstage. I tried to make as many of their shows as I could, especially if I wasn't working.

I once had a musician friend tell me that the hours coming down from a show were the loneliest he'd ever felt. *"You go from a hundred miles an hour to ten. One minute everyone is screaming for more, the next you're at home in your boxers folding laundry and making yourself toast."* I wanted to ask David if he ever felt that way, but he wasn't the depressive, melancholy type. Even now he was cleaning up our coffee mess with a small smile on his lips. I suddenly had a hankering for toast and beans, and I was about to ask him if he had any when he walked out of the kitchen.

"Take off your pants and lie on your back. I want to taste you."

My eyes glazed over, toast dreams forsaken. I didn't need those extra calories anyway.

My favorite thing about David's condo was the taproom connected to his building. It was one of those trendy joints that has a mini-pretzel warmer and five gazillion types of beer. Hipster Christians had Bible studies at the tables downstairs, and there was always at least four men wearing slouchy beanies and plaid. On rainy nights we'd walk over and sit under the strings of Edison lights, drinking pint after pint until they shut the place down. We made a lot of noise when Ferdinand and Brick joined us— sometimes they brought girls who reeked of fruit perfume and cleavage and said *fuck* a lot—that always made the Bible study guys pack up early and leave. When we were sufficiently drunk, we'd stumble the ten paces back to his building and make grilled cheese with the nasty cheese slices that come in plastic sleeves. I bought a nice hunk of fancy cheese from Beecher's in the Market, but it molded in his fridge and eventually I threw it out.

I learned that Americans have nostalgia for taste buds. This was proven to me when I lived in Miami. A girl I bartended with who was originally from Ohio suggested a road trip to Georgia. She was craving White Castle, she told me, and was willing to take a three-day road trip to eat it. I'd expected magic, maybe In-N-Out on crack, but after my first bite I'd put my sandwich down and asked her if we'd really driven to Georgia for hamburgers or if there was something else going on.

"*Yara,*" she'd said. "*In America, we feed our obsessions. We don't care if they're not practical.*" She'd then eaten my sandwich and three of her own then ordered a dozen to go, which she put in a cooler in the trunk of her Prius. "*They're not as good heated up, but beggars can't be choosers.*"

I'd gone home wondering if we'd made some sort of drug run I was unaware of. I mean, who drove up the Florida Panhandle and went to another state just for hamburgers that tasted like dirty feet? When I got home, I'd searched the internet and found that people were quite passionate about dirty feet burgers. It was a thing. Also, if you put cheese on anything, they'd eat it: coated, stuffed, sprinkled, saturated—you name it. Cheese sells as well as sex.

We frequented JarrBar across the street too. It was a closet more than it was a bar, barely large enough to host a dozen well-fed people, but it reminded me of the intimate neighborhood bars in England. Sometimes we went after I got off of work. We shared a bottle of Lobo and ate anchovies until our tongues were raw from the salt.

"Am I your type?" I asked him one night as we were walking back to his place. He looked at me like I had just said the craziest thing.

"Of course you're my type, baby." His voice was raspy and the wind caught it and carried it away.

"Who did you date before me?" I asked.

I expected him to laugh it off, say something to deflect, but instead, he gave me his memories.

"My last girlfriend was Italian." He pronounced it Eye-talian to be funny. "She was jealous. If I even looked at a bank teller when thanking her for my most recent transaction, she'd not talk to me for a week. I was scared of making eye contact with any woman over the age of eighteen and under the age of fifty."

I laughed even though I knew he was sort of being serious.

"You're not talking about Elizabeth, are you?" I asked, remembering the poor girl he'd broken things off with around the time he met me. We passed a couple of drunk guys on the sidewalk, and David quickly crossed from my left side to my right, placing himself between me and them.

"English, I've told you that Elizabeth and I were not a couple." He pretended to be upset, but it was a farce. We argued about Elizabeth all the time. He insisted they'd never been a couple and I insisted they had.

"My last real girlfriend cheated on me," he said. "That's why we broke up." He grimaced. "She was cheating the whole fucking time we were together. That's the reason she was always accusing me of something— because she was so damn guilty, you know?"

"What did she look like?"

He made a face at me. "Ah, I see where you're going with this." He reached out to tickle me, but we were crossing the street and I danced away from him.

"She had dark hair, dark eyes. Curvy."

"What about the girl before her, what did she look like?"

He grinned. "She was a redhead. I went through a redhead stage in college."

"Thin or curvy?" I asked.

"Thin. Tall."

We reached the door to his building and he pulled out his key.

"What were you saying about your type?" I laughed.

"I don't have a physical type." He shrugged. "Is that what you were looking for?"

"Yes, as a matter of fact I was."

"I like smart women, English. Cultured women. Funny women. Kind women. I like that type in every color and size."

I liked that.

"When was the last time you had a blonde?" I asked. We were up the stairs and almost to his door.

"Last night when I had you."

"That's not what I mean, Lisey."

"You're my first blonde," he admitted.

"So you're going through a blonde stage," I joked.

"No," he said. "No more stages. I found what I'm looking for."

And then I was stunned into silence, playing his words over and over in my head.

"This is the most beautiful my life has ever been," David said. "This is what I want."

I wondered about that when I was away from him. David had barely left the Pacific Northwest. I'd traveled all over the United States and a little bit of Europe—yet I never felt like I'd arrived at a significant moment. I chased that moment so hard I could barely stay still in one place for more than six months, yet he could eat anchovies, his teeth stained with wine, and tell me it was the most beautiful his life has ever been. It was innocent and simple, and all the things I wanted to be. That's when I realized that David was who I wanted to be. Someone who hadn't necessarily mastered his art, or his life, but was goddamn trying with everything in him. There was this creeping feeling that sneaked up on me, mostly when I was alone, it made my throat close up like I was eating too many crackers without anything to drink. He was too much and I was too little.

17

BEANIE GIRL

I LEARNED THAT DAVID cared about everyone. The homeless man on the corner of Union and 2nd that he bought sandwiches for, the crying forty-something woman walking out of the sushi restaurant that almost bumped into us, the girl with the piercings who sold hand-knitted beanies at the Market. He wanted to discuss their plights in detail.

"You don't just end up on the street. He had a mother, a family. Someone loved him, so what happened?"

I thought him naive. He could have been a foster kid. He could have had a disinterested mother like me.

About the beanie girl, he said, "She has the saddest eyes I've ever seen…"

Beanie Girl, she was the one that bothered me most. I couldn't quite put my finger on why. We had to pass her to reach the sausage shop we liked, and once David bought two beanies from her just to see if she would smile. Pink and a mottled grey. He took the pink one and gave the grey to me, though I stuffed it in a drawer as soon as I got home.

"Do you think she knits beanies because she's sad, or that she's sad because she has to knit beanies?" he asked. He always looked really stressed out when he spoke about her. I was rather annoyed by it.

"Well, first of all, you need to stop staring. It's making her quite uncomfortable. And why does she have to be anything? She makes beanies, end of story."

"She's sad. Have you looked in her eyes?"

I gave him a look. "Have I stared in Beanie Girl's eyes? No, David, I have not." That wasn't exactly true. She had very, very blue eyes—startlingly so. She wore a kohl eyeliner around them which made them pop out even more. *Look at us!* they said. *We're so vulnerable!*

"Well, that's where she keeps it all." He made circles with his fingers and lifted them to his eyes like they were binoculars. "Everyone has a story." He took my hand and squeezed it as we walked.

"So I've heard," I replied tartly.

The last thing I wanted was David sniffing around some pierced, blue-eyed Olivia Newton-John lookalike. One with sad eyes at that. Men had a thing for female vulnerability. They wanted to be their hero.

It was a Sunday morning, the boys were playing a gig two hours away in Bremerton, and I had all day to be alone. That was one of the things you forgot to miss when you were in a relationship, how good it felt to be uncoupled for a time, to enjoy your own company. I chose a book from my shelf, one that I'd been promising David I'd read, and carried it to a little Asian tea bar that sat under the Market. Colorful stools made their way around a low circular bar. Today most of the stools were filled. I spotted an empty seat and made my way over. I didn't recognize her right away—her hair was hidden underneath a bright yellow bandana. She glanced up at me as I shrugged out of my jacket and I startled for a moment when I recognized her face. I slid into the stool and cleared my throat wondering if I should say something. No. That was weird. I ordered my tea and pulled my book from my bag. I'd read a few chapters and then we could talk about them tomorrow when he got back. It was then that Beanie Girl looked over and asked if my book was any good.

"I just started actually. My boyfriend has been hassling me to read it, so I thought I'd give it a go."

"It sounds…hostile," she said, staring at the cover.

"I suppose it is a bit, yes," I said. And then I added, "He likes violent art. I think he's drawn to it because he doesn't know how to make it." I was surprised that I said something so honest to a complete stranger. I thought about how mortified David would be if he knew that's what I thought about him and I felt ashamed.

She smiled. It was a sort of faraway smile that didn't reach her eyes. David was right. Nothing reached her eyes.

"Hey," I said. "You have a stand in the Market, yeah?"

She looked up sharply and studied me like she was trying to place my face.

"Something like that."

I figured she'd closed the conversation, shut me down, but then her face lit up in recognition.

"You're with that musician. You come to the Market every Thursday!"

I shrank a little in my seat. What I said was even worse now that she knew who he was.

"I'm good with faces," she shrugged. "I saw him perform once at The Crocodile."

Ah, the good ol' Crocodile. I smiled and changed the subject. What else was there to do once you've made an arse of yourself?

"You off today?"

She nodded. "A friend's covering for me. Broke up with my boyfriend and couldn't stand the thought of sitting there all day. So, I'm sitting here."

"Bad guy?" I asked.

I was already thinking about calling David to tell him he was right. That would probably make him more sympathetic to her though, and I finally realized why I'd never liked the looks of her. *Oh my God, you're jealous!* I told myself. That wasn't part of what I did. It was something new for me and it made me uncomfortable.

"Yeah, you could say that. We've been on and off for a few years," she said.

"What does it take to find a good guy who's not a total pussy, you know?"

She looked at me suddenly and smiled. "But, you have one, don't you?"

I finished off the rest of my tea and stood up. "It was nice chatting with you—"

"Petra," she offered.

"Right. Lovely meeting you then, Petra." I saw she was about to ask my name and I wanted to get the hell out of there before I had to tell her.

And then I slung on my coat and hurried from the shop like I had somewhere important to be other than with my insecurities. I didn't tell David about my run-in with Petra aka Beanie Girl, and the next time we were at the Market, I insisted on walking a different way to our lunch spot. How did she know we were there every Thursday anyway? What a creep. The kind that looked blonde, and edgy, and slightly innocent, but would fuck you in every position known to man.

"How many girls flirt with you on any given day?" I asked him one day as we were walking to meet the guys for dinner.

David rumbled with laughter.

"What? That's a legitimate question. You're a musician. You're supposed to philander."

He raised an eyebrow then announced, "You're jealous!" with extreme excitement. "That's my new favorite thing about you, English."

"No! David, no. I'm most certainly not jealous," I lied. "It's just a question."

He rubbed a hand across his face as he thought. "I don't know how to answer that. I'm around women all the time. They're mostly friendly—chatty even—but what's the line between being a friendly person and flirting?"

"Do they inspire you?"

"Pussy is very inspiring, Yara." He laughed.

I punched him in the arm and that made him laugh harder.

He was so naive. He grabbed me by the waist before I could say anything else and spun me around to face him. We were in the middle of the sidewalk, our arms wrapped around each other—mine more hesitantly. A man in a bowler hat played a movable organ a few feet away.

"What does it matter? You're the only one I want."

"Pussy is pussy," I said. "When women offer, men take."

"Not true," he said, frowning. And then—"Ah, well I've felt yours and there's no going back."

I smiled grimly, his words not offering me comfort. And why did I need comfort? David and I had a deal. I was here to inspire him, not fall for him.

"It's not you I'm worried about," I told him, somberly. "It's all the slags who want to shag you."

"Slags who want to shag me," he repeated, his eyes glowing.

"Yes, David. You're a musician. When you hold your guitar, women treat it like you're holding your dick."

He held his stomach as he laughed.

"Why would I want anyone else? That cute accent and ass," he said.

"There are plenty of cute accents and asses where I come from," I told him.

"Oh shit, well let's never go there then," he said.

I shook my head at him.

"I want you, English. I think about you all the time—no—scratch that. I obsess over you all the time. You're my muse. Wasn't that the deal? You're worth every penny."

I didn't know what to say to that. I liked it. I liked it so much I stopped to make out with him right there on the sidewalk.

"Dumb," I said. "Ridiculous." But I meant to flatter him with those words.

"Why you gotta be that way, English?" he said, reaching down to cup my backside. "When we have babies can they talk like you?"

I smacked his hand away. He was so good at this.

18

PETRA

PETRA AKA BEANIE GIRL did not evaporate from our lives like I willed her to. On a Friday night in August, she came to The Crocodile in fishnets, a rose gold miniskirt, and a black wife-beater. She'd dyed her hair silver like those uber posh too-cool-for-school Suicide Girls, and in her sweaterless state I could see the ink all over her arms. Her whole look screamed—*I don't give a fuck because I'm a sex kitten.* And I really resented that. Some of us were not sex kittens. Some of us wore proper pants and didn't scribble on our skin, and we didn't exactly know where our place was in life, but we actively tried to find it. Girls like Petra undermined the process. They made us feel dumpy and plain. They perhaps made our boyfriend think we're dumpy and plain. Who knows? I didn't want David to see her, but that was like asking for a rainbow to not be seen.

Throughout the night she carried around a bottle of organic beer. She watched out for herself even when getting drunk. Honestly, I wanted to puke at the sight of her. It didn't feel right—her being here when David was playing. What exactly was she playing at? The band came on around ten after the opening act, and maybe it was my imagination, but I felt like she crept closer to the stage. She'd been dancing for the last hour with a careless abandon I didn't possess, like it was just her in the room. David probably wouldn't recognize her, she had different hair, and she wasn't wearing a beanie. He'd be in the zone, ready to perform and probably high. He'd be looking for me in the crowd, not her. I was blowing things out of proportion. Plus, the more the merrier, right? We wanted to fill their shows, pack the house, get likes on the Facebook and Instagram pages. I found a spot in the back where I could watch everyone watch David and clutched my warm beer in my hand. I felt too sick to drink it. My favorite thing about coming to their shows was the effect they had on people. It was addicting to watch. *He's mine!* I wanted to scream.

They were halfway through a song called "Babylon" when he recognized her. It was subtle. I'd only known him a few months myself, but I'd seen his eyes light up when he found me in a crowd. So when his eyes lingered on her a second longer than normal, and I imagined they made eye contact even though I couldn't really be sure, I got chills all the way down to my toes.

Petra was there to steal my man. I threw my warm beer away and sulked along the back wall, listening to songs I'd heard a dozen times before.

After the show, I beelined over to where David was standing surrounded by people. *What people?* I thought, straining my neck to see. The room was still packed and I had to push my way past the crowd of drinkers to reach where he had hopped down from the stage. The soles of my shoes stuck to the floor where drinks had been splashed. When I was just a few feet away, I saw the backside of Petra's silver hair as she stood in front of

David. She was nodding vigorously, as vigorously as her little neck would allow her.

"Absolutely," I heard her say. "That's the thing about art, isn't it?"

I wanted to snort, I wanted to reach out and yank her fairy hair until she screamed from the pain. *Stop talking to my boyfriend about art, you cunt.*

David spotted me and everything changed. First he smiled, a deep smile that reached his eyes. Then he excused himself from the group that was gathered around him and pushed toward me.

"Hi, English." He grabbed my face and planted a good one on me. I hoped that Petra was watching.

"Hi back," I said. He smelled like sweat and adrenaline. I wrapped my arms around his torso and hugged him. The whole band was on fire tonight.

"That was fantastic," I said. We stayed like that for a good thirty seconds with all of the disgusting liquor-soaked bodies bumping into us.

"There was an agent here," he said. "On vacation with his wife. They happened to wander into this shit-hole and heard us play. He wants us to fly out to LA to meet some people."

"Oh yeah?" I said. I searched the crowd for a couple with an LA vibe, but all I could see were sweaty, liquor-bloated faces.

"We're going out for a drink to celebrate." He motioned for the guys who'd finished packing up the equipment and were looking around for him. I felt so relieved. That's why he was practically glowing, not because of Petra. I pictured a record deal and how many more Petras there would be.

"I'll wait for you outside," I said.

I was desperate for fresh air—all the people, all the things, smelled. He nodded and turned back to help load up Ferdinand's truck while I headed toward the doors. I hadn't caught sight of Petra since I walked up on them, and when David came toward me, she had disappeared from my mind altogether. He was so reassuring in the way he touched, and kissed, and doted on me. I felt silly for being worried about Beanie Girl. I didn't want to think about her name anymore. That made her presence in our lives too personal. She was just Beanie Girl, the silver-haired slut from the Market who looked at my boyfriend with bedroom eyes. I almost felt foolish about the whole thing when the doors to The Crocodile opened and David walked out with Petra at his side. They were smiling—no—laughing about something, and for a second I thought he was going to take her arm and walk right past me.

I turned away so neither of them could see the look on my face. Ferdinand's truck came bouncing around the corner and I headed toward it in a hurry. I didn't know if David was driving, but right then all I wanted was to be tucked away in Ferdinand's beater so no one could see my face. He called my name, but I pretended I couldn't hear him as I ran for the truck. Ferdinand saw my face and opened the door for me without a word. I saw him look over his shoulder at Petra and David and he shrugged. David looked confused, but then Petra said something and they walked to where his car was parked on the street. *Great!* So now they're riding together. That was probably the dumbest thing I could have done. Ferdinand looked at me in the rearview mirror. All I could see were his eyes.

"What? Have you never seen a jealous girlfriend before?"

"Didn't you know that David only dates jealous women?"

"Shut up," I said. And then—"Are you pulling my leg?"

He made a sharp turn and my head smacked into the window. I rubbed it as he opened a bag of beef jerky and offered me some across the backseat.

"You could have sat in the front you know."

"I know," I said, taking a piece.

"It's his pattern," Ferdinand said. "We all have patterns. David likes batshit crazy girls." He glanced at me in the rearview again. "No offense."

"None taken."

"I think he gets off on someone wanting him that bad. He's the middle child."

I'd never bought into the whole birth order business, sounded like a load of bloody excuses to me, but I leaned forward to hear what Ferdinand had to say.

"I'm not jealous," I told him.

He laughed, his large shoulders bouncing up and down.

"And I'm not stupid."

I sniffed sulkily and stared out the window. "I'm not. Girls just throw themselves at him. It's disgusting."

"Look," he said. "You're only what? Twenty-four? Twenty-five?"

"Twenty-five," I said.

"Yeah, so you have plenty of time."

I didn't know what he meant by that. Plenty of time for what? To figure myself out? To learn how to not be jealous?

"If it makes any difference, he likes you more than he's ever liked another lady."

I grinned at Ferdinand because I really liked hearing that. And no one had ever called me a lady.

When we got to the bar, a place called The Boheme, David's car was already there, parked along the curb. They'd had enough time to go inside and find seats. Ferdinand helped me out of the truck and we walked together toward the door.

"What is this place?" I asked.

"The Boheme," he said like I couldn't read the sign myself. "I come here when I eat shrooms, the place is a trip."

The Boheme was indeed a trip. The minute we walked through the doors I felt like I'd stepped into a Lewis

Carroll novel. Every color, every texture, every pattern was thrown onto the walls. There were simple wooden booths in the bar and some high tops where people sat and drank out of colorful glasses. David waved to us from the back of the bar where he'd secured a large round booth. Petra was sitting toward the back and center with the girl I'd seen her come into the club with. She looked like a pierced, pink-haired Doris Day. I ignored both of them and gave David a tight-lipped smile when he walked up to me.

"Where'd you go?" he asked. Then he poked Ferdinand in the chest and pretended to be angry. "She's mine," he said.

Ferdinand shot me a look. "Are the other two yours as well?"

I covered my mouth to hide my smile. In two seconds Ferdinand had become my new best friend and favorite person on the planet.

David flushed. "I forgot to introduce you, Yara." He turned his back on the girls and mouthed. *"That's the beanie girl from the Market."*

I tried to look amused.

"The other one's her best friend, I think," David said under his breath. I looked at Ferdinand, who raised his eyebrows and shrugged.

"But why are they here?"

"Petra is an artist," he said. "She used to be in a band. I thought it would be nice for her to be around other artists." He leaned toward me. "She just went through a bad breakup."

I wanted to tell him that I knew, but instead, I chose to not be predictable. Ferdinand thought I was another one of David's jealous girlfriends and I wasn't.

"Okay," I said, walking toward the booth with a smile.

"Hi, Petra," I said it loud enough for everyone to hear.

Ferdinand the unbeliever laughed behind me as I scooted into the booth determined to not be that girl. The

same girl as the ones he'd had before. My new resolve
lasted approximately ten minutes.

19
DRINKS AND DOUBT

PETRA WAS ONE OF those girls who didn't even know she was flirting with your boyfriend while she was flirting with your boyfriend. It was sort of delicious to watch her if you weren't on the shit end of it all. She was mostly composed of sex and casual advances. When she took a sip of her beer, for instance, she licked her lips like the gods' own ambrosia had dripped on them. And when she had to think about something she bit her goddamn bottom lip and eye-fucked the air in front of her. This was her norm. I imagined she grew up with a slut for a mother and a completely absent father, and this was the only way she knew how to talk to men. I was wedged in-between her and David, but sometimes they talked around me because artists had so much in common. When she spoke, her pillow lips moved sensually and in rhythm with her doe-eyed blinking.

Ferdinand, who was sitting across from me and next to her friend, Beatriz, was watching her with just as much rapt attention as I was. It was hard not to, honestly. If I were a guy I would have had a boner. Brick arrived ten minutes after us with twin sisters in tow. And then the LA couple arrived, their LA-ness shining off of them so hard I wished I'd brought my sunglasses. The wife was wearing neon pink pants. Everything else was monogrammed in Louis Vuitton. The big shot music guy was wearing tan chinos and had a lot of chest hair peeking through his white button-down. Not the nice kind that David had, the unruly kind that needed a trim and a good conditioner. We all crowded into a booth and the big shot ordered drinks all around. I rubbed David's dick under the table to distract him from Petra, while the guy's wife talked about their recent vacation to Italy. None of us had been to Italy so we all nodded and sipped, nodded and sipped. Finally the boys started talking shop and Petra and I took each other in.

"So, how long have you and David been together?" she asked.

I translated her question to: how easy would it be for me to steal your boyfriend?

"Two years," I said.

"That's a long time."

"It feels more like two months." I nodded. "But that's how it is when you have a good thing, yeah?"

She looked away and took a sip of her drink. "I wouldn't know."

Oh yeah. A breakup. I remembered the day in the tea shop when she spilled her guts to a British stranger.

"How have you been doing with that?"

She shrugged.

"Do you and David live together?"

"Practically," I said. "Though we keep our separate places."

She tilted her head to the side. "Funny, two years together and you still haven't moved in."

"People don't need to live together to be together," I said. "We like our space."

She smiled. It was a condescending smile, not sweet or friendly. I spoke girl like a fucking boss, you know?

"When I'm in love I can't stand to be apart from the person. He's like a drug. Pure addiction." She looked up at the ceiling like she was having an orgasm and lightly touched her neck. I wondered what it was like to be that kind of addicted to a human being. I looked over at David who was watching Petra with a glazed look in his eyes. I removed my hand from his crotch, annoyed.

David gave me a disappointed look and turned back to Mr. LA.

"It must be a whole thing to date a musician," she said, softly. "Being on the other end of all that passion and creativity. Being someone's muse."

My eyes needed to roll, they asked to roll, but I kept them focused on Petra. *Steady, girls.* I wanted to tell her that I'd evaluated her and knew what ran through her psychological veins.

You want to be someone's what-if, I told her in my mind. Be beautiful enough and important enough to inspire someone who had actual talent. It was more of a glamorous job than being the artist.

"I see him as David," I told her. "The artist is part of the person, not the total sum of them."

Petra looked perplexed. "You must not be an artist." She smiled faintly.

She was playing games with me, trying to make me think I wasn't right for him. I was heated, fidgety in my anger. The LA couple was sliding out of the booth, bidding us farewell. I moved my sharp response away from her and said a mechanical goodbye. Petra's words were ringing in my ears. I wasn't the angry type. It took a bit to rile me up—get under my skin— but her flippant insinuation that I don't understand him pricked a rather large nerve. David put his arm around my waist, but I was stiff and uncomfortable as I watched the LA couple walk

111

toward the doors. I was so distracted I hadn't even learned their names.

"Do you want to stay for another drink or go to my place so I can fuck you?" he asked, quietly.

I looked over my shoulder, at Petra. She was staring at us, and I was sure she'd heard him. I decided to make the most of it.

"Let's go fuck," I said and then kissed his neck.

I could see the goose bumps erupt across his skin. We said goodbye and slid from our places at the table. When we walked out his arm was still firmly positioned around me.

When we got to his place I settled myself on the sofa while he went to the kitchen. When he came back he was carrying a bottle of champagne and two glasses.

"What are we celebrating?" I asked.

"Our two-year anniversary."

I felt myself flush with embarrassment. "Oh, you heard that, did you?"

"Well, I was sitting right next to you."

"Supposed to be talking to your fancy LA producers, not eavesdropping!" I laughed.

He set the champagne and glasses on the floor and sat down next to me.

"She was showing a little too much interest in you. I needed to set her straight."

"With a lie?" He was smiling which sort of lightened the situation, but I was still annoyed at being called out.

"I figured she might avert her eyes if she knew we were two years deep," I said, plucking on a string that was hanging from my shirt.

David pulled me onto his lap so that I was straddling him.

"What did you say about deep?"

His voice was gruff, it made me soft and pliable. I pressed my forehead against his and moved my hips so that I was grinding against him. David moaned into my neck and grabbed my waist to help.

"You aren't attracted to her, are you?" I asked.

"Who, Yara? Why are you asking me this right now?"

I stopped moving and his eyes snapped open.

"Petra," I said. "The Suicide Girl."

He groaned. "I'm attracted to you."

I moved a little and he perked up like he was in the clear.

"And who else?"

He stood up, lifting me with him and started walking toward the bedroom. "I have it bad for Courtney Love…"

I pushed away from his chest and tried to wriggle out of his arms.

"That's bloody foul," I said.

"Just kidding, English! Seriously. You're the one who brought up Suicide Girls."

I decided to let it go. For now, because he was laying me down on the bed and kissing my thighs.

20
HAPPY BIRTHDAY, PETRA

THE NEXT TIME I saw Petra it was in my territory—the hollow ting of freshly washed glasses, the smell of orange rinds, and the chatter of people who were momentarily happy, their real miseries forgotten in the company of friends and food. A good place, a safe place. I was bartending on a Friday night, lifting warm glasses from their drying racks and shelving them. I didn't usually work Fridays, but the guys were playing a show in Bainbridge and I'd picked up the extra shift to stay busy.

I'd moved into David's condo the month before, as he'd appealed to my finances, saying it was a smart move to live with him and save money. I thought that was a smart move on his part. Petra came in with a group of friends, each of them carrying a brightly wrapped parcel in their hands. A birthday party, but for whom? They sat in the dining room in earshot of the bar. I strained my ears to hear them. And speak they did. Petra's tongue was loose and liberated by the strong drinks I was making.

It was her birthday and she was talking about David. I could make out the excitement in her voice even over the din of the Friday night crowd.

"You just…you have to see him to know how talented he is."

"I guess we'll see tonight," a male voice said. I could hear the mocking in his voice.

"Petra's boyfriend," someone else laughed. "She wishes," someone else called out. I heard them all laugh, including Petra who didn't deny it.

I winced, walked to the opposite side of the bar so I couldn't hear any more of it. I'd not been in this position before where a woman was actively pursuing the man I was seeing. Her worship of him made me feel untethered. I didn't know how to react or respond. David would blow it off if I told him. Men did that, treated female fawning like it wasn't a thing, like a woman couldn't lure them away with cunning and pussy. They could. I'd done it myself a time or two.

Since Petra had arrived in David's life I'd taken to buying lingerie. I'd never felt the need to prop up my tits, decorate my ass with lace and ribbons until a much prettier, much more self-assured woman came along. And now the frilly garments were a spreading disease in David's condo, filling drawers and hanging on doors, littering the bedroom floor in blacks, pale pinks, and deep oxblood. Every time I put one on, I felt cheapened. David didn't pay much attention to any of it. He liked what was underneath the lace and silk. He'd push them aside, pull them off without looking. He wanted the warm soft skin, and yet I kept buying them, a shield against other women. I was sexy, I was kinky, I was the type of girl who got trussed up to have sex. It became so bad that on my birthday David handed me a box. Inside was a lilac nightie cocooned in floral tissue paper. I wanted to cry when I saw it. Another nightie, another stupid, uncomfortable nightie.

"Do you like it?" David asked. "I know you like that sort of thing…"

That sort of thing. He thought the nighties were about me. Love for him thrived inside of me, his willingness to buy ridiculous getups because he thought I enjoyed them. I held it close to my chest, nodding.

Petra's friends all knew about her infatuation with David. They were going to his show after dinner, the show I was missing because I had chosen to work. I pulled off my apron and set it on the counter, then I went to find my manager. I'd feign illness, I'd tell him I'd been wanting to vomit all night and that if he didn't let me go I'd…

He let me leave. I was out of there before Petra and her friends had finished their dinners and watched her unwrap her presents. It was wrong what I was doing. But, I needed to see for myself. I thought about wearing a costume, something to hide my face—a wig perhaps, but it seemed so contrived and silly. So, I went as myself and waited near the bar which was as far away from the stage as you could get.

They arrived after me, pierced and tattooed, roots in need of dyeing. Petra moved toward the stage while her friends went to the bar to get drinks. Birthday princess. I watched them order a round of shots and carry the little cups to their boyfriend-stealing queen. What had been in those brightly colored packages? Lingerie…? Lipstick…?

David set down his guitar and pulled the mic stand up to a stool. One leg propped on a rung of the stool, he spoke while lowering the mic, telling jokes to make the audience laugh. I smiled despite myself. He was good, he was getting better every day.

"We have someone special in the crowd today," he said.

I was roped, looking around like everyone else. Would we know the someone special if we saw them? He'd not said anything to me about there being a special guest watching the show tonight. Someone opened a door nearby and fresh air rushed in, light fingers over my heated skin. I closed my eyes for a minute wishing I'd not come, feeling foolish about my paranoia. It was me David loved, me David came home to every night. There would always be women who'd lock their affections on him.

Musicians were the gods that gave melody to pain, summed it up in rhyme and rhythm. It was easy to feel connected to the person who strummed, or keyed, or sang recognition into your existence. And it was easier to believe they wrote songs just for you. *This is mine, they're singing about what's mine.* How much more extreme did this feeling become when the person singing your pain looked like David Lisey?

I opened my eyes trying to guess which song was next, what he'd play for the special guest he forgot to tell me about. When he sat on the stool something intimate would be played. His only instrument would be his voice and sometimes his guitar. But his guitar sat neatly beside him as he spoke into the mic, searching the audience with his eyes.

"Someone special," he said. And then my flesh crawled, my head spun.

"Where are you, Petra? Happy Birthday. Let's all sing 'Happy Birthday' to my friend, Petra."

The crowd erupted in a badly timed, badly chorused version of the birthday song while Petra rocked happily in front of the stage, staring up at David adoringly. Her friends wrapped their arms around her shoulders, taking videos on their phones. I moved toward the door, my head bowed, my heart hammering. When I was free of the club I took deep gulping breaths of air, but I couldn't get enough; my lungs felt small and shallow. I walked to the corner of the street, then turned around and went back to the club. I'd stepped in a big wad of gum and my shoes stuck to the sidewalk leaving webby trails of pink. I'd go backstage, wait for the show to be over, and confront David.

How had he known it was her birthday, or that she was coming? Did they text each other? Did he see her in the day while I was at work? Did she come over to the condo? I turned around at the last moment, requesting an Uber. In two minutes I was tucking my legs into the tight space behind the driver's seat, asking to be taken to the ferry. I was a passive aggressive coward. That sort of thing clung to your flesh like a smell, rot turned inside out. People could sense it on you; it caused them to be distrustful. It was hard to make friends when you had the smell, hard to keep them when you did make them. You held back from them and they held back from you, an even trade of nothingness. It was a wonder David ever got past it, but now he was there, in the middle, unaffected.

The condo was dark when I got back. Usually David left the light on in the kitchen when we weren't home. He said it was depressing to come back to a dark house. But, this time he'd turned it off before he left. I wondered if it was an omen. I changed out of the jeans and shirt I was wearing and back into my uniform. David texted me an hour later and said he was on his way home. He never stayed out with the guys anymore, who went for drinks after. He came home to me, tired and sweaty, smiling so big I couldn't help smiling myself.

When he walked in the door, I was counting my tips in the kitchen. I hadn't turned on the light, I wanted to see what he'd say.

"Why is it so dark in here?" he said.

"You forgot to leave the light on."

My voice sounded accusing but it wasn't because of the light, it was because of Petra and the birthday song he sang to her.

"Did I?" he said. "A mistake."

He kissed me on my temple and I could smell the cigarette smoke in his hair and on his jacket. Could I smell Petra? Had she hugged him before he left, said thank you for the song? I breathed deeply trying to smell the truth, but there was only David.

"How was the show?" I asked.

"Great."

He moved over to sort through the mail, distracted. I waited for him to say more, tell me that Petra and her friends had shown up on her birthday, but he didn't. Weren't we the couple who shared things about our day, our observations? Hadn't we texted or come home many times to say to each other: *"I saw Ferdinand walking down the street today. He looked rough..."* or *"That girl, Ginger, the weird one who comes to every show, she was at the gelato shop today; she ordered carrot gelato."*

We were information sharers, conspirators, psychoanalyzers of our friends, so why then wouldn't he tell me that he saw Petra, that he sang her a song?

Something had changed.

21

ADDICTION

I DID A LOT of drugs in high school. Everything depressed me: the dull brown bricks of the school building, the white walls of the flat I shared with my mother, the way the girls at my school left the top button open on their uniforms to draw attention to what they would later feed their babies with. We were no different than animals, pursuing little nests and little families. Preening, pretending to be something we were not to draw a mate, tits pushed forward, lips wet with gloss. Drugs softened the harshness of the world, put a blanket over my senses.

One of my teachers, Miss Mills, saw me strung out in the hallway once and pulled me into an empty classroom to tell me that I had a bright future ahead of me and I was on the fast track to ruining my life. She was the sort that wore her dull brown hair in a low pony every day and looked forward to weekends so she could use her label maker. Her fingernails were always painted, a sign of too much time on your hands. My own fingernails held chipped black polish, bitten down to the quick. In my opinion, she'd already ruined her life, so who was she to judge mine? I'd peeked into her classroom one morning to see if my friend Violet was in there, and I'd seen her bent over her desk shoving biscuits into her mouth. Not even homemade, the kind out of the tin. I used drugs, she used biscuits, practically the same thing. As soon as the words were out of her mouth, I blew her off, laughed in her face.

Nobody said the right things about drugs to kids; the lingo was stale and the arrow dull. Drugs were for right now, right here. When you're told that you're going to ruin your life you aren't in the place to be thinking about the rest of your life. Does it even exist? Maybe you were not excited about the rest of your life because what you'd lived so far had been absolute shit. You just can't threaten kids with their futures when they don't understand the gravity of time. I'd stopped doing drugs when I'd come to terms with the world. I had a professor in university that told me that the spectrums of pain were meant to be felt and that they were beautiful in their own way because they caused change. At first, I'd been appalled—who wanted to experience pain? And then I'd thought of all the girls I'd gone to high school with. The ones from the good, wholesome families. They'd already begun the process of setting up families for themselves. In ten years they'd have an identity crisis. They'd be so tightly wrapped up in their husbands and children they'd not know who they were. They'd experience their own pain. My pain had already caused me change, I knew who I was and what I wanted because of it. I made peace with having a bad mother, and not having a father, and I stopped the whole *"this isn't fair"* mentality, which caused me to medicate. Sure, life wasn't fair. A complete no-brainer when you weren't being a narcissist. But, doing drugs wasn't going to change my world. Acceptance was. I'd decided I wanted to feel the full spectrum. But, that didn't include men. Men could make you hurt harder than your parents, or friends, or anything else could. I'd hold them at arm's length. My drug was wanderlust. I got high by starting over. We always had a drug. We could replace one with another, but humans were addicts.

"Yara…Yara…?"

"Yes?" I was at the window watching the rain fall over the water.

"Sometimes it's like your body is here, but you're not," David said.

I smiled. "That's exactly it."

"Where do you go?" he asked.

He came up behind me and kissed the spot behind my ear. I shivered. His warm lips conjured up dirty thoughts no matter where we were or what we were doing. His lips knew how to do things.

"I used to do a lot of drugs," I told him. "Now I do you. And sometimes I think about that."

He laughed into my neck, the spicy smell of him all around me.

"Does this life bore you? Living together, the familiarity?" He started to dig his fingers into my ribs in an attempt to tickle me. I wriggled out of his grip and turned to face him.

"No," I answered honestly. "I bore me."

"That can't be possible," he said.

His tone was light but his expression was serious. In his love for me, he couldn't fathom the idea of me being boring. He was obsessed with me as he often said.

"I have the same thoughts over and over. I'm tired of it."

"So stop thinking them, think about me instead." He leaned in for a kiss, but I turned my head so that all he had access to was my cheek.

"Why didn't you tell me that Petra came to your last show? That you sang 'Happy Birthday' to her?"

It took him a minute to catch up. He was still talking about one thing and I'd moved on to another.

He frowned. "I don't know," he said.

I believed him but that wasn't good enough. I needed him to know.

"You do know and I need an answer."

"All right," he said, slowly backing away from me.

He went to sit on the couch and I stayed where I was at the window, facing him. As I watched him work through his thoughts, the strangest image came to mind. An elderly woman who'd come into the bar with her daughter. She'd been wearing a wig but it was crooked, a garish red/pink color. She'd worn a pinky ring, thick and chunky. It looked odd on her age-spotted hand, the skin thin and wrinkled around it. But I liked her right away, the brazenness of her.

"What are you thinking about?" David asked me.

"An old lady with a pinky ring," I said.

"See, how could you bore anyone, let alone yourself?"

I tried not to smile. "Don't change the subject," I said.

He nodded seriously.

"She's been coming to a lot of shows."

"A real-life groupie." I rolled my eyes.

"I knew it would make you uncomfortable."

"So you're keeping things from me because you think they'll make me uncomfortable?" I folded my arms across my chest. I was battle ready. I wanted to fight.

"Yes," he said. "I'm in the wrong. I'm sorry and I won't do it again."

He was a natural diffuser. I wasn't ready to stop. I felt things and I wanted to express them.

"You sang 'Happy Birthday' to her, made her feel special…validated. It's like you want her to fall in love with you."

"Come on, Yara…" He turned his face, dismissing me.

"No, you come on," I said. "That's exactly what you did."

"I'm a performer!" he said. "I please the crowd. That's something you signed on for being with me."

"No, I signed on to being with you, not your career."

"It's a package deal," he said that through his teeth.

I could hear the ebbing anger and it excited me. David was rarely upset with me.

"I think you have a thing for her," I said, and David balked. "You have a savior complex, David! You've said so yourself."

He stood up, walked toward the kitchen, away from me, and then stopped.

"Do you even believe what you're saying?"

"You knew what you were signing up for when you wanted to be with me."

He looked at me long and hard. "I did," he said. "I don't know how any man or woman could grow accustomed to unwarranted accusation. It's not good for the heart."

"Why did you sing 'Happy Birthday' to her?"

"Because it was her birthday," he said simply before walking away.

I started to feel the withdrawals right then and there. I'd replaced wanderlust with a human. That was a terrible mistake.

New addiction, new problem.

DEEP SLEEP

IT WAS A LITTLE THING, like a pebble in your shoe. Sometimes you knew it was there and sometimes it moved out of the way of your toes and you forgot. That was Petra and her presence in our lives. A lingering uncertainty in my mind and possibly David's.

David got depressed. I called it the deep sleep. Not to him, but that's how it was in my mind. It wasn't often, but it was powerful, and during our year together I learned how to watch for signs of its approach. I didn't know how to manage him when he was like that. There was no manual, no website that gave firm answers. *Be supportive,* they said. *Depression is chemical, and you can't just expect them to snap out of it.* I felt inadequate, like anything I said or did wouldn't be enough. I touched him so he knew I was there, and I fed him because I was afraid he would forget to eat. He wouldn't talk to me when he was like that, but occasionally when I was walking by he'd grab onto my hips and bury his face in my stomach. I'd drop whatever I was holding, a laundry basket, a roll of paper towels, and hold onto his head. I tried to talk to him even if he didn't return the words. Just nonsense about TV shows or customers that came into the bar. The more nonsense I spoke, the shallower I felt. I wasn't saying anything to help him—I was just trying to fill the silence.

I'd watch him from the kitchen, sitting in the chair by the window, knowing that I didn't understand his depression. And maybe it wasn't for me to understand; humans always want to fix things. Sure, I got the blues like everyone else, but this was something more. To David, depression was a tidal wave, not something that could be fixed with a new day and perspective.

I was in the kitchen cleaning up after dinner when someone rang the doorbell. I peeked around the corner just as David opened the door. He was shirtless and in his sweats, a Seahawks hat backward on his head. I had a brief thought about how comical it would be if I opened the door that way, just as I dipped the last plate into the soapy water. I felt somewhat accomplished tonight. My risotto had made David feel something. He'd said it was the best he ever had. I dried my hands on a dishtowel and stepped into the living room. It was Ferdinand. I was glad he came. David did better when he was around. I stopped short as I rounded the corner. Ferdinand wasn't alone...with him were Petra and a girl I didn't recognize, though she seemed to recognize me. I watched her exchange a look with Petra and I had the feeling I'd been the topic of one of their conversations.

"Yara," David said. "Look who came to see us."

I glanced at Ferdinand who ducked his head, apologetic. He was one of the few people who knew how I felt about her.

Petra waved sheepishly as her friend looked on stony-faced.

"Drinks," I said, clapping my hands. David winked at me, which caused a flurry of butterflies to erupt in my belly. *Yes, yes, yes!* I wanted to say. *Come back to me.*

I went to the kitchen to fetch a bottle, the smile dropping from my face as soon as I was around the corner. I was wrong. I had no reason to dislike these people. My insecurities would push David away. I needed to put them away.

When I came back in carrying a bottle of wine, they were all sitting around the living room talking. David was animated, his smile contagious as he took the bottle and wine opener from me and got to work opening it.

"I'm not as good at this as Yara," he joked, and I bent down to kiss his head.

I went to get the glasses, glancing at Petra and her friend who were on the couch sitting in the place where David and I most often made love. It felt like sacrilege to seat them there. David and Ferdinand had pulled up chairs from the table we'd recently chosen together. When I walked back with the glasses, David jumped up to help me. He'd put on a shirt, but the damage was already done, an image engraved in their minds. I'd prefer they not know what's under my boyfriend's shirt. I'd prefer they wonder. Once you got the image of shirtless David in your head, it was hard to get it out.

I watched the girls suspiciously, over the rim of my wineglass, looking for signs of adoration. Of course, they adored him, who didn't? He was the type of person everyone wanted to be around. I got another bottle from the kitchen and poured more wine, smiled. David was smiling too. I wondered if it was genuine or if he was faking like me. Everyone smiling like we weren't all dying of our loneliness. David and I were less lonely because we'd found each other, but there were wolves like Petra who wanted to take.

In university, there'd been a girl in my Psychology 101 class who'd given us a lecture on men versus women. *"If a man introduces his male friend to his extraordinary new girlfriend, his friend will think—I want a girl like that. If a woman introduces her new boyfriend to her female friend, the friend will not think—I want a man like that, but rather, I want that very man."* I'd never put much stock into what she said, after all, I had never coveted a friend's boyfriend, but here I was watching as Petra listened with rapt attention to every word that dripped from his mouth.

Drip

Drip

Drip

David was talking to her, as the rest of us sat and listened. She asked about his process. Such a cheap way to get an artist going. Everyone knew that if you asked an artist about their process, they'd oblige and quite happily. It's like she knew without knowing. I watched them and my stomach rolled. Were they leaning toward each other or was it in my head?

He sat in front of one of the large bay windows, a silhouette against the dying light, giving his expertise.

"And when sudden inspiration comes does the depression lift?" Petra asked.

"Not always, but sometimes it's enough."

"Do you have a muse?" There was quiet in the room as he turned to look at me. And then all of my uncertainty dropped away. It was just David and me in the room when he looked at me like that.

"I do," he said, not taking his eyes from me. He smiled and despite the jealousy I was feeling, my lips curled upward. A sweet token of ownership on both our parts.

"What is it about Yara that inspires you?" Petra asked.

There was a genuine curiosity in her voice. That's not what bothered me, what bothered me was her motive for asking the question.

"Just look at her," David said.

All eyes turned to look at me, but it was David's I focused on. Heat in my belly. He looked like my David, not the shell of a human he'd been these last weeks. We were okay. I felt like I could breathe.

Petra moved onto something else seamlessly, steering the subject away from me and onto something new. That's when I realized the type of woman she was. She tested for weak spots and took notes. She was unfazed, undeterred.

We finished the second bottle and Petra's friend, Kelsey, offered to run down to the store and grab another. The thought of having to spend more time with them, a fake smile plastered across my face, made me feel ill. David must have seen the panic in my eyes.

"Maybe another time," he said, looking at me. "Yara and I have plans to meet up with some friends for drinks." He said each word meticulously. That's how it was when he lied—like each syllable, each letter, was more convincing if spoken with perfect emphasis.

A lie. I was grateful for it.

I nodded at them apologetically and they all stood at once.

I bid them farewell while David saw them to the door. It hadn't even crossed my mind yet that Petra now knew where we lived.

When they were gone, David pulled me against his chest and kissed the top of my head as I cried.

"I'm so sorry," he said, over and over. "Yara, I'm so sorry. I'm back."

I didn't believe him. He left me without warning and with ease. It was like he was stuck in a soundproof room and no amount of effort on my part could free him. Even as he held me I was afraid it would come again. And what would I do next time if Petra wasn't there to help me?

23

MOTHER MOTHER

"TELL ME ABOUT YOUR MOTHER," he asked.

It had been a week since Ferdinand brought the girls over. A week of consistent, happy David. I was putting away laundry, small neat piles into drawers. I'd denied his request to meet his mother twice. I wasn't ready for that yet, and now he was asking about mine. I'd rather meet his than talk about mine, but I didn't tell him that. My back was to him so he didn't see the look that crossed my face at the mention of my mother.

David always wanted to know things. *Who was your first kiss? Who was the first guy who gave you butterflies? Where were you when you found out Heath Ledger was dead?* I answered his questions with a mixture of caution and thrill. No one had ever asked me these things before, but there was the lingering feeling that his questions were a trap, that he was trying to find something not to like about me.

"Your mother," he said again. "You have one, don't you?"

It was meant as a joke, his voice light, but it stung. Yes, I had one, but barely.

I felt creaky and old when I thought about my mother, phantom hurts like an old chain from the past was tugging on my ankle. But David was asking and I'd found myself more and more unable to say no to David.

"She had another baby," I said. "When I was seven or eight. I can't remember." These details—the ones I thought he'd want to know. I was his muse after all; my brokenness could feed him. I wiped my hands on my jeans, they were sweating. I moved toward him, wanting reassurance. I didn't come from what he came from. I had nothing to offer.

He looked steadily on like this didn't faze him at all, rubbing little circles on the skin of my arm with his thumb when I went to stand near him. I relaxed. Anything that had to do with my mother made me feel shame.

"I remember her belly growing. At first, I thought she was getting fat, but I hardly saw her eat. Then one day she was in the kitchen and she grabbed her stomach with a yell and said it was kicking. I asked her what was kicking and she grabbed my hand and held it to her belly. She hardly ever let me touch her, she said my hands were always sticky." I paused to watch his face, his eyes slightly narrowed now like he couldn't imagine the world where a mother would think her child's hands were too sticky.

"Her stomach was so hard, that's what I remember thinking, how fat people had such hard bellies."

He smiled, sort of, and nodded for me to keep going.

"She didn't come home one day, and the neighbor came to bring me food and check on me. I wasn't even scared to be alone in the flat at night, I was so used to it. And then she came home and her belly was gone, her stomach was flat, flat, flat—like it used to be. When I asked her where the baby was she wouldn't tell me."

"Do you think she gave it up for adoption?" he asked.

I shrugged. "For all I know it could have been stillborn, or maybe the father took it, or maybe yeah—adoption."

"She could have been a surrogate," he said.

"Yeah, that's not really my mum," I said. "She's never been into the selfless, giving lifestyle. But, your guess is as good as mine."

He rubbed my shoulders, kissed me behind the ear.

"Are you asking about my mother so you can find out why I'm detached and avoidant of commitment?" I laughed.

"Yes," David said.

My mum. She had almost no neck. That's what I didn't tell David. Those details felt like they were only mine. It perplexed me how her head was attached to the rest of her. I spent a lot of time trying to figure it out. Just a lobbing ball of blonde hair on a torso. Her hair was like mine, people stopped to admire it. But there was too much of it, thick and heavy. It diminished her necklessness further. She wasn't abusive, though from a young age I knew she was disinterested. She liked men; they kept her interest. Her life was a quest to find the perfect mate—the one who wouldn't leave her. And yet she left me. A cycle.

I was a project gone wrong and now she had better things to do. I preferred it that way. My friend, Moira, had a mother who criticized everything she did: *you should wear lipstick; you're pale. You wear too much lipstick; you look like a whore. If you exercised more, you could have a lovely figure. Why do you spend so much time drawing? You should exercise or you won't find a man.* Moira was a lesbian, so lucky for her finding a man wasn't a priority. She complained about her mother in great detail, which I found fascinating. *A mother who cared too much about every little detail...tell me more.*

Mothers—bad mothers especially—made their children feel guilty for existing when they were under stress. *"I gave you life"* was a popular one, as well as, *"I work hard to put food in your stomach!"*

You wanted to have a baby, or maybe you didn't and just chose to keep your baby, it still wasn't our choice to be here, so stop throwing it in our faces that you have to maintain us.

My mother was shouting at me one day. It was after the man she'd been seeing suddenly broke up with her, and her mascara was streaked down her swollen face. I'd answered a question she'd asked me with a grunt and she lost her shit, lobbing a loaf of bread at my head.

"Don't you talk to me like that!" she screamed. "I gave you life. I put food in your belly!"

I'd had enough. I'd been feeding myself for years, working the till at the local grocery mart. Half the time I was feeding her.

"You brought me here," I said to my mother. "You wanted a buddy, something to love you, right? Should have got a dog, Mum. Lot easier than a fucking human. Now feed your mistake without feeling like a savior." I'd marched off to my room and left her standing in the kitchen, arms slumped at her sides, defeated.

She'd not apologized and neither had I—neither of us was sorry. And that's how we parted ways eventually, both a little relieved to be done with each other. Carrying on with our merry lives.

24

MONDAY MEMO

IT WAS ALL SUPPOSED to be a pit stop: Seattle, David, the relationship. I reminded myself of that on Mondays when I stumbled into work crashing hard from the weekend. But by Friday I was fully immersed in my life with David, my memo forgotten in the throes of the happiness I found with him. *Perhaps this time is different*, I'd tell myself. This was my artist, not just any artist—the one suited for me.

Four days a week we went for a run around Lake Union. On Tuesdays I cooked, on Thursdays he did. I did the laundry, he cleaned the bathroom—we fought about the dishwasher. We made love every day, the newness of that hadn't worn off yet. We brunched at Pike Place Market on Sundays and ordered late night takeout on weekends when David had a show. He bought me flowers every week. I'd come from my shift at The Jane and there'd be a bouquet from the Market on the small table where we ate our meals, and an open bag of Cheetos, staling out, as he called it. We watched *Homeland* and *Game of Thrones*, a bowl of kettle corn between us. We fought about money (he wouldn't take any from me), and his late night bar trips with Ferdinand were a subject of contention (Ferdinand was an alcoholic). It was all so beautiful—my life with him—and unlike anything I'd had before. And then Monday would come again, and I'd remind myself that this would all have to end soon. I couldn't live this life forever. Monday, Monday, Monday. I hated it for different reasons than everyone else.

And then, on a Monday in November, a year to the day he pulled the splinter from my finger, he asked me to marry him. It went something like this…

I was sitting on the floor in front of the fire, my back resting against the sofa and my legs spread out in front of me. David's head was resting in my lap, and as we spoke I played with his hair.

"It's a completely different language," I joked. "When I first got here I had no idea what you guys were talking about."

"Come on," he said. "It can't be that different."

He had a bowl of sweets balanced on his chest. They looked like gems in the firelight. He took turns putting them in my mouth and then his. I felt perfectly chubby, and happy, and content. He was shirtless, his jeans sitting low on his waist. I could see the logo strip of his boxer briefs. I ran a hand down his warm chest before saying, "All right, American boy. Are you ready then? For a true lesson in British lingo?"

He dropped a couple of M&Ms in his mouth and winked at me before singing a few lines of "American Boy." I waited for him to finish before I said:

"Skin and blister means sister."

"Da fuck?" he said. "How'd they come up with that?"

"I don't know. Sisters rub on your nerves, I suppose." This seemed to appease him because he nodded solemnly. He'd told me that his sister tormented him throughout their childhood.

"It gets better," I said, "so hush. Apples and pears...are stairs."

He sat up. "You're messing with me." His hair fell over his eyes and I wanted to touch it and leave it at the same time.

I laughed. "I'm not. Lie back down." He did as he was told, but he had a funny look on his face.

"Pete Tong means wrong."

"Okay, give me that one in a sentence." He put a red M&M between my lips and I frowned as I chewed.

"This whole situation's gone Pete Tong," I offered.

"Poor Pete," David said. "What did that guy do wrong? The whole of England is taking the mick out of him."

"Yes," I said. "Imagine how Jesus feels. He's a word for disbelief. Seems rather ironic."

"I'm not ever going to take the Lord's name in vain again," David vowed, a hand over his heart. "You should stay away from Pete Tong. That poor fucker."

He set the bowl aside and rubbed the inside of my thigh with one of his hands. I knew where this was going.

"Girls say *spend a penny* when they need to piss. I need to go spend a penny."

"That's fantastic. That's my favorite," he said. "Now, are you up for a shag?"

I threw back my head and laughed. "That's the only one you know."

He flipped over until he was on his stomach and he kissed slowly up my thighs.

"You. (Kiss) Are. (Kiss) Right."

And then out of nowhere he grew serious. "Your work visa expires soon."

My hand froze in his hair. It was true.

"Yes," I said.

"Marry me, Yara."

I thought he was just throwing out an idea, and I was just about to shoot it down when he produced a ring from the bottom of the M&M bowl. My mouth fell open.

We knocked the bowl over as we both stood up and jewel colored ovals skittered across the floor. I turned my head to watch them, my shock palatable.

It was a mistake—saying yes. I knew it even as my eyes traveled from one M&M to another: red, and blue, and yellow. I'd remember them scattered across the floor like that forever, his proposal still wet on his lips. The earnest fire in his eyes.

"We're precise chemistry, Yara. We're so good this feels like a dream. I want to marry the shit out of you."

And in that exact moment, I thought of Petra, the way she was creeping toward him, and my mouth opened to say yes.

"Yes, David," I said, my eyes filling with tears.

And then he slid an oval diamond onto my ring finger. I stared at it as it caught the light, too beautiful for words. He kissed me and I wrapped myself around him, euphoric, my Monday memo forgotten—everything forgotten.

25 MARRIAGE

THERE ONCE WAS A GIRL who never dreamed of a wedding. Weddings, and marriage, and commitment were for people who wanted the same thing for a long period of time. The same person. I mocked that sort of mindset, the basicness of it. Those dreams were sweet vibrations of stability that lulled you into a deep, psychological sleep. I didn't want sleep. And it all started with flowers, and silk, and stiff-faced cake toppers holding hands. I knew that I wanted to be awake. I wanted my wit and my sense, and by God, I wanted to own my own heart. So when David asked me to marry him, I was surprised when I said yes. And not just any yes, but the type of yes a girl who's always dreamed of a wedding would say. I let him slide the ring on my finger, and then I threw my arms around his neck, climbing his body in excitement until my legs were wrapped around his waist. I held up my hand behind his head so I could see my new ring. And then I rewrapped my arms around his neck and squeezed and squeezed until he told me I was choking him.

"Get used to it," I'd said. "This is your life now."

We got matching tattoos the next day to celebrate. David suggested it and I liked the permanency of my mark being on his body. They happened on our shoulder blades, his right and my left.

"Now there is love marked on your skin," he said to me after, kissing the spot.

"Are you sure?" I kept asking him.

For weeks after he gave me that ring I was still asking, *"Are you sure?"* on a daily basis like he was the one doubting rather than me. Our tattoos scabbed and healed, and I'd ask him, *"Are you sure?"*

"I'm sure," he'd say—steady, anchored—completely and unequivocally sure. We decided we didn't want a large wedding. I didn't have much in the way of family, just a few close friends I'd collected over the years, and David had a very large family, most of whom he said would either get too drunk or not drunk at all.

"I've seen them ruin weddings before," he told me. And then he listed them off like he did every time: "My cousin Lydia, my brother, my great aunt Angela...they get drunk off their asses, or judgmental off their asses, and start fighting about stupid shit. And then there's Sophia, but that's a whole other issue."

And then like always, fascinated by the concept of family, I asked: "And what did they fight about? What did the bride and groom say? How long did it take for them to reconcile?" I was most interested in Sophia, so I asked about her too.

He answered all of my questions patiently, his voice rumbling in his chest, even though I'd already asked them a dozen times before. As his full lips formed words, he traced the spaces between my knuckles with his fingertips. We were always touching, we couldn't stop touching. I'd never been in love before, not like this. I thought I had, but everything before felt like a lie.

"My cousin Sophia had an abortion when she was twenty, she marches in pro-choice rallies," he explained. "My aunts are Catholic. Sophia's own mother has disowned her. Sophia refuses not to come to family things because of them. I think you'd appreciate her—she has the same *I don't give a fuck* thing you have going on."

"How do they treat her when she shows up?"

"They ignore her, whisper, make rude comments."

"And how does she react?"

"She doesn't. She just lives her life."

Sophia was stronger than me, I decided. I wouldn't even bother going. If my family treated me that way—with conditional love—I'd disown them too. She was the one showing real love: showing up, not retaliating.

"And what do you say about all of that?" I asked him.

"I don't think there's anyone right or wrong. We have to let people be who they are. Sophia does a good job of that, you know? She doesn't fight with them or condemn them. She leaves them be."

"But, what about your aunts? To them she committed an atrocious sin. You can't ask them to come down to her level, a level they don't believe in."

"I'm not. No one is. I'm asking them to come up a level actually. To show love instead of judgment. Because if they're right about their belief system, there is an ultimate judge anyway, isn't there? We don't need human judges."

Fact: I liked him more every day. Usually the more time I spent with someone the less I liked them. A good sign. By the time we were sixty I'd be so full of love I'd be ready to burst.

I bought my wedding dress from a consignment shop in Queen Anne: white lace with long sleeves and a deep V-neck that almost reached my belly button. There was a spot of blood on the hem—two dark red droplets. When I told Ann she made a disgusted face.

"Gross, get it dry-cleaned."

I nodded, but there was no way I'd wipe off someone's history from my dress. How did it get there? Was it in love or lust, anger or joy? I spent so many days imagining that scenario that I was almost tempted to go back to the store and ask about its original owner. I decided not to dry-clean it, to wear it as is with all the bad or good still attached to the fabric. We planned on marrying in Vancouver, a favorite city for both of us, just a few friends in tow. David found a blue velvet suit in the back of his aunt's closet and told me he would wear it. David told me that Lazarus Come Forth would sing a cappella as I walked down the aisle.

"What aisle?" I asked him, and then he told me that he booked a church and a restaurant for after we'd taken our vows where we could all celebrate. I hadn't done a thing, hadn't lifted a finger. It was like he could sense my hesitancy and rushed into action making the plans.

"Is there anyone you'd like to invite from back home? Like a friend…some distant family?"

"No," I said quickly. "My life is here now, my people are your people."

"Yara," he urged. "You can't just cut people off when you feel done with them. They're part of your tapestry."

I watched his lips as he spoke. It was mesmerizing the way they moved. He licked his lips often and I always wished he were licking something else.

"I don't want anyone else to come," I said with finality.

I felt guilty. I thought of Posey, who didn't even know I was getting married. She still texted me once a week and I told her about everything but David. There were a handful of others I could call. They'd all be excited and shocked to hear the news—some of them would even offer to fly out for the wedding. But, in the end, I chose to tell no one. What I had with David felt private, like it needed to be protected from the outside.

Atheists Who Kneel and Pray

And then it was time to meet his parents, who were angry with David and suspicious of me. I didn't blame them. He asked a girl to marry him, a girl they'd yet to meet. They didn't know it was my fault and not his, that I'd been dodging their dinner invites and weekend trips for almost a year. But I took the ring, and bought the dress, and now it was time.

PART TWO
THE E-MAIL

Dear Yara,

The band's in London November 12th. Want to catch up?

David

I RE-WRITE IT TWENTY-FOUR times before I send it. I don't even know if she uses this e-mail anymore. If she answers, it will hurt. If she doesn't answer, it will hurt. She replies three days later.

Hi David,

Yeah, sounds good. Let me know when and where.

Yara

She's so cold.

.

26

I REMEMBER

I REMEMBER THE SMELL of her clothes, her perfume, her skin. The tilt of her chin when she was offended and the way her mouth pulled in at the corners when she was wary of your motives. I remember the way the tip of her tongue peeked out and touched her top lip when she was having an orgasm. And the way she'd hold the first sip of wine in her mouth for what seemed like a full minute before swallowing it. The way she closed her eyes and moaned when she swallowed…the wine. And me. I remember how she wouldn't take shit from me or anyone else. She didn't care what you thought about her, she cared what she thought about you. She wouldn't let you in just like that. You had to prove it. I remember the open bags of Cheetos, all lined up in her pantry. The first time I saw them all lined up like that I'd pulled a couple rubber bands off my wrist and started closing them so they wouldn't go stale.

"What are you doing?" she'd said, when she caught me tying one up.

"Someone left them open," I'd said. "They'll go stale."

"That's the point." She'd taken the bag from me and pulled off the rubber band, handing it back to me.

"Stale Cheetos are my favorite." She'd pushed it between her lips, wagging her eyebrows at me.

And then as she was walking away, she'd said, "Are you going to write a song about it?"

I remember the way she'd always say: *Are you going to write a song about it?*

And I'll never forget that I did write a song about it. All of it. And those songs. I wrote one song, I wrote two songs, I wrote three songs, I wrote four songs. Yara gave me one gift: endless inspiration. One song, two songs, three songs, four songs go platinum. We make money, we acquire fame, we travel all over the world and live the very dreams we dreamed.

But I'm poor.

I have nothing but money.

And her sweater, I still have one of her sweaters. Her smell has long since faded out of it, but if you look closely at the cuff of the sleeve, you can see tiny flecks of orange trapped in the wool. Cheeto dust.

I lift it to my nose before every show, trying to find her somewhere. It comes with me when we're on tour. I keep it in a box that looks like a coffin. The guys give me shit about it, but I don't care. There was one time I forgot the box in a dressing room in Albuquerque;I only realized it by the time we reached Reno and we were getting ready to play a show.

"I'm not playing," I told them. *"Everything will go to shit without the sweater."*

Sometimes a man gets carried away, but what does it matter? That's a man's business. They convinced me to go on anyway; hard slaps on the back and looks that made me feel like I was overreacting. The sound went out during the first song. It had worked fine during rehearsal, but I didn't sniff her sweater, so it stopped working. Then during the middle of the show, the stage manager started violently throwing up. She was rushed to the hospital in the middle of our set after passing out and was later diagnosed with the norovirus and severe exhaustion. Again, the sweater. Then Ferdinand broke three guitar strings, and I forgot the lyrics to "My Wife's Wife." By the time we left the stage and were back in the tour bus, all the guys were convinced about the sweater.

"No more shows without Dave's sweater," Brick said.

He stank of beer and sweat and I didn't want him anywhere near Yara's sweater.

"Do we need to sniff it too?" Ferdinand asked.

Ferdinand somewhat understood my grief over Yara—having watched the whole relationship unravel, he never questioned it.

"No one sniffs the fucking sweater but me," I said.

So the sweater became a sort of Ark of the Covenant for us, with me as its handler and the guys as firm believers in its magic. We didn't go on tour without it, and it's on the cover of our second album. Sometimes we tell the story at our shows and the crowd roars. They want to see the sweater. But Yara's worn grey sweater is only for me. I wonder if she's ever seen our album cover and recognized it—I wonder that too often actually. The most twisted thing about being an artist comes when you understand you're creating for one specific person. The painful part is realizing who that person is, and the devastating part is knowing the compulsion will never go away. And they mostly stem from a death: emotional, physical—it doesn't matter. They die to you and their things become sacred. She doesn't deserve it; she's a coward. But trying to control who controls you is like dictating what the weather should do every day.

We moved from Seattle to LA to pursue the music. Ferdinand, Brick, and our newest member, who we call Keyboard Carl. Carl came last but I like him most. He has greasy hair hanging around his face that reminds me of Kurt Cobain's, and he wears 90's boy band T-shirts. He gives Lazarus Come Forth a nice solid rock & roll vibe.

The guys found the transition to LA easier than I did. I was leaving behind memories; they were wanting to make new ones. In truth, they've always loved the idea of fame harder than I do. I just love the music.

We signed with a small indie label: a husband and a wife named Rita and Benny. They are so passionate about music they do little but eat, sleep, and talk music. They make me feel inferior but well taken care of. Everyone has a nickname in our circle, so we call them The Musics. We stayed in their house when we visited and by the end of the long weekend, they believed in us and we believed in them. I guess the rest is history.

Ferdinand buys his mother a lake house in Chelan, and Brick buys his girlfriend new tits the size of cantaloupes. Keyboard Carl says he's saving his to buy an island. I think that's an excellent idea, but there's no one I'd want to take to the island with me, so I deposit my checks and try to forget that the money is in there. Some guys would use it to ease the pain, I guess, same way as some people use drugs. I want the pain to stay where it is, hard and heavy. It makes me feel close to her. I am inspired, but I am empty. The month after the tour ends, Ferdinand comes to my condo, which I had purchased from my aunt.

"You have a beard now," he says, scratching his head. "How do you eat pussy with a beard?"

I laugh and we hug in the way men do with a few firm hits onto the back. I've always thought it funny that even in hugging, men show aggression. Ferdinand stays with me for the week and before he leaves, he tells me I need to find Yara.

He's nervous when he tells me. I've seen him play to crowds of eighty thousand not even breaking a sweat or vomiting like Brick did before a big show. He sits now on the arm of my sofa, his legs spread. His body is bent so that his elbows are resting on his knees, his hands dangling between them. He looks me in the eye, but he's having trouble doing so.

"Look," he says. "I have a friend in London. He came to one of our shows once…"

"Which one?" I ask.

"Red Rocks. He came to Red Rocks and I asked him to keep an eye out for Yara."

"How does one keep an eye out for someone they've never met, in a city with millions of people?"

"I showed him her picture. He writes restaurant reviews for a blog, so I figured if he was frequenting London's bar scene he was liable to run into her."

"And did he?"

"No."

I can't hide the disappointment from my face. "So why are you telling me this?"

"Because I don't really give a fuck who you fuck. But, you changed after she left, and fucking all those girls didn't help you. Neither did the album's success, man, which I suspect was mostly written about her."

I pause to think about "Atheists Who Kneel and Pray." The night I had fallen drunk on a stranger's lawn somewhere in North Bend, on my way back from a bar. The snow was falling around me, shocking my face and hand with little pinpricks as it landed. I'd stared up at the sky and thought about how I didn't believe anymore—not in God or his creation. Definitely not in love. She'd come as a thief in the night and taken it all away. How could a person do that? How could they have so much power? And as I lay there, in a drunken state of heartbreak, I'd written the song that had put us on the map.

"You need to find her," Ferdinand says. "You need closure, man. Or something else. Find her and tell her it was all for her. Whatever you need to do."

Ferdinand's mother was a shrink. I take it that he gleaned all his wisdom from her.

I rub my hand across my face. "Okay, man," I say. "Okay."

27

TRASHY E-MAILS

I CHECK MY TRASH for her e-mail. When she used to send me e-mails they went straight to my trash, I never figured out why. I tried to make it so they went to my inbox, but she'd send an e-mail and it would be sorted into the trash. A forewarning perhaps. The e-mail I'm waiting for is the one where she offers me a sincere and heartbroken apology. It gives me a decent reason for walking out on me six weeks after we were married.

I imagine I'll read her e-mail and go, *"Aha, I get it now. Thank you for explaining everything so well that I don't have to hurt anymore."*

Every day I check my trash for that fucking e-mail, but it never comes. Do the guilty not send e-mails? I'm checking my e-mail one day (the trash) when I see a title in the subject bar that says: NEED A PRIVATE EYE, I'M YOUR GUY. I open it partly because it's cheesy and I think this guy, Ed Berry is his name, could come up with a better slogan for his business. Ed claims he can find anyone, and he can do it to fit your budget. I don't know where Ed gets off thinking anyone would call him after that awful slogan, but I call him because I figure Ed needs someone to believe in him. I leave a message and he calls me back within two minutes.

"What can I do you for?" he says in a dirty accent. I can't tell if he's from New York, Texas, or Minnesota. "All three," he tells me later. "I'm a man who moves around."

I almost hang up on him, but I remember what Ferdinand said about needing closure. Yara and I celebrated our second wedding anniversary last month. I got a tattoo to commiserate, and then I got drunk. Where is my wife? That's Ed's job now. I needed a private eye and he is my guy.

I tell Ed that I need to find someone and he tells me that international work doesn't come cheap. I assure him I can afford it. When I hang up the phone, I know I've crossed a line there's no coming back from. When you set out to find someone, you don't stop until you do. And then you have to deal with what you find.

Ed sends me photos. Large 8x10 ones. He also sends the files to my e-mail. They do not go to my trash. I check the trash before opening the files. Nothing.

In the photos I see Yara behind a bar. No surprise there, she had a master's degree and refused to work as anything but a bartender. I see her walking down a street with plastic shopping bags, her chin tucked to her chest. I see her smiling as she sits at an outside table with another woman. Ed labels each photo with what she's doing. Female subject eats at The White Knight at eleven hundred hours. Is joined by another female. They leave together walking west on....

I don't like that he calls her *female subject*. She's Yara.

I check my trash for her e-mail.

I know where she is, now it's just a matter of actually going. My tattoo gets infected. I consider having it lasered off. Bad juju when the tattoo you got to commiserate your second anniversary with your runaway wife gets infected.

When it heals there is a spot in the middle where the ink disappeared. It's perfect in a crippling way, so I keep it. When I check my e-mail, I rub that empty spot in the middle of my tattoo. It's not something I was aware I did until Brick pointed it out. Brick can be painfully observant when there aren't women around.

"Dude, why do you do that? It's like the same thing every day."

I shrugged it off, but it made me think. There was a story of a man whose wife died. He went to the graveyard every day, picked the same flowers, wore the same tie. He sat next to her grave and told his dead wife about what he'd had for breakfast, how the neighbor had raised her hand in a wave as he walked by. This was the way he grieved the love of his life, with ritual and consistency. It was a grab at control after the uncontrollable happened. Death. Me touching the blank space of my tattoo, me searching for her e-mail in my trash. I was lost forever in my grief.

I hate being home, home being my family home where my parents have a lime green golf cart that they drive around the property proudly numbered 12. My sister keeps toys for her children to play with when she brings them over on the weekends. The house always smells of apple cider vinegar, which in turn smells like dirty feet. My mother has become a consumer of apple cider vinegar.

"It kills the bad bacteria in your gut," she tells me.

To illustrate this, she pats mine right where the bad bacteria live, then points to her own. I take a shot of it to appease her and I gag. No one talks about Yara, that's the rule. We carry on like she never happened. Sometimes I can tell my mother wants to talk about it, ask if I've heard anything, but she holds the questions in her eyes instead. For the first time in my life I'm grateful that we're the type of family who avoids talking about things.

It's the sound of my sister's children riding their tricycles along the pavement in front of the house that bothers me the most. I always wake up to it and put a pillow over my head to kill the sound of plastic wheels on hot asphalt. The grating roll of them, the laughter. I hate it. It reminds me of a happiness I won't likely ever know—a family of my own, small humans who call me Daddy or Papa, a woman who I want to make them with. When I kiss my mother goodbye after the weekend and ferry back to the city I am inordinately relieved. Who am I anymore? Not the man who used to like hanging out with his family. Not the man who was thirsty for music. I go to sleep in my own condo; the hum of engines lulls me to sleep and it's the best sleep I've had in days. Next week will be better. Next week I will try harder to get on with my life. Next week we play a festival in Seattle.

I check my trash for her e-mail.

FANGS

SHE HAD FANGS. Figurative ones, but also her incisors were sharp which made her look like a vampire. The first time I saw her I thought of the books all the girls were reading when I was in high school, the one about the beautiful vampire who falls in love with a mortal girl. I was the mortal boy and this girl—godlike—made me feel plain and insufficient. Later she told me that I made her feel the same way, and maybe that's the way it's supposed to be— two people in awe of each other, who feel lucky to be with each other. I came back to see her again, thirsty for her attention. I wasn't exactly starved for attention, but lately hers was the only attention I wanted. Maybe the first time was a fluke, an off night for my masculinity. But when I went back I felt the same thing—if not stronger. I flirted with her and she flirted back, but not with the soft pliability that most women flirted with.

"*Hey splinter guy,*" she'd say because she knew it annoyed me. "*Are you going to write a song about that?*

She threw barbs, they were well aimed and they made me laugh. If I were a different man I'd have a bruised ego. I took her jabs and molded them to me. She was something I knew existed but had never met: the Loch Ness Monster, Bigfoot, the leprechaun at the end of the rainbow. Terrible analogies, I know.

Yara

And then she told me, after a lot of prodding—Yara.

Her name was music.

I'd leave the bar and think about her hair. Not her tits or her ass—her hair. What the fuck was that? I told my best friend, Ferdinand, about her hair and he called me a little bitch.

A little bitch I was.

"Do you want to run your fingers through it?" he asked. "Stick your face in it and get that good smell?"

I did.

"Fuck off," I said, but he'd just laughed.

"I'd rather have my fingers and face somewhere else, but suit yourself."

I invited her to my show. Once, twice, three times. I'd never had to beg a woman to come to one of my shows before. And then to make matters worse, she never came. Each show I'd climb onto the stage and look for her, her blonde hair—even if it was tied back I'd be able to see it. And then I'd climb off stage disappointed. She didn't work the same way other women did. Other women had dials, knobs; nothing was labeled. Yara had only one switch and it was either Off or On. I wanted to speak her language. I wanted to be her language. This was obsession and I welcomed it. A nice change to not feeling anything at all or to feeling disappointed.

We played The Crocodile the last Saturday of the month. I'd invited Yara again, but by then expected her not to come. We usually sat around in their greenroom drinking until it was time for us to go on. But, on that particular night, I couldn't sit still.

"Give David a hit of that," Ferdinand said to Brick, who was smoking a joint.

I waved it off.

"It's like you're strung out on something, man."

Ferdinand knew me pretty well, but I didn't want to talk about it. Yara had been different with me the last few times I went into The Jane—not as talkative and friendly. I took a shot to appease them a few minutes before the show started.

"Who are you looking for?" Ferdinand asked as we walked onto the stage. Ferdinand knew who I was looking for but he liked to ride me about it.

"Yara," I said, without thinking.

"The one you've been obsessing over? Dude…"

"You haven't seen her. You don't know. Actually I don't want you to see her." I picked up my Charvel and ignored the way he was looking at me. Ferdinand was the bassist, but he got more ass than I did. As the face of the band, lead singers got the most ass; their name was the one most called out and remembered. He was six foot four and wide like a bull, women thought Ferdinand was a combination of mysterious and dangerous. In reality, he was a man of few words who had a kitten screensaver on his MacBook. He didn't like to talk unless it was about music or his mother, and he cried when he got a nosebleed, but hey, the illusion was half the fun. It worked out well for his social life.

"Who's that?" Ferdinand asked.

He jutted his chin toward the bar as he turned the E peg on his Fender. I lifted my eyes, tried to see past the bright lights that shone on the stage. A flash of platinum hair, but it could be anyone. Girls with that hair color were a dime a dozen. Her hair was so long it kissed her hips, hips that sashayed when she walked.

"A blonde," I said. "Wrong one."

161

"There are plenty of blondes you can pick from right here," Ferdinand said. "An entire buffet of blondes."

I flipped him the bird and picked up my guitar. A buffet. Right. That's what it had become. You could swipe left or right, go on two hookups in one night. If you didn't like one there was another. Around and around you went, fucking groupies, girls on Tinder who said they wanted to have a good time but were looking for a husband. You could fuck your way through the Pacific Northwest if you were halfway decent looking and carried a guitar. It was all unfulfilling. Barren experience after barren experience.

Time to start. Brick was on the drums. "One...two...three..."

It was her. I realized that halfway through our first song. Energized, I moved around the stage with new vigor. Ferdinand raised his eyebrows, tilted his head slightly toward her as if to ask, *That her?* I nodded. He pursed his lips, dipping his bass guitar and closing his eyes. This was his favorite part of the song. What would be Yara's? I sang, played to impress. I didn't want to scare her and for that reason I didn't make eye contact until we were three songs in. She was here, she had come. I was into it. She wasn't just going to be my muse, I was going to make her my wife.

A lot of good that did me. A lot of fucking good.

29

BEGGARS

I COUNT THE DAYS she's been gone. I count them until it becomes painful to know there was an actual number pushed between us—a number that only grew. Would only grow. Days, then months, then years. They tell you it gets better but it doesn't. I make a list of things I want to forget because it hurts to hold them in the forefront of my mind.

That one time she cussed out my brother when he told me to get a real job.

That one time we were playing a show and I saw her in the crowd with her eyes closed and her hands raised like she was worshipping.

That one time she was so angry with me she threw a loaf of bread at my head and told me to choke on it.

That one time she licked the tears off my face and said she was craving something salty.

That one time I felt sorry for myself and told her I was a lousy artist and she told me to write a song about it.

That one time she filled the vodka bottle with vinegar and when I started coughing and choking she told me I needed to stop drinking so fucking much.

That one time she convinced me to let her wax my balls and told me it wouldn't hurt at all.

That one time she drew boobs on my face with a Sharpie while I was sleeping and then I had to play a show later that night.

That one time she sang to me when I wouldn't sing anymore and it was so bad and so good at the same time.

That one time we got married.

That one time she left.

When does it get better? Can someone give me a time frame?

If someone doesn't want you, the only self-respecting thing to do is to let them go. Truth, honest to God, I'm not lying to you. It's that or a restraining order. I've seen those guys who wouldn't let go. Their girls would peace out and they'd lose their shit. Man, those fuckers reminded me of beggars; stooped shoulders, watery eyes like they'd just hit a joint. How do you let yourself get to that point, man? That's pathetic. What bothered me most about those guys was the type of girls they were grieving. Shallow girls, cover girls, too much lipstick—girls, none of them even a little bit like Yara. I judged those guys so hard and I guess I shouldn't have. We all have someone to grieve even if it's not Yara.

I made a new list of things I wanted to forget.

The way she cooked my meals when I was a zombie and carried them over to me, placed the fork between my fingers, and told me in her gentle voice to eat.

Her cold fingers when they smoothed the lines on my face.

How she never complained about the months when I disappeared, she never brought them up after.

The way she'd lash out at me, accusing me of cheating on her.

Those girls, the ones who were not Yara, their speech was fickle, their voices high and twangy. They never asked a real question, just hinted around it. They sounded cheap, like those plastic recorders they teach you to play in middle school. I'd had those girls, I'd listened to them speak, and say my name, and ask me non-questions. Yara's voice was deep…elegant. Her accent was regal and her tone matter-of-fact. I added something I wanted to forget to the list of Yara's questions.

Why fuck a girl and lead her on if you have no intention of being in a relationship with her?
Why are you whining that you can't write a song when you haven't tried to write a song?
Why do you let your brother speak to you like that?
Why do you want to marry me anyway?

After a relationship ended and you went through the initial grief, it was time for the groveling (or bargaining as the shrinks called it). Groveling was a rite of passage. It's where you got to look so pathetic no one would want you anyway, but you were sad enough to try. I didn't know where she was to grovel or I would have. Fuck, I would have gone the whole nine yards with the groveling, been a beggar. I skipped that stage and went straight to the asshole stage. That's the best one. You get to drink a shitload—and you don't even care what you're drinking. There's a lot of *"Fuck that bitch."* And, *"I'm better off without her."* When you get tired of the hangovers and your dick won't get hard anymore, you stop drinking and you medicate with fun new things: friends, the gym, brown rice and chicken breasts perfectly portioned, and random hookups with girls you meet at the gym.
Grief without the fights, grief without the apology, grief without the closure. Thick, suffocating grief wound tightly around one woman. And with as much pent-up grief as you have

for one woman, you're sticking your dick in another one. It's sick.

Pride, I had too much of it. If I really wanted to I could have fucking found her. I know that now. I should have begged and groveled, crawled to her on my hands and knees so she could see the effect she had on me. Maybe I could have brought her back.

The pen was there that day, lying on my nightstand. I didn't recognize it, where had it come from? It was a tourist's pen, something you'd buy at the Market: a skyline of Seattle behind a tiny plastic dome. There were flecks of glitter in water. I picked it up, watched it snow over Seattle. And then, just like that, the words fell into my head.

Are you going to write a song about it?

Why yes, yes I was. I called the song "Beggar." It was the second song I'd written about Yara and it took twenty minutes to get it out. It had her rhythm: *soft, soft, hard, hard.* When I was done I felt…less. Just less, like I'd transferred some of my grief into a composition book instead of letting it sit in my chest. This was what Yara had told me would happen if my heart broke. I hated the song because of that—I hated every song about her, and they all were about her. I hated the girl that made us famous. I hated myself for loving the girl that made me a beggar. Bitter, bitter—like orange rinds. She'd done this to me purposefully, hurt me with intent. I changed for her, but she hadn't changed for me. That was the difference. She'd just left me behind.

I checked my trash for her e-mail.

30
LOOKING

I HAVE A DREAM that Yara is locked in a closet and calling my name. When I wake up I'm covered in sweat and my heart is pounding. I glance at my phone. It's five o'clock in the morning. I do the numbers in my head as I swing my legs over the side of the bed. Two years this month, that's how long it's been since she left. I take a shower, make myself a pot of coffee, but I can't shake the dream. I could see her so clearly, her long hair braided down her back, her red-rimmed eyes. I make a point not to look at old photos because every time I do it feels like I'm back at day one—the first day after she left me—but I can't stop the dreams. They bring her face back to me in detail. My friends tell me that I need closure. Before the residue of the dream has worn off, I book a one-way ticket to London. It's now or never, I tell myself. I pack a small bag and leave without telling anyone.

"Business or pleasure?" the woman in the seat next to me asks.

She fastens her seat belt and then looks over at me expectantly. I have no plan to spend the flight talking to a stranger.

"Business," I say.

"What sort of business?"

"I'm going to find my wife." And then I lean my head against the window, the pillow propped against the glass, and fall asleep.

I stay in a hotel she once told me about, on the Strand. She bartended there for a few months before she decided to adventure in America. What are the big differences between London and Seattle? The weather is the same. As I put one foot in front of the other and steer my body through the streets, I am rained on the same way I am rained on back home. I don't walk with my head down like everyone else because I am looking in their faces, the people who carry umbrellas (we don't really do that in Seattle, carry umbrellas). I am searching for Yara, who no longer works in the same place Ed Berry reported. Rainwater drips down my face, into my mouth because I won't bend my head against the rain.

I am looking for Yara. I am looking for Yara...

I think about calling Ed, but I'm already here. I can find her. That's what I say to myself as I walk through the streets. Even before I met her it seemed I was looking for Yara. I knew that she struggled to accept love. I was too young to understand consequences. I thought everything would work out in my life, that the wrongs would right themselves and that eventually she would be okay. That's not how it works. I know that now.

The bars here are all named things with a *The* at the beginning: *The* Porcupine, *The* Imperial, *The* Glassblower, *The* Oyster and Mirth. I look into their windows, eyeing the bartenders. I am looking for Yara.

She is everywhere and nowhere. I see her in the people. She Americanized herself to fit in, but now I see that she is London. How can a person be like a city? Her attitude about life is damp, but she pushes forward with an old elegance. She doesn't complain about what's happened to her or why. It's the damp she lives in, it's part of who she is and she's fine with that. I've seen so many others question, and cry, and rage against the whys of their life. Yara doesn't waste time on that. She has somewhere to be and she goes. She grew up with adjectives. She's interesting and old like the gothic buildings that line the street. If you go inside many of them they're modern and young—that's like Yara too.

I love London.

In the afternoon I am tired of walking and looking, looking and walking. I find a place to sit and eat called The Counter at the Delaunay. There is a blue and white pattern on the floor that I can't stop looking at. I sit across from grandparents who have brought their young grandchildren for lunch. We're all in a booth by the window. The boy and girl look like twins.

"Can I see your lovely smile? Show me your lovely smile," the grandfather says as he holds up a camera.

"Do Mister and Missus Grumpy need to go to the toilet?" the grandmother asks. "You'll let me know, won't you? Perhaps a little later then."

I'm fascinated by the way they speak to each other, the attentiveness and tone.

We don't speak to our children that way in America. We don't direct as many adjectives at them. I think of the songwriters I love, all from here, this place of giant red buses and gothic spires. Steve Mac; Camille Purcell; Paul Epworth; Goddard, Worth, and Lennon. Their grandparents must have taken them to lunch and told them to show their lovely smiles, and offered them bites of their bacon roll—*"Would you like a tiny bite, then? It's crispy on the inside, but the bread is very soft and warm…my word! Look how many swirly twirly shapes and designs are on this table! You're very posh, aren't you, my lovelies! Posh and perfectly darling…"*

I understand Yara more by listening to her people. The longer I walk, and listen, and stay, the more she makes sense to me. Tigers don't make sense in a zoo—they conform to the zoo, but they don't make sense. I order a tea the way she used to drink it, and something called porridge and banana. The girl who brings them to me asks if I want honey for my porridge.

"Yes, please," I say.

Yara used to put honey on her oatmeal, I remember that. I'm doing this all to feel close to her. Maybe then I can find her.

The porridge is delicious. How did she ever eat oatmeal when she was used to eating this? It's creamy and decadent. I get honey on everything—my hands, and the table, and my clothes. I want to write a song about that too—following your girl to London and getting honey on everything. She causes me to write songs without knowing it.

On the fifth day I'm there I get a call from my mother. My father had a heart attack. I run to my hotel and toss everything into my luggage. Everything is a blur after that—the cab ride to the airport, the flight home on which the wifi doesn't work, the hot coffee I spill on my pants. My cousin is there to pick me up. Her face looks grave. I don't think about Yara again until after the funeral. Then I feel more desperate. People die. We are not permanent. We have to hurry if we want things.

31
THE PAST COMES BACK

WE PLAY BUMBERSHOOT IN SEPTEMBER, six months after my father died. It's a largely acclaimed art and music festival in our home state, something we've been dreaming of for years. We climb the stage and can only describe the experience as one of the most surreal moments of our lives. Just a few years ago we were bright-eyed and hopeful, standing in the audience and dreaming of the day we'd be on the stage. And now we are. The weather is gracious, the sun pounding down on Seattle in her full majesty. I glance up and eye the scrappy little clouds that dot the sky. There will be no rain today. My mother and sister are in the crowd too, wearing matching red visors. They jump up and down and wave when they see me looking. They're wearing their Pixies shirts and I know they're headed to the reunion show after this. It's from the stage that I see another familiar face. I remember a fight, yelling, Yara throwing a loaf of bread at my head and telling me to choke on it. It sounds comical now but at the time it wasn't. The anger that spun out of her tornado-like, ripping up what we'd been building together. She said things that night that I'd rather not remember, horrible things about me and the band…my family. It was a painful memory, a gateway to the end. I catch Petra's eye and she smiles as she sways to the music we've already started playing. Her hair is an ashen yellow and she's dressed in a sheer white dress. I can see her outline underneath the fabric, the dark circles of her nipples. She wants me to recognize her—she wore that dress so she'd have a better chance of it. Women use their bodies like weapons.

After the show Petra waits for me at the back of the stage. There are a lot of people there calling my name, but she stands quietly, her hands clasped in front of her body like she already knows I will stop. If I couldn't see her goddamn nipples I'd say she looked saintly. I stand in front of her even though security has me by the balls. A big burly guy in a leather vest says, "We need to keep moving."

"Hello, Dave." She pushes her hair behind her ear and looks at me shyly.

It's so intimate, the way she calls me Dave. It triggers something, maybe my deep loneliness, and that's why I lift the barrier and wait as she ducks under it to join me. She waves to her friends like this was the plan all along and links her arm through mine.

We don't speak until we're in the trailer we share with two other bands. Since they're performing we have it to ourselves for a few hours. The guys pull beers out of the fridge and wipe the backs of their necks with plush white towels, while Petra and I move to the tiny back room where there is a double bed. I sit on the edge and she sits next to me.

"I'm not trying to sleep with you," I say. Though saying it out loud makes it seem like I am.

She smiles that closed lip smile that she's mastered and shrugs like she could go either way. I have a thought that I'm ashamed of: what if I should have been with Petra all along and Yara was the mistake? Well, clearly Yara *was* a mistake, but I'd always blamed Petra for the initial frays in our relationship. Wholly unfair perhaps, but that's what Yara put in my head: *Petra was there to cause trouble, Petra was waiting for us to break up.* Petra had been quiet in those days, trailing the band from show to show, showing up so often she became one of our entourage by default. Then the thing had happened with Yara. She came around for a while after that, but one night after I'd had too much to drink, I'd ordered her the fuck out of my condo. According to Brick, in a drunken slur I'd told her that it was her fault Yara and I had broken up. I think of that now as I sip water from a bottle and watch her studying me cautiously. Is she looking for anger?

"I'm sorry," I say. "About what I said. I was hurting and I wanted to fuck everything up."

"That was a long time ago." She shrugs. And then she says, "She had this way of making you crazy. It was like she enjoyed torturing you."

I stare at her. Maybe it was true, but no one had ever said it out loud before. I don't want to talk about Yara. She must see it on my face because she stands up and grabs my hands, pulling me to my feet.

"Let's get out of here," she says. "I'll buy you dinner."

I only hesitate for a moment. I haven't been with a woman in a year. That was after the initial year when I slept with anyone who was game. I like holding her hand, but more than that, I like the way she looks at me.

It's the first day that I don't check my trash for Yara's e-mail.

32
MEET THE FOLKS

THE EXCITEMENT AROUND A wedding was contagious. Everyone wanting to know the details. Plenty of congratulations, slaps on the back, and unwarranted advice. While I was basking in the happiness of it all, my future wife was looking more wilted by the day.

"What is it, Yara?" I asked. "Do you not want to do this?"

She looked shocked by my question. "No, no," she assured me. "I'm just not this person...who plans a wedding, you know?"

I did know and I liked that about her.

"I'll make all of the arrangements," I promised, kissing her on the forehead. "It will be small. Tiny. Just close friends and a handful of my family. Is there anyone you want to invite from back home?" She was shaking her head before I'd finished the question.

"I was a bridesmaid once, right out of uni—I mean college," she said. "A girl I'd gone to high school with, pretty and popular back then. Her name was Angie. She was out of my league in high school, and I was out of hers when I moved to London. I didn't realize we were friends until she asked me to wear a high-waisted mint dress and hold a handful of wildflowers."

"You'd never hung out?" I asked.

"No. And I was about to turn her down. I felt awkward about being her bridesmaid when we weren't even real friends, and then she told me that she'd always admired me, and while the rest of them cared about stupid things I did my own thing. Truly, I think her real friends had all moved away and abandoned her in a way. They saw her early marriage as something that could be viral. Anyway, I did it. I was her bridesmaid. I remember feeling panic for her as she walked down the aisle, even though she didn't feel it for herself. How did she know everything would be okay, that he would take care of her, that she'd remain herself? I know now that she didn't, that love was a leap of faith, and that love was just a word until someone gave it a definition."

I nodded slowly, not wanting her to stop speaking. It was so rare that she shared things from her past like this.

"I don't know if John, the man she married, fulfilled her in the way she was hoping, if he was a good husband and father. We never spoke again after her wedding. But sometimes I have these sharp moments of realization that this is my wedding, and that I am to be married. I think of Angie and wonder how much I can trust all of this."

I couldn't relate, though I did my best to understand her. I came from married people, hard and unwavering Catholic dedication to family. It was what you did, and it was what I'd always wanted.

"Do you worry that I'll disappoint you in some way?" I asked.

She smiled. "No, I'm worried that I'll disappoint you in some way," she answered. "That I won't be enough."

I pulled her into my arms and held her so tight. "Impossible, Yara," I said. "You don't have to be enough for me or anyone. I love you as you are. I don't want you to ever feel pressured to be something for me. That takes the ease out of real love."

She'd looked at me hard, like I'd said something outrageous.

"That isn't the deal we made, is it?" she asked.

"Deal? What deal?" The ferry docked and I shifted my car into drive to follow the line of cars off the boat.

"The one where I date you to inspire you," she said quietly. "Be your muse."

I'd forgotten about it. How long ago had that been? How much had happened since then?"

I looked over at her and she was staring out the window, her fist pressed to her mouth.

"Yara, I never was part of that deal," I said. I reached out and squeezed her knee. "I only played along to get you. If you recall, I was talking marriage before I knew your name."

"Oh, I recall," she said.

I was worried. I didn't like when she locked me out. I decided to change the subject, away from weddings, and my family, and her anxiety over both.

"We should go away for a few days," I said. "Go somewhere to relax and just be together."

Her hand dropped back to her lap and she turned to look at me.

"Really?" she said. "Where?"

"Somewhere where it's just you and me."

She nodded. "Yeah. I'd like that."

We were walking through the front door of our condo when my phone buzzed in my pocket. A text. I didn't recognize the number.

> *Hey, hope you don't mind—Brick gave me your number. It's Petra.*

177

I glanced up at Yara, who was walking toward the bathroom. Yara didn't like Petra, she'd made that abundantly clear. Despite my better judgment I typed: *Hey! That's cool. What's up?*

The bubble appeared to let me know she was typing, but then I heard the bathroom door open and I jammed my phone into my back pocket.

I don't know why I did it. Why I didn't tell Yara right then and there that Petra had texted me. A stupid choice.

"What's wrong?" Yara asked when she saw my face.

"Nothing," I said. "I'm just tired."

She nodded like she understood, and it occurred to me what a long day it had been for her. I walked up behind her and rubbed her shoulders as she stood in her favorite spot staring out of the window that overlooked Elliott Bay.

"Take your clothes off and get into bed," I said. "I'll give you a massage."

"With your tongue or hands?" she asked.

"Both."

She raised her eyebrows at me and then walked toward the bedroom.

Before I followed her I pulled out my phone. Petra hadn't sent a follow up text after all. She must have changed her mind about whatever she was going to say. I deleted her text and put my phone on the charger before following Yara into the bedroom.

33
THE WEDDING

THERE WERE SEVERE THUNDERSTORMS on the day of our wedding. We got married in February in a little chapel in Vancouver. The church had a bell tower that they promised they'd ring once we were married. We'd expected rain, but nothing like the torrential downpour we got.

"Relax," said the photographer. "Rain on your wedding day is good luck."

So I relaxed. We needed all the luck we could get. The streets were overwhelmed with puddles and our handful of guests had to play hopscotch to reach the church. My mother came into the room where I was getting ready ten minutes before the wedding was to start. She kissed one cheek and patted the other.

"I've never seen you so happy," she said. "That warms my soul."

"Is Sam here?" I asked.

She nodded.

"Your brother wouldn't miss your wedding, my boy." She smiled. "I know you butt heads but he still loves you."

I shrugged like it didn't matter but it did. The relationship I had with my brother wasn't my choice. He always hated me, even as children, and over the years his resentment had just deepened. When she left I texted Yara.

You still want to do this, right?

WHY?! She texted back right away. *Did Ferdinand say I was a flight risk?*

I laughed as I stared down at my phone. He had.

Even with all of her trepidation about the wedding I never doubted she'd show. Ferdinand asked what her flight risk was, and I brushed him off even though I knew he was serious.

I'll be there, Lisey. I love you deeply.

When Yara walked into the church, her shoulders and face were spotted with raindrops. She looked ethereal…glowing in the dim lighting of the chapel. My heart beat wildly in my chest and I smiled so much my cheeks hurt. She looked steadily on as she walked down the aisle, her eyes fixed on my face, holding a small bouquet of white flowers. She didn't smile back at me, her face neutral. It looked like she was trying to be brave, but I didn't see that at the time, that was something I realized later.

As we took our vows, we were interrupted by the rumbling sound of thunder. I had to pause twice just so she could hear me. And when Yara said, *"I do,"* the lights flickered and everyone gasped. What foreboding. The only time she was herself the entire night was when we were alone for a few minutes in the bathroom while I held up her dress so she could pee. She giggled and hid her face while I teased her for being helpless. We kissed at the sink as she washed her hands. And then later when we walked hand-in-hand back to our hotel instead of hailing a cab, letting the rain soak through our wedding clothes so that when we finally got to the lobby we left puddles all over the floor.

I booked a suite on the tenth floor; the elevator ride was long and excruciatingly cold. When we reached the door, I stopped her so I could carry her inside. She made a show of rolling her eyes and acting irritated, but I knew she liked it.

"That was fun," Yara said, once we were inside the room.

"The wedding?" I asked, only half serious.

"The rain," she replied simply, turning around so I could unzip her dress.

I had an idea. "Can you go stand right there…by the window?" I shrugged off my suit jacket and tossed it over a chair.

She narrowed her eyes, but surprisingly did as I asked, walking stiffly to stand in front of the wall of glass. Behind her was the city, the lights colored and twinkling. I took a picture of her standing there, her mascara running, and her white dress plastered to her body. I could see her nipples and the pink of her thighs where the material clung to skin. Long tendrils of her hair were stuck to her neck. She was more beautiful than she'd ever been in that moment, and I had to look away so she wouldn't see the emotion on my face.

"Yara Lisey," I said, setting my phone down.

When she smiled her lips puckered as she tried to bite back laughter.

"It sounds nice," she said. "Like a musician's wife." She wiggled her eyebrows and put her hands on her hips.

"Help me take this thing off, will you?"

She turned her back to me again and I unzipped the dress, licking rivulets of water off her neck and back. She shivered and I wasn't sure if it was from the cold or me. When she turned around there was that hungry fire in her eyes, so I kissed her good as she flicked open the buttons on my shirt.

Later we lay in bed, waiting for our room service and touching each other almost shyly like we'd never done it before.

"You're a husband," she said. "Is that weird?"

"No, not even a little bit. I knew I would be as soon as I saw you, English."

"You haven't called me English in weeks," she said. "I missed it."

I thought back, trying to remember why. "I guess we've just been busy."

"Busy?" She frowned. "Too busy for nicknames?"

"Too busy for affection. Isn't that fucked up? The weeks before a wedding all of the softness in a relationship goes away." We hadn't fought very much, but there had been days of quiet stiffness when neither of us chose to speak to the other.

She laughed. "Well it's over now, thank God. We can get back to living."

"Yara Lisey," I said.

And then the doorbell rang with our food and I stood up to put my robe on. I was happy, so happy; the way you feel when you realize that out of the billions of people on the planet you've found your one.

She didn't stick around long enough to change her name.

34
THE CASE

BACK THEN YARA CARED more about Petra than I did. I thought her fixation would stop after we were married. But I think Petra is ultimately why she left. Or maybe I just need a reason to understand why she left and that's the one I chose.

"Do you think she's pretty?" she'd ask.
I did.
"Yes."
"Do you think she's into you?"
I did.
"Yes."
"Do you think she understands you better than I can?"
I did not.
"No."
"Why are you asking me these things, English?"
"Because I know you'll tell the truth."

She was right. It was hard for me not to tell the truth and she used that against me. Sometimes it felt like she was building a case with my truth. I started being an omission kind of guy, to field off Yara's truth searching. I told myself I was protecting our relationship. For the first six weeks after we were married I was happy. Yara seemed happy too. She took to baking, which I'd never seen her do before. When I asked her about it, she blushed and said baking was what you were supposed to do when married.

"I think that was in the nineteen fifties." I laughed.

Yara waved a spatula at me. "So what do we do now then?"

I came up behind her and kissed her neck. "We fuck," I said. "It's the new baking."

She threw her arms around my neck, still holding the spatula. I felt cake batter drip down my neck as she kissed me.

"Good," she said when she pulled away. "I hate baking, it's such a fucking bore."

I saw Petra a few weeks after Yara and I were married. I was at Ferdinand's house with a couple other people watching a Seahawks game. Yara was working the nightshift at the restaurant. I'd forgotten about the text until she walked in, and then I felt guilty. I'd deleted it so my wife wouldn't see—or rather so she'd not have a reason to be angry with me.

I was sitting on Ferdinand's couch between Brick and a guy Ferdinand grew up with named Erick. When Erick went to the kitchen to grab another beer, Petra took his spot next to me.

"Hi," she said.

"Hey."

"Sorry about that text," she said, ducking her head. "I was drunk."

"Drunk texting is never good," I said. I was trying to make things light, but she nodded somberly and looked down at her hands.

"I know. One of my friends took my phone from me before I could send another." She laughed and I smiled stiffly wishing the game would come back on and give me an excuse to end the conversation.

"The truth is I needed to say this in person." She cleared her throat and looked around nervously. I did too. The guys were all in the kitchen with their beer waiting out the commercials.

"I…uh…well, I am in love with you, David," she said. "I know you're married, and I know this must be awkward, but I needed to tell you."

I stared at her. Why did this feel like a set up?

"Why did you need to tell me?" I asked.

Petra looked stricken. She opened and closed her mouth and then glanced over her shoulder to see where everyone else was.

"I thought you should know," she stammered.

"I'm in love with Yara. I'm married to Yara. Why would I need to know that?"

It looked like she wanted to cry. I softened my tone. "Petra, I'm with Yara."

She stood up abruptly and nodded her head. "I see," she said. "I just thought…"

"You thought wrong," I said firmly.

She left before I could say anything else. Ferdinand came over as soon as she was gone.

"What was that about, man?"

"Nothing," I said. "Listen, I'm going to take off. I think I'll stop at The Jane so I can see Yara."

He nodded still looking at the door.

I needed to touch her. See her face. She'd been right about Petra—even though she'd never come out and directly accused her—she'd acted suspicious of her since they'd met. Female intuition, my mother always said, was never wrong.

When I walked into The Jane I didn't get the welcome I was expecting. Yara spotted me right away, but instead of greeting me, she turned her back and walked toward the kitchen. I grabbed the only available bar stool, telling myself it was busy and she hadn't meant it. I waited for her to come back, my unease climbing by the minute. When she finally emerged around the corner, she was carrying a tray of food and wouldn't look at me. This wasn't like her. No matter where we were, we caught eyes. I always found her from the stage when she was at one of our shows.

"Yara," I said when she walked back around the bar. She grabbed a glass and glanced over at me while she poured a beer.

"You seen Instagram?" she asked.

"No."

"Well, I have."

I opened the app and there it was, the first picture that popped up was a group pic Brick had posted thirty minutes ago, right after I left. I hadn't even realized someone had taken a picture. Petra was sitting next to me on the couch and she must have just said something because we were looking at each other. I ran a hand over my face and glanced at Yara, who was leaning over the bar talking to a customer. She pointed something out on the menu and then turned her head to look at me. I could see the hurt in her eyes. I tried to see the picture as she saw it: Petra in very short shorts, leaning toward me in what looked like intimate conversation, one shoulder exposed when her shirt slipped down. My mouth was slightly open as I said something to her. It looked like we were having a grand ol' time instead of how uncomfortable the situation actually was.

I stayed until the game was over and the bar cleared out. Yara still hadn't come over and I didn't entirely blame her.

Understanding comes with knowledge. Knowledge comes with time. I tell myself that in time Petra will do for me what Yara did. Fill the void, consume me with her quirks, and love will override the doubts.

She does not. But that's my fault, not Petra's. It's not true what they say, that you can only give your heart away once. That's the philosophy of the young. The old know better, they know it's not the heart that you give away, but the mind. Fuck…shit…the mind is a powerful thing. It controls the heart, but most people don't know that.

I have to find her.

PART THREE
THE E-MAIL

Dear Yara,

The band's in London November 12th. Want to catch up?

David

SO CASUAL. SO NONCHALANT. You'd think we were only acquaintances, that we'd once sipped a couple of beers together instead of tattooing love on our skin and reciting marriage vows. I read the e-mail again and analyze the shit out of it. How can I not? I count out the words: thirteen. The punctuation: four. His name, my name. They used to go together. A flippant, casual turn of phrase: *catch up*. In the end, there's only so much psychoanalyzing you can do to a thirteen-word e-mail. I move on with my life, feeling rather pathetic. But not before I e-mail him back. And okay, sure, I don't move on with my life. I am stuck. What does moving on entail? Forgetting? Forgiving?

Being happy? Besides, I know what he wants to talk about. I know why he's coming. He wants his divorce.

> **Hi David,**
>
> **Yeah, sounds good. Let me know when and where.**
>
> **Yara**

My e-mail is a word shorter.

I'm that petty.

Why now? It's been three years. He's met someone. I can feel it.

35

WATERMELON

A YEAR BEFORE THE FUCKING E-MAIL

IT'S FRIDAY NIGHT. I put on my only dress and a pair of ripped tights, and head to Posey's for her monthly get-together.

"Look nice," she'd told me. *"None of that Seattle grunge you've been wearing."*

The weather is getting warmer, people are wearing fewer layers and more smiles as they walk about the city. It's comical to see, everyone clamoring for the sun. We look like children gazing up at the faces of our parents, dim smiles and glassy eyes—winter's presence still paling our cheeks. I've known Posey since grade school. She kicked a boy's arse once when he told me I was ugly. Right there on the playground. She was suspended from school for a week, but that hadn't mattered to her. Even when her mum took away her Gameboy she'd insisted that he deserved it.

I still remember the shock and glee I'd felt watching it all unfold. Someone was standing up for me.

"Who's ugly now?!" she'd screamed, standing over him, staring down at his bloodied face.

Even back then Posey had worn androgynous clothes. I remember the long sleeve black button-down and the black jeans hanging limply on her skinny frame, an emo child warrior with blood on her knuckles. She's insane but those are the sorts of people you cherish. After we graduated I went to university for boring shit—business classes—and then switched my major to hospitality management, while Posey got a degree in art history and now ran a gallery in central London. Her life is beautiful, a reflection of everything she is. My life is also a reflection of everything I am, and that's quite embarrassing.

I stop at a flower shop a block from her flat and pick up a bouquet to take with me: Marsala calla lilies mixed with grape hyacinth—she'd be more impressed with their names than the actual flowers. Posey lives in a flat right on the river, just a ten-minute walk from my place, which is significantly less posh. Her parties are always the best. She gets the top shelf liquor and plays only eighties music, which is fine by me. Dancing drunk to the eighties is life. But, more than that, she makes a point of inviting handsome men as an incentive for her girlfriends to attend. I'd be fine with just the expensive booze, but I suppose the scenery is a nice plus. When I arrive, the party is in full swing. A man I've not seen before is dancing with Sharon, the sluttiest of all of my friends. She has her leg propped up on his hip and is swinging an invisible lasso over her head as she grinds against him. He's into it, biting his lip and staring at her jiggling tits. They aren't good tits, they're just tits. When he sees me he stops dancing and runs a hand through his hair like he's forgotten where he is. Sharon doesn't notice, she spins around and grinds her backside against him, whipping her hair from side to side.

We stare at each other for a moment, the *Dirty Dancing* soundtrack is playing and I feel like I should be carrying a watermelon. I break eye contact and squeeze past them to find Posey. She's in the kitchen taking a tray out of the oven, a cigarette stuck between her lips.

"Who's that guy dancing with Sharon?" I ask.

"Fuck," she says. The movement of her lips makes ash fall from the tip of her cigarette and onto the tray she's holding. Something sizzles.

"I fucked up the appetizers again. Oh, that's Ethan," she kicks the oven closed with her foot, "a work wanker. Cooks the gallery's books. He's sexy but sort of an arse, if you know what I mean." I know what she means. And then she adds, "I hear he has a massive Moby."

Moby Dick is my favorite book. She knows it bothers me when she makes penial references around it.

I ignore him because every other girl isn't. I'm not one to feed into fandom. Eventually, toward the end of the night, when I'm getting ready to leave, he walks over looking sloshed and holding a beer. He looks at me expectantly. I glance over my shoulder, but there's no one there. It's me he's come for.

"Haven't you noticed?"

"Noticed what?" I ask. I'm surprised he's broken away from his fan club. I look around him to see if there are any girls trailing behind him.

"I've been eye-fucking you all night. I thought it was obvious."

"Hmmm," I say, setting my drink down and digging in my purse for my lipstick. "I've noticed you eye-fuck yourself in almost every mirror and reflective surface you pass. I must have missed that part. Thank you for fitting me in, by the way."

I drop the lipstick back in my purse and look away, bored. He's very good looking. It's almost hard not to look at him.

"Your name is Yara Phillips, you were born in Manchester, went to school in London, and traveled all over the US just for fun. Your friends say you're a city whore, and also a man-hater, but that if I asked nicely you might say yes."

"Ask what nicely?" I ask, raising my eyebrows. And my friends were fucking traitors. They could fuck off, the lot of them.

"I haven't decided," he says. "Dinner…drinks…a good fuck."

He's drunk. I decide not to be too hard on him. And besides, he took the time to gather some information on me. Not a complete narcissist, yeah?

I eye Ethan warily, the scruff on his chin, the deep-set eyes, the too-cool-for-school haircut. This boy/girl dance is exhausting. It feels the same each time: flirt, sex, date, disappoint, break up. I'm made of glass not steel.

"Let me decide for you then," I say. And without another word I move past Ethan as he stares after me forlornly. I have to say goodbye to Posey before I leave, so I push past a couple making out and have to step over a drunken guy slouched against the wall. Ethan follows me into the living room where Posey is sitting on the couch half sprawled across her girlfriend. Her white blonde hair is combed back in a low ponytail and her eyes are sleepy either from the liquor or the joint she smoked earlier. I lean down and kiss her on the forehead, promising to call her next week to set up a lunch date. All the while Ethan lingers awkwardly behind me.

"You taking this one home then?" Posey says, jutting her chin toward him.

I glance over my shoulder before shaking my head.

"No," I say. "I don't take advantage of drunk men."

Posey laughs and reaches her hand toward me. I take it and she squeezes my fingers.

"He's not always an arse," she says. "He's quite kind if you look really deep. Really, really, really deep."

We all laugh, even Ethan who curses colorfully at her before she shows him the finger and tells him to get the fuck out of her house. And then we're walking out of the flat together, down the stairs, and past the doors with their bright white paint and shiny gold numbers. The minute I push open the doors to her building, the song of London greets me: cars, music, laughter drifting out of a pub, the sounds of people as they love, and flirt, and play. Ethan grabs my hand and I don't pull away. I figure I've given him a hard enough time.

"I'd like it if you walked me home," he says. "Just to be safe."

I roll my eyes. "Where do you live?"

"Over by Paddington Basin," he says. "Next to Selfridges."

"You've got to be kidding me. I'm not walking all that way. I'll call you an Uber." I pull out my phone but it's dead.

"Shit, do you have yours?"

He shakes his head.

Such a fucking liar, I think.

"Battery died hours ago."

I notice he's not slurring anymore. The wanker was faking.

"I can just come to yours then," he says, cheerfully. "I don't mind at all."

We're trudging through the streets now. It's started raining. I shoot him a dirty look. Part of me wants the company, but I'd prefer to be the one to suggest it.

"Is this how you get women to sleep with you? Because it's pathetic. I don't take strays in, I'm not the bloody pound."

He laughs. "No, actually. I never have to work this hard. I'm trying a new tactic where I sort of beg and act like a loser and hope you feel sorry for me."

"Right," I say. "Unfortunately that won't work for you. You might want to reconsider."

"Your friends said nothing would work." He shrugs. "They reckon you're still hung up on that David guy."

I recoil at the sound of his name. It's like someone just tasered me. How dare they tell him about David! God, I desperately need new friends.

"Who's David?" I ask.

"Exactly," he says.

I open the door to my building. *Time to move on, Yara,* I tell myself.

36

SKYLIGHT SEX

I LIVE IN A whitish building with ten units and worn
espresso colored floors. The place is old, but the floors are
new, made to look old. I love those floors, how they try to
be something they're not. The flats are four to a floor,
except for the third floor, which only has two units. That's
where I am, in the attic space that has been converted into
two small studios and divided by a thin sheetrock wall. My
side has the skylight; my neighbor, Bidi, has a slanted
ceiling and a window seat with built-in bookshelves. I'm
jealous of her window nook, and as far as I know she is
too busy fucking the guy from 5M to use it. I've been in
her place once to return the vacuum she loaned me and
spotted five varieties of bongs on the shelves that were
meant for books. I bought my own vacuum after that. I
won't be taking loaners from someone who desecrates
bookshelves. The room came with a single bed and a
dresser that is so worn and chipped I'm not even sure
what color it had originally been. I papered the drawers
and packed away what little I had. You'd think someone

who traveled America for as long as I did would have…more. But, I don't. I shed things like a snake shed its skin. When I left I didn't take anything with me but some clothes.

Ethan kisses me as the rain tinkers softly against the skylight in my living room; the one good thing about my sad little flat is that small piece of joyful sky. A slice of light. He undresses me slowly, which puts me at ease;his long fingers flick across the buttons on my dress, popping the little beads out of their assigned holes. He doesn't say stupid shit about how hot my body is, I appreciate that. Maybe he doesn't think my body is hot, I don't really care. We're here now and on the way to orgasmic glory. I need time to acclimate to this new man who is touching my skin and breathing hard against my neck. I know that once he's inside of me I'll have taken a step away from David and toward my future. It's all for the best. Or at least that's what I tell myself.

I breathe him in. A new smell. Maybe I've missed this: the first smells, and touches, and kisses. It's so different with each man. Ethan's not at all what I thought, quite gentle actually. I imagine it's all a show with him, the fucking, and flirting, and whatnot. He goes full bravado like a Hollywood action flick and then settles into a romance once you're impressed. It's a grand tactic and a great relief. Bad boys are only fun when they're threatening to break your heart. There isn't a hair on his chest, just smooth, white skin and lean muscle. I try not to remember the dark hair I liked to run my fingers through. Another man, another lifetime. I hadn't known I liked hair on a man's chest until I saw David's. Ethan is going to make love to me—I can tell by his movements. There won't be any fucking tonight. Tonight? I think maybe it's morning. He licks my clavicle. He's the sort of guy who wants to stare into your eyes as he pokes around inside of you. A literal fucking romantic. And in ten years, when someone asks how we met, he'll tell them that he tried to play it cool, but he was in love with me from the first moment. This was how beautiful things started, I assure myself—at the tail end of something else.

Ethan leads me toward the bathroom and I have to redirect him to the bedroom, both of us laughing. I kick open the door. Before he pushes me down on the bed he turns on the radio. I almost laugh except I'm caught up in the moment, the potential for love songs and lovemaking. I want to believe again, to feel. The adverts are on: a car dealership, and then a dating service. He takes off my bra while a woman with a smoky voice talks about the husband she met online.

His mouth is on me when a jingle about Nando's chicken plays; first one breast and then the other. The irony is sort of hilarious. I arch my back because it feels so good to be touched after such a long hiatus. Why did I ever stop doing this? He rubs me through my panties and then suddenly yanks them off. I lift my hips to help him and he tosses them somewhere over his shoulder. Finally a song comes on. I haven't heard it before, but it has a nice beat. A sort of ra ta ta ta that makes your heart accelerate.

I relax as Ethan settles himself between my legs and I curl around him. I like this part. I get lost in it, my eyes rolling back, my hands gripping his too-cool-for-school hair. The song plays, but I'm too lost to hear it. His tongue keeps beat with the music. And then he crawls up my body until his weight is on me. And it's the very moment Ethan is pushing himself inside of me, while I'm moaning into his mouth, that the song reaches me. I recognize the voice, and I listen to the lyrics as a strange man moves in my body.

Atheists who kneel and pray, the voice sings. *Begging for just anything. Non-believers bitten down to the core. Pass them a word, give them a string. When you're dying you cling. Yara, Yara, the god of disbelief. I worship between your legs. Pray to your fallacy, pray to your winter. You kill everything.*

Ethan at first thinks I'm having an orgasm. He speeds up, pushing into me harder while he bites at my neck and shoulder. I convulse against him, my grief so profound I shudder. Thousands of miles away, and David has crawled into bed with me, crawled right in the middle of Ethan and me and punched me in the gut. I feel him release into me and I wonder dumbly if he put a condom on. Drunk was bad. Drunk was irresponsible. Drunk was potential pregnancy or STD from a stranger.

Stupid, stupid, Yara, I think. And then David is on his second verse, accusing me of ugly things.

We're all just atheists who kneel and pray, you made me believe and then erased the day. Fallacy, Yara, a molten idol. A flesh and blood god, not a god at all. A girl who calls you just to kill. Yara, Yara, the god of disbelief.

Ethan is looking into my watery shocked eyes and I notice that his are weatherworn blue. Like an old pair of denim. Had we made love? Had we fucked? Was I pregnant and riddled with STDs? He rolls off me and I breathe a sigh of relief when I spot the condom. I want to cry from relief.

Yara, Yara, the god of disbelief.

I curl up on my side, too wrung out to even pull up the sheet. He does if for me before climbing into bed and molding his body against mine. I don't tell him to fuck off and leave. I don't want to be alone, I'm afraid of what I'll do. I did it. I did what I'd set out to do. I wanted to break a man's heart for his art. Rip his belief system to shreds so he'd have to rebuild it. And that was the thing about a scorned artist, wasn't it? Their new medium was you. Just ask Bukowski, ask Plath, ask Taylor Swift whose blood they used for ink. David was going to hate me for the rest of his life. But, he was going to make beautiful music. He already had.

"Yara," Ethan says softly.

I pretend to be asleep.

37

BRONTE

A BAR. THE BASICS: you restock, pour, clean, pour some more, have entitled servers tap their fingers on the bar top you just wiped down while shooting you dirty looks.

"I need it now," they say. "Can you hurry? I fucked up the order."

You listen, you nod, you pour. You smile, and frown, and cut citrus until your fingers sting. You soak the guns, clean the speed racks, count your drawer. The coins go *ting, ting, ting* as they shuck out of your hand and into the plastic dividers. You tell off a server for ruining your liquor count with their overly generous pours, you ignore the manager who always looks at your tits unless he's handing you your paycheck. You are extra nice to the hostess so she ushers the best people into your section. You eavesdrop on conversations that are none of your business.

I used to be into that sort of thing.
Her husband gave it to her then left.

I'm obsessed with that show. Have you seen it?
I've been trying to get rid of you for years.
Pass the salt, you salty bitch.
He fucking worships her, the cow.
One tit looks like a cantaloupe, one tit looks like an avocado.

At night I still hear them speaking, broken bits of their conversation passing through my dreams. I consider another occupation, but bar life is the only life I know, and I quite enjoy it. I'm offered a job at Bronte, right off Trafalgar Square and situated on the Strand. I worked with one of the managers before I left for the States, and he told me if I were to ever find myself in these parts again to look him up. It's an airy setup with floor to ceiling windows, decorated with the sort of color palette that Posey's grandmother would have worn on her face: peaches and golds. I imagine most of the writers of old would have steered clear of the place, but it made non-writers feel charming to come here and sip cocktails named Billy Bones or Sgt. Pepper.

I keep a low profile, but eventually my friends hear I'm back and pass through for drinks. Some of them come in twos; some come alone. People I went to school with, or worked with, or tried to forget. They all ask the same questions: What was New York like? Did I shag anyone famous? Seattle's just like London, yeah? *No,* I think. *Seattle has David. London is lacking.*

I hear his song—my song—on the radio all the time. I want to shut it off, but I reckon I deserve the punishment. I listen each time, to the words, his hurt, his anger, and let the ache build in the pit of my stomach. If I listen too hard, I start to remember the way his lips felt—the soft, wet comfort of them. *Fuck this life*, I think.

"I love this song," someone always says.

My name is in the song, but nobody notices. No one but Posey, who jokes one day as we're having lunch in

Camden Town: "Did you fuck the guy who wrote this song? While you were across the pond?"

I stare at her, and she sits up in her seat, ramrod straight, her eyes becoming large.

"You can't just fuck celebrities and not tell me, Yara," she says.

"He wasn't one. Not then. He was just a guy who came into the bar and flirted with me."

"And what did you do to deserve a song like that?"

I picked at the bun on my burger and stared at the floor.

"Look, I don't want to talk about it," I say. "It's bad enough I have to hear the bloody song everywhere I go."

"I'm so impressed," says Posey. "I always knew you were a muse, but you got a song on the top ten. Epic shit right there."

"Posey!"

"All right, all right. When you're ready, yeah?"

"How are things with you and Samantha?" I ask, trying to change the subject.

She gives me the side-eye. "How many girlfriends have I had in the last five years?"

"Too many to count."

She points her fork at me. "Exactly."

"So what are you saying? You're going to break up with her?"

I pictured them the night I was at her house for the party. They'd seemed really into each other: affectionate, comfortable. But, maybe I'd been too drunk to see the truth. And wasn't Posey always affectionate? That was just her thing. Even if you weren't a hugger and she forced you into one, you'd suddenly make an exception.

"I don't know. For now we're okay."

I want to ask more, clarify what she means, but I don't think she knows yet.

"Ethan talks about you a lot."

The conversation shifts again, back to me. I hate this ritual of information sharing. When you're a bartender you can listen to everyone's dirt without having to be personally involved. That's the way I like it. Can't we just sit here in silence and enjoy each other's company that way? She drains the last of her beer, slams the bottle on the table, and looks at me expectantly. I blink at her, not sure what to say. The morning after he spent the night I'd told him I had a dentist appointment and had to leave. He'd gotten dressed, and so had I, and then I walked him downstairs, waiting until he was around the corner before returning to my flat.

He's called a couple times since then, texted too. But, I've been firm about my rejection. I am in no way, shape, or form willing to date someone. I don't know that I ever have been. Most people move through life looking for some elusive soulmate experience. I am trying my hardest to avoid it. Does that make me fucked up or wise? Who knows, who cares?

"He's not my type," I say, looking around for the server. If Posey is going to be launching questions for the rest of lunch I need to top off my wine.

"So, this David Lisey guy is…was—?"

She's baiting me. I shoot her a dirty look and slouch down in my seat.

"I don't have a type. That's the honest truth. I believe in connections, and yes, I had one with him."

Posey has sleepy eyes. If you didn't know her, she gave you the impression that she was incredibly bored with whatever you were saying. When she smoked pot her lids drooped even lower, and it looked like she was sneering at you. But, at the mention of David, her eyes are wide open, like someone has just thrown water in her face.

"Did you fuck him?"

It's a trigger. I see myself lost beneath him as he moves over me. His smooth skin beneath my fingertips, hot and damp. He's not constrained like other men, he's not trying to be careful with his reactions. Each time he pushes into me, he moans, his face flashing expressions that ranged from pain, to relief, to shock. I felt like music the whole time. I was an instrument and he was reveling in the way I played.

"Yeah," I tell Posey.

She smiles. It takes a minute for me to be back in this dingy pub, the windows filmed over with a layer of scum. I can still taste him on my lips, smell his skin.

"When did you run?"

I shrug.

"I'd always meant to. So, I just stuck with it."

"Has he tried to find you?" She drained the last of her beer, licking her lips and staring at me expectantly.

"There's no way, really. I don't have a Facebook, my number changed when I moved home. He knows very little about me."

"But, he wrote you that song," she says. "He's trying in his own way."

I turn away. "He's angry with me. That's why he wrote the song."

"He's angry because you left. He's not angry you're you."

"That is me, though, isn't it? I leave."

Posey's mouth pulls into a tight line. "Stop trying to convince the world that you're more damaged than anyone else, Yara."

The words come out immediately, an electric denial. "I'm not," I say. But, maybe that's exactly the narcissistic thing I was trying to do.

"You broke a man's heart because you thought your love was so important it would damage him beyond recognition. And what's a true artist anyway, Yara? What you say it is?"

I don't even know how she's figured that. I guess one just has to listen to the lyrics of the song. I could be angry with him for outing me like that, but the truth is I deserve it.

"I don't understand why you're being like this. You asked and I told you. It's not fair that you're attacking me for it."

Posey touches my face like she's searching for me underneath my skin. I don't like when people touch my face, but when Posey does it I don't pull away. There are too many years, too much familiarity. Her finger is on my forehead, pressing.

"You're too much in here. You want to be a poet and you're not. By the time you realize you're not doomed, your life is going to be over and you'll never have taken any risks."

"You're paying today," I tell her, snatching up my bag when she drops her hand. "I won't pay to be tortured."

38

SLOW ROTATION

I'VE ALWAYS TOLD MYSELF that it was only a matter of time before he found me. I study my face in the mirror as I put on my makeup. Do I look like I did the last time he saw me? My hair is shorter and I suppose my face is more lined. Posey claims that I look hollow. He's coming for a divorce, I remind myself, not a reunion. But we had something real, and surely he wants to shout at me a bit, tell me what a worthless human I am, tell me about all the pain I caused.

I suppose there's a chance that I may not be that important to him anymore. For the most part, men are better at moving on than women. When people come looking for you they want one of three things: closure, revenge, or money. I'm sure David has more money than he knows what to do with, so I can at least stand still and be a good target while he takes the other two. At the very least he's coming for my signature.

Yara, Yara, the god of disbelief…

I meet up with Ethan for dinner. We've been seeing each other for around six months, and other than David's e-mail, my feelings for him have been uninterrupted. When I see him my stomach always does this fluttery thing other girls like to call butterflies. To me it feels more like resolve fluttering to death in my belly. I wasn't supposed to fall in love again, and while I'm not sure I'm there yet, it's getting close. Posey assures me that we aren't meant to fall in love only once.

"You can do it again and again," she says.

But, she's broken up with Samantha or whatever her name is, and I think she's just trying to be hopeful for herself. In the end, Samantha wasn't ambitious enough…or maybe she wasn't interesting enough. I can't remember. Posey always finds something wrong with them. I always find something wrong with me.

"Hey girl." Ethan stands when I near the table, all six feet of him.

I eye the way the fabric of his shirt stretches across his shoulders. The muscular arms he has by going to the gym four days a week. I can't go anywhere four days a week, I'm not that disciplined. He leans over and kisses me on the mouth. Not a peck either—his tongue slips between my lips and he moans a little when I kiss him back.

Just then David's song begins to play across the restaurant. I break free of Ethan's lips and have the urge to wipe my mouth with my napkin. Wipe Ethan away because David is watching me. Is it David's song or my song? It follows me around, pissing on everything—the shops, work, walking down the fucking street. I tap my fingers on the table and search for the server. I need a drink, a very large, very strong drink. Ethan sings along as he studies his menu, and as always, I tense, waiting for him to realize the song is about me.

"So I was thinking," he says.

"It's never good when you do too much of that," I interrupt.

He makes a face at me, the kind a stern father makes to threaten his wily offspring.

"I was thinking," he begins again, "that it's time to get married."

I stand up. My chair grates across the concrete floor and people turn their heads to look. Ethan is laughing, every one of his bright white teeth showing as he throws back his head and holds his stomach.

"I'm just joking, Yara," he says.

I sit back down, but I scoot my chair back a few inches. He lost my trust with the "M" word.

"I was thinking it's time to move in together."

"Oh my God," I say, clutching my heart. "Why would you do that to me?"

"Because now moving in together doesn't feel quite as scary. You just escaped the dreaded 'M' word."

"Clever," I tell him. And I mean it. Moving in together doesn't sound half as scary as it would have if he hadn't brought up marriage first.

"Why?" I ask him.

"Why do I want to move in with you?"

"Yes," I say.

"Is this multiple choice or essay?"

"Essay," I tell him.

He clears his throat. "All right. I want to move in with you because I love you. I mostly hate life, except when I'm with you, that is. I was a mangy sewer rat before, a deplorable. Now I feel like a teenager. Up here," he taps his temple, "and down here." He moves his hand to his pants.

I laugh.

"Seriously, Yara. I just want to be with you all the time. I am committed. I want to share more than the occasional dinner date and Sunday stroll through the park with you. I want to have a fucking Christmas tree and Easter ham with you."

"All right," I say. "Top marks for that excellent essay."

He gets up to kiss me, and you'd think by the expression on his face that I *had* said yes to a marriage proposal.

"Where will we live?"

"We'll find somewhere new," he says. "Where I haven't fucked dozens of hos."

I choke on my water and he has to stand up and hit me on the back—a completely senseless thing people do to make themselves useful when someone else is choking.

"Well, when you put it that way…"

"In hopes that you'd agree, I've already been looking up flats to rent. There's one quite near here. I can ring the agent and see if we can have a look before someone else snatches it up."

"You're pulling my leg. What an eager beaver."

But, he already knows he has me. The thought of getting out of my grubby little flat is thrilling. The thought of starting something solid with a man I love and respect feels like movement forward. It makes the past a joke if you can somewhat behave in the present. Like it didn't really matter that I walked out on a man and a marriage, or that I've never managed to stay in a relationship for longer than a year. Moving in with Ethan will make me legit.

"Call her," I say. "I'm excited."

"I love when you're excited," he says. "You wear it like a child."

I don't know if that's a good thing, but I smile at him over my wineglass as he pulls out his phone to text the agent.

After dinner we catch the train to Embankment and walk the short distance to a stately limestone. The Eye is lit up to a neon pink and I wonder if we'll be able to see it from the flat.

"I always thought this was a hotel," I say to Ethan.

The agent is waiting for us outside, looking put out and checking her watch like we're already late. He gives her a little wave to let her know it's us she's meeting.

"A stickler," I whisper to Ethan. "Let's annoy her."

He winks at me conspiratorially and we step forward to do our handshaking and name giving. Her name is Lucinda, or Lucretia, or some shit like that. She sums up my bag and my shoes, usually a telltale sign of a woman's wealth and stature in the world. I'm carrying a secondhand Gucci bag Posey gave me. I seem to pass the test as she glances at it appreciatively and leads us into the building.

"This one is going to go very fast," she says, walking toward the lifts. "Being so centrally located and all. It's just a short distance from the Tube and there are some wonderful restaurants and shopping nearby."

I take in the chandeliers, the heavy wood paneling, and the crisp uniform of the doormen.

"I'm afraid there's quite a long application process as well," she says. "Only the cream of the crop allowed in here." She glances back at us to see if we're afraid.

I nod solemnly. When her back is turned I make a face at Ethan.

We get off on the seventh floor and she leads us down a wide carpeted hallway, stopping at 37G. She types into a keypad and there is a click as the door opens.

"Keypad entry," she says over her shoulder like we were too daft to notice.

The space is 1,200 square feet of perfect. We *ooh* and *ahh* as we walk through the small rooms and come to a stop in the kitchen. Three identical windows face the Eye, the Thames spread out before it, glittering like black magic. I give Ethan a look. Ethan gives me a look.

"Can we afford it?" I ask softly, doing a tally of money and bills in my head.

He smiles like that's the silliest question in the world.

"Yes, Yara. Do you want it?" he asks.

"Very much so, but shouldn't we look at some others? It seems so hasty to jump into the first thing we see." I glance at the agent who is pretending to investigate a cabinet while she eavesdrops.

"That doesn't sound like you at all," he says. "You're a see it, want it person. Usually you've decided within the first few minutes."

He's right, of course. I knew the minute I walked in that there would be no need to look further.

"I suppose I'm trying to be responsible," I tell him. "Not so hasty."

"No. Don't change. The way you're sure about everything makes me sure too."

"All right then," I say, looking at Lucinda. "We'll take it."

She nods.

"So how did you two meet?" she asks as she pulls an application from the folder she's holding.

"I was working the corner," I said. "I had a brown wig on that day and he picked me up in his convertible and took me to a hotel to fuck me. We just hit it off, you know? Been together ever since."

Ethan's eyes are wide, his hands shoved in his pockets. I don't know if he wants to laugh or chastise me, but he plays along, nodding his head.

Lucinda looks from one of us to the other, her doughy face strained. It's like the dumb bitch has never seen *Pretty Woman*.

"Thank you," Ethan says, breaking the silence. He pulls the application from her fingers. I shrug and wander over to the window to watch the Eye in her slow rotation.

It's time to stop waiting, isn't it? To be ready. For life to start. I'm not even sure what I was waiting for. Very soon I will see David, and then I can say a proper goodbye and get on with my life. He deserves that and I do as well. I made mistakes in my youth, but it is time to move forward.

39
THE FLAT

ETHAN AND I TAKE the flat. Or we fill out an application and turn it in with our twenty quid, hopeful and positive. He is positive because he wants the flat. I am positive because I want to want the flat.

When Posey questions my lackluster enthusiasm I freak out on her.

"Oh my God! I want the flat, I freaking want the flat, all right?"

"But, do you want the flat alone or with Ethan?" she asks me.

I have to think about that one for a minute.

"You're evil," I tell her. "And I hate you."

"It's okay to be you, Yara," she says. "The people who love you will work with your shortcomings, not against them."

"What does that even mean?" I ask her.

"If you're in a relationship with Ethan, you should feel comfortable enough telling him that you're freaked."

"If I tell him I'm freaked, he will get freaked," I say.

"Then he's not strong enough for you, is he?"

I give her a dirty look as she moves the subject on to something else. Harrods. She's talking about Harrods. Posey is two extremes. She's either too deep or too shallow. There is no grey area, no middle anything. It's exhausting being with her because you're either listening to asinine shit you don't care about or she's tearing your psychology apart and making you cry.

Who is really equipped to deal with someone else's reality? It's why we're all so afraid to show ourselves, the vulnerability of being left once our truth is discovered. Also there is no way I'd date me. If I were a man I'd date another man. Men cry less than women.

Ethan and I are at a cafe one afternoon having lunch when he tells me the agent has left a voice message on his phone. We press our faces close together so we can listen at the same time, and he holds the phone between us. She informs us in her hoity-toity voice that we got the flat.

"Congratulations," she says. "It will be a lovely place for you to begin your…er…lives together."

"She sounds quite surprised," I say to Ethan, pulling away to look at him.

He smirks and shushes me as she rattles off the address where we're to drop off our deposit check. I laugh as soon as he sets down his phone.

"She thinks I'm a prostitute," I say. "She hates that we got it!"

"Former, my love. You gave up that lifestyle to be with me. I can't believe we got it. Fate, don't you think?"

"Absolutely," I say.

I reach for my glass of wine, already imagining where I'll put my record player and my small collection of potted plants. Ethan is so happy he orders a bottle of champagne to celebrate. I hold my glass and smile, smile, smile.

I'm on autopilot; there are things to be done so I do them. I turn in my notice and carry home an armload of boxes to start packing. Ethan texts me pictures of dining tables and bookcases he finds online. I like white and he likes wood, so we settle in the middle and buy grey. I am euphoric, so into this shit. I imagine mornings in the spacious kitchen, cooking breakfast with a view of central London before me. I can almost smell the coffee brewing around my perfect life. The coffee brewing brings back a long suppressed memory and I move it away. Be gone, memory! I have a beautiful, centrally located flat!

I hum as I tape the boxes and wrap my things in newspaper. I don't have much, mainly books and a few records I brought with me from the States. You'd think they'd remind me of David, but they don't, they just remind me of me. Our move-in date isn't for another four weeks, but I have to shave down my belongings, decide what comes with for my new, domesticated couples life. It's not a marriage, but it's close, the joining of belongings and lives, the determination to merge existence with another human being.

I don't know if it's because I'm on the verge of committing in a big way—a bigger way than I've done in ages—but I find David's face in my mind. His smile, and his eyes, and his laugh, which always seemed to be directed at me. I'd liked being laughed at by David. He found me effortlessly amusing. I do what a woman in my position shouldn't do, but often does anyway—I make comparisons between Ethan and David.

They are very different, but also very similar. Ethan's playfulness and self-deprecating jokes remind me of David. But, Ethan is a businessman. He was a womanizer by choice, seeking out the ones he wanted to sleep with— or in my case—be in a relationship with. Women just fell all over David without him having to ask, and he dealt with it all in good humor. It almost bored him. He was committed to the music, and he'd been committed to me.

Perhaps that was the highest praise I'd ever received. Ethan is more set in his ways, a contractual man who likes to have everything in order. David was an artist, there was no order. I love Ethan, but in a different way than I'd loved David. Perhaps it's because I'm a different person than I was three years ago. As you age, your propensity to love changes and evolves with your personality. You gain in either selfishness or selflessness. What I do know is that I didn't give David what I could have…I wasn't able. And now we'll never know what we might have been together.

That's why I'm determined to make things work with Ethan. I won't play games. I won't flake. I will be good to him. And besides, I've never felt quite like this before. Ethan isn't as good and isn't as bad as the men I've dated before. He lies somewhere in the middle, which cushions all of my needs and gives me some assurance that I've broken free of all of my daddy issues. Who did I compare men to before David? There's been a man I've run out on in every city, and yet none of them have been worth a fond remembrance.

I check the calendar for the date. My meeting with David is two weeks away. There's a distant throb in my heart when I think about it, but I push it away and focus on here and now. My life is good. There is a doting boyfriend and a buffet of possibility spread out in front of me. I will not be arriving at my meeting with David as some lonesome girl, empty-handed and speckled with regret. I am moving forward. No, I am charging forward.

40

I RISE

I ACCUMULATE WRONGS. There's never one big thing. One big thing could happen and I'd move right past it like it didn't. But those little wrongs, my God, I collect those. I can look back now and see what a hoarder I'd been in my relationship with David. What we had was almost too good and I needed to sabotage it before it sabotaged itself. At least I kept control that way. Even as I pack my things into boxes readying myself to start a life with a new man, and even as I mentally prepare to see the man I left behind, I replay those last months in Seattle over and over.

In the weeks prior to our wedding, I rose up against David. He never had a chance and that's the truth. I rose like a wave and he was a ship, and I just kept collecting wrongs and climbing higher. It's sink or swim when you're on that ship, and I don't know if he would have fallen to the bottom of the ocean or showed off his breaststroke because I didn't stay to see. He talked me down, most days—rationalized, assured, loved. He did everything the right way, but my wave was growing.

I showed up for the wedding, I give myself credit for that even if everyone else does not. I wore my dress with the splash of blood on its hem, and I held my flowers and walked down the aisle in a quaint little church. David was so beautiful he made my eyes hurt. He wore a blue velvet suit over a white shirt. His shoes were black snakeskin. Iridescent when you looked at them closely. I didn't feel the trepidation until after we were married. Isn't that something? With the rings securely on our fingers, the contract signed, we went to the hotel after the small party and just looked at each other. David liked to say "my wife." He said it every chance he got. But, it felt like an accusation to me. How was I to be a wife? How was I to deal with not just one Petra, but thousands of Petras? I didn't have the strength. And then, about four weeks into our wedded life, I stared to wonder if he was up for the taking? When he realized who I was, wouldn't he turn to another woman for comfort? I collected the looks Petra gave him, and I wondered if I married him to own the looks he gave in return.

"Why did you speak to her after the show? It should be me you speak to first, I'm your wife."

"You posed for a picture with a group of girls and allowed them to press themselves too close..."

"When I told you I was sad, you hugged me instead of discussing the problem."

"You went for a beer with the guys when I wanted you to come home."

"You made love to me with your eyes closed, who were you thinking of?"

"You don't care if I orgasm, you only care about yourself."

"You wish I were more like your mother, soft and supportive."

"You love your art more than you love me."

A barrage. I rose higher and higher. If he didn't look at me the right way after a show, I'd be hurt. If he looked at me too much, I'd feel smothered. Be with your fans.

Don't be with your fans. You don't love me enough. You love me too much. I rose.

I knew that the problem was me, and yet I couldn't control my feelings. David drove me mad, or my love for him did. And then I saw the photo of Petra and David at Ferdinand's house, sitting so close together it looked like their knees were touching. David came to the bar later, the guilt written all over his face. He tried to explain, but he couldn't climb the walls I'd erected. He hadn't even known they were being built. That's not quite fair, I know that now. It took two more weeks. During which time I drove myself mad. It was a mistake, falling in love with him, staying when I knew I needed to leave and go home.

There was a note written in my own hand. All I could find was a pen with red ink. It was in the kitchen drawer and the end of it was chewed on. I didn't want my letter to him to look angry or aggressive, I wasn't either of those things. But, there was only a red pen. So I wrote it as gently as I could if only to quell the red ink.

I'm not who you think I am, I told him. *I can't be who you need me to be. I have to go. Forgive me.*

It was weak to leave a note. He deserved words, a fight, closure. But, I was afraid he'd convince me to stay. And even if I stayed for a time, it was inevitable that I'd eventually leave. I was too insecure to allow David to love me. I didn't trust him, despite what I said. What I was feeling would never go away. Words can only temporarily soothe a discord in psychology. I did not expect him to give up his music for me, just as much as I did not expect me to give up my insecurities for him. So, I resolved to take my leave and leave him be. And as I walked away, I said it over and over—

Forgive me, forgive me, forgive me, forgive me, forgive me, forgive me, forgive me.

41

BAD REUNION

THE RESTAURANT WHERE I'M meeting David isn't what I pictured. Why had I imaged something quaint and romantic? A brick building with a rose trellis, wooden floors, and plush plum colored seating. That's how reunions are supposed to go down, isn't it? The way they did in the movies. But, this isn't really a reunion. I'm trying to romanticize it to help myself along, a crutch of sorts. It's a warmer day than I expected too, and I can feel a line of sweat roll down my back as I walk toward the front doors. When I step inside, the first thing I notice is the minimalistic design. I shiver. The stark whites, modern light fixtures, and boxy tables and chairs. There is nothing warm here, and it occurs to me that David chose this place specifically as my interrogation room. An elegant, middle-aged woman greets me, a menu in her hand. Her long gazelle-like body is draped in a black kimono.

"Welcome," she says.

"Hello. I'm meeting—"

"David," she finishes for me.

"Yes. How did you—?"

"This way," she says.

She turns before I can reply and I understand that I'm expected to follow. My stomach is knotted as we walk through the mostly empty dining room. I can't see past her shoulders, though I suspect David is there, watching her as she approaches. Is he equally as nervous? Angry? At any moment I'm going to see him and I'll be able to read it on his face. I could always read everything on his face. My heart is beating so wildly it hurts.

When she steps aside to show me the table, David isn't there. I stare at the empty seats and feel sharp disappointment.

"He called ahead," the hostess says. "He will be here shortly."

She leaves me there with my oversized menu, and I feel childlike in my aloneness. I cross my legs, uncross them. Straighten my hair, wonder if there's lipstick on my teeth or if my mascara is clumped over my eyelashes— stupid, shallow thoughts. I chose to wear something casual: a pair of dark jeans and a slouchy T-shirt under my leather jacket. What's the point of not being yourself and giving people the wrong impression? I come as I am. I sip at my water until I spill some of it on myself, then I'm dabbing my white shirt frantically with my napkin, cursing my clumsiness.

When he steps inside the restaurant, the atmosphere changes. I can feel him before I see him. I set my napkin down and sit up, alert. And then he's there, moving like water toward me. Everything goes quiet in my head. I have the urge to weep, and then I'm standing to embrace him. I have to reach up on my tiptoes to get my arms around his neck. We don't let go right away. Anger, resentment, the dire need for answers—is put on hold for...one... two...three...four...five...six...seven...eight—seconds. I can feel his warmth and smell the fabric of his shirt—and through that, the spice of his skin. His body is curled around me, his hands heavy on my back as he holds me to himself. I am so lonely in that moment—so aware of the fact that I have never healed or moved on. When he steps back and we're no longer touching I feel inordinately sad.

"Hello," David says softy.

I study his eyes to know what he's feeling, but he's guarded. Who has walls now?

"Hi."

He motions for me to sit down. I do, never taking my eyes off him. He's different. I suppose that happens after people are apart for a length of time. They become more themselves while you cling to who they used to be.

His hair is shorter, shaggy—more styled; the smile lines around his eyes are more pronounced. He's wearing a lot of money: starched light blue shirt with a popped collar, slim jeans that emphasize the length of his legs, and a camel colored jacket. He also hasn't looked at me once since he sat down, which you could see as quite odd, or quite telling.

"I'm going to need to order wine for this. A bottle. So you choose either red or white."

"Red," I say, softly.

My fingers find the straw wrapper from my water and I hold it between my fist for support.

"Okay."

He sets about studying the wine menu while I sit solemnly, my hands clasped in my lap. When our server comes to collect our order, David rattles it off without consulting me. *Another way he's changed,* I think. I wouldn't say less considerate than I would say more self-assured. When we're alone again he finally looks at me. There are many notable things about David: his good looks, for instance, his deep voice, the John Wayne gait—but the most pronounced thing about him is the expression he's unable to hide from his eyes. It hurts him to look at me, and suddenly I feel such shame. Shame at who I am, who I was with him. I feel dirty underneath his very clear, very honest eyes.

"How have you been?" he says. He doesn't really want to know. He just needs warm-up questions.

"I've been well," I say, cautiously. "You've made quite a name for yourself. It's wonderful."

His lips pull into a straight line and he nods, an attempt at a smile.

"Why? Why did you go, Yara?"

"I didn't imagine it going like this," I say. My straw wrapper is mangled so I twist and untwist the napkin in my lap. My hands can never be still when I'm upset.

"How'd you think this was going to go down?" he asks.

One of his elbows is resting on the table. His posture is casual, flippant, like he doesn't care to be here, but must. He's running a thumb across his lips as he stares at me.

"You meet me here, we have a few drinks, we chat about where our lives are now, and then we hug as we part ways and say 'let's do this again sometime'?"

"I—I don't know, David. I came because you asked me to and I thought I owed you that."

"How long has it been since you left?"

Since you left. Not—*since we last saw each other.* He's not wrong to say it that way, but the phrasing still hurts.

"Years…three years…"

"Three years, two months, five days," he says.

I don't respond. How can I? I feel like he's trying to prove that he cares more.

"Beat me up," I say. "Say anything you like if it makes you feel better." I lean back against my seat. "I deserve it."

"That's not why I asked you here," he says.

"Why did you?"

"I'm in love."

I feel as if I'm in a snow globe and someone's shaken me around. Of course he's been loving other girls, fucking other girls—but to hear it.

"I want to marry her, but I can't because I'm still married to you."

Our wine arrives. Perfect and terrible timing. We're locked in a cold stare while it's opened and poured. David accepts his small taste and nods to the server, never taking his eyes off me. She, in turn, pours me a glass and discreetly disappears. He drains his glass and pours himself another. I wish for something stronger as I lick my lips.

"Who is she?"

He's shaking his head already. "You don't get to know that. You left."

I feel a rise of anger that I'm probably not entitled to. But I came, I met him, and now I also want answers.

"I do get to know that, because you want me to sign papers. That's why you're here."

He considers me for a moment and then says, "Tell me why you left, Yara." Before I can answer or even process his words, he rephrases them. "Tell me why you left me."

It's more painful when he says it that way. It's also the truth. I didn't just leave Seattle, or the States, I left him—a person, the human I claimed to love.

I imagine the look on my face is awful because David almost looks sorry he asked.

I haven't taken a deep breath since I saw him, so I do that first, then I say, "I always said I'd leave, remember? I knew you'd be better if I was gone."

"Better at what?"

I shake my head. My hands are trembling. "Better. Just better."

"A better man, a better human, or what was it…a better artist?"

That's when I know it was her, that ashen haired bitch with her love-drunk eyes. She's the only one I'd ever said that to other than David.

"Petra," I say.

David doesn't confirm or deny. He looks on, his face expressionless. He's rehearsed this, I realize. You don't just march into a conversation like this one without considering every possible outcome.

"Was it going on before I left?" I ask.

He looks momentarily taken aback. "Of course not. She's—we've been together for almost a year now. She came to a show…"

He's already told me more than he was planning to.

"All right," I say. "So you're here for a divorce."

"Don't, Yara," he says. "Don't say it like that. Where you're suddenly the victim. I'm just giving you what you've wanted since the beginning."

"What you want," I correct him.

He leans back in his chair. The stem of his wineglass is perched between two of his fingers. I'm afraid he's going to drop it and get it all over his shirt.

"We both know that's not true." His voice is low, angry.

"Why didn't you find me then? Before now."

He says nothing. We're staring again. Our server reappears. She wants to know if we've looked at the menu. I can't look at her for fear I'll burst into tears.

"We'll both have the rib eye," he says. "Medium rare."

It's what I would have chosen for myself. He knows that, but it was still unnecessary to order for me. He's showing me that he still knows all those small things about me, like how I like my steak cooked. What he's doing works, because I feel another pang of deep loneliness.

Finally he says, "So, you were never in love with me. You just wanted to play God with my emotions."

I can see the muscles in his jaw working. He can't play this game with me. We both struck our deal that night in

Seattle. Words were exchanged. He's acting like he had no part of it.

"That's how it started. You know that, David. It was a game, but then all of a sudden I was very much in love with you. Very much. It got to be too much. I didn't know what to do with it."

He nods slowly. "Why didn't you talk to me about how you felt? You could have told me and I would have understood."

"Would you have?" It's the first time I have to actually think about that. David was so sure about everything back then he rarely checked to make sure I was sure too.

"Well, it worked, didn't it? A platinum album. I guess I should thank you for that."

"Don't," I say. "You were always worth a platinum album—"

"—Not quite. Not according to you who needed to break my heart for the sake of art. Not worth anything unless I was as jaded as you."

My eyes well with the tears I swore to myself I'd not cry.

"You're right," I tell him. "I left because I'm a jaded coward and I tried to pretend I was doing you a favor."

He's quiet as he considers what I've said, then he reaches into his back pocket and pulls out his wallet, tossing a hundred pound note on the table and standing up.

"I'll be in touch," he says.

After he's gone I stay to drink the rest of the wine, but leave the food untouched.

42
BACKPEDALING

FOR DAYS AFTER I'VE SEEN David at the restaurant I can do nothing but cry and wander around my flat touching the boxes that were taped shut and stacked near the doorways of each room. I feel restless, unsettled. I haven't told Ethan that I'm still married to David, and I know that's a conversation we should have already had. I keep expecting David to show up at my door with the papers he wants me to sign. I send Ethan's calls to voicemail until he leaves messages saying he's worried about me. I text, tell him I'm under the weather and I'll call soon. I don't want him to hear my voice. He'd know right away that something is wrong and I'm not ready to tell him that I've seen David. I make more excuses—a sore throat, exhaustion, packing—but finally after a week, he shows up at my door wearing a look of deep concern.

"David. You've seen him then?" he says once I step aside to let him in.

"How did you know?" I ask.

Ethan looks distraught for a second, like I'd confirmed his worst fear.

"His band is here, there are posters all over the city. They're talking about it on the radio and at work."

I turn away so he can't see my face and put the kettle on. David used to make fun of me, he said the Brits thought they could solve everything with a cup of tea. And we can.

"Yes, I saw him." I move toward the canister of sugar and squeeze my eyes shut, willing Ethan away. *It doesn't work like that, Yara. You have to deal with things head-on.*

"Did you fuck him?"

I spin around, disgusted. "Are you fucking with me? That's the first thing you ask?"

"It's important," he says firmly. "I want to know where your heart is."

"Well, it's not in my pussy," I shoot back.

Ethan looks immediately sorry, but it's too late.

"Listen, Yara, cut me a break here. Your rock star ex-boyfriend comes into town, the one who wrote a song for you that plays all over the radio, and I'm not supposed to be concerned?"

He knew more than I gave him credit for.

"No. I did not fuck him. And he wrote that song to humiliate me. It isn't exactly a love song, Ethan."

"It is a goddamn love song. He wants you back—that's why he wrote the thing."

I laugh. I can't help myself. I'd never thought of "Atheists Who Kneel and Pray" as a love song. I guess it was a song about love.

"He doesn't want me back, trust me."

"Why not? How can you know that?"

"Because I left him six weeks after our wedding, Ethan. I never spoke to him again."

Ethan stares at me, his mouth slightly ajar.

"I've not told anyone that until now," I say softly.

"You married him? I thought you didn't believe in marriage."

"Yeah, I thought so too. That's why I ran."

"I don't know what bothers me more, that you did that to someone, or that you never told me you did that to someone."

The kettle whistles and I hide my tears by turning away to switch the burner off.

"Listen, it happened, and it's the truth. I'm sorry for all of it, but I'm the one who has to live with the things I've done, not you."

He looks like I've slapped him across the face. "Is that the way you see it? Like I factor in very little?"

The image of pedaling backward on a bike flashes through my mind. I can backpedal but I'm tired. I don't want to defend myself to make Ethan feel better. I don't want to talk about this anymore.

"Think what you like," I say. "But if you're even questioning me, we shouldn't be together."

Ethan leaves and then it is just me. I wonder if it will ever be any different. I don't think about my mother often, but when I do, her memory is always accompanied by feelings of loneliness. She left me alone in our tiny flat when she went to work. She worked nights at the front desk of a hotel. I'm not sure how old I was when she first started leaving me alone, but I remember feeling tiny. I couldn't reach the cupboard with the biscuits. I'd have to drag a chair to the kitchen and climb on the counter. What would have happened if I slipped and fell? My mother would have come home to a very small, dead child. No one would have even come to my funeral because there was no one we knew. My mother was from a small village in North England. When she got pregnant with me she left the village. As far as I know, she's gone back and lives there now, but I haven't spoken to her in years. When I asked her once if I had grandparents she'd said, "It doesn't matter." And that was valid, I suppose, because I

231

technically don't have a mother either, and it doesn't matter. People live without things and they thrive.

My mother gave me a gift. It works against me, not for me. She was always irritated that I was around. As a child I tried to stay out of her way as much as possible because she didn't like me to ask her questions. When she was home I watched her keenly, eager to please, always wanting to earn a half smile or any sort of acknowledgment. If she was reading and I'd drop something in the kitchen, her head would snap up and she'd glare at me. I'd feel like such a failure in that moment, like I'd failed her in the deepest way. She never hit me, and she rarely shouted. It was her quiet that was distressing. As an adult I am racked with guilt when I feel I have inconvenienced someone. That's how it works against me. If I walk into a cafe and take the seat by the window, I feel guilt for being selfish, for taking the best table in the house when someone else could have it. If I buy a new pair of shoes and then see someone with no shoes, I want to strip mine off and walk barefoot for the rest of the day. Why should I have anything when someone else does not have what I have? I wonder if this affected the way I thought about David, because I always knew I had someone who was far better than anyone else. When Petra showed interest in him I lost my mind. Petra needed him more; they were more alike than we were. I could survive alone, but Petra needed healing and David could make the lame walk with his never-ending faith. In a sick way I thought I was doing everyone a favor.

It was wrong. I was wrong. I deserve love, but it's going to take me a very long time to learn that.

43

BEST AMERICAN ACCENT

IT'S LUNCHTIME AT BRONTE. The front bar is busy and I've not had a moment's break since my shift started. The juicers hum and the smell of fresh fruit is so strong in the air my mouth is watering. They make us wear these waistcoats with ties. It's unbearably hot. It's been a week since I met with David, four days since I last spoke to Ethan. I'm feeling quite sorry for myself, a little rejected, and alone actually. Yesterday I bought a paperback from the corner shop and wandered around with it under my arm, intending to find a bench where I could read while I sunned. There were plenty of benches, plenty of sun, but I kept thinking there'd be a better option if I walked a little bit further. Before I knew it, I'd walked four miles and the sun was dipping low in the sky. I missed my chance and I never found a bench good enough. *Hey, girl, hey—you're an asshole.* It's good to know these things about yourself so you don't go around blaming others for your fuckups.

I'd bought a bottle of wine on my way home and drank the whole thing sitting at my living room window watching the traffic. When I looked in the mirror this morning, my teeth were stained and my skin so sickly looking I'd been frightened. What was I doing to myself? Drinking bottles of wine to cope with my inner turmoil. I've been back home for three years and I've not felt the need to leave again. Perhaps my wandering days are over, or perhaps I found what I'd been looking for and then lost it. Either way, it finally feels like I have settled in the right place, the place where I started. Except now I question everything. The urge has appeared. I am considering running away again, packing up my things, and going somewhere new. But, how many times can a person start over?

"I thought you hated lunch shifts."

I'm so deep in thought I almost drop the handful of lemons I'm holding. I clutch them to my chest and look up in alarm. David is sitting on the stool directly in front of me next to one of the regulars, an older lady we call Penny. His skin is brown like he's been out in the sun for the last week and he's wearing a white V-neck and ripped blue jeans. So simple and yet he looks like a rock star. I think of my sallow wine-flushed skin and panic.

"They've grown on me," I say, trying to hide the tremor in my voice. "What are you doing here?"

I search the bar in front of him for papers, but there are just his hands, clasped on the bar top. I set my lemons down and reach up to touch my hair. I hadn't bothered to do anything with it this morning, just slung it up in a messy knot on top of my head. My tie feels like it's strangling me. This is ridiculous; my fixation on the way I look. What does it even matter? The man is here to divorce me, not ask me on a date.

David clears his throat. "I figured I was a bit of a wanker to you the other night. I threw a spanner in the works and what a cock up that was, yeah?"

I'm laughing before he's finished. "Dude, you've totally been practicing," I say in my best American accent.

He grins as he rocks on his bar stool from side to side. For a moment I'm transported back to Seattle where he used to rock like that on a different bar stool and flirt with me. I thought it was endearing the way he had the enthusiasm of a little boy, but looked like a man. We grin at each other, but then my heart starts to hurt and I don't know what to do with my hands or face. I turn away, make a juice for a customer: guava, lychee, mint, and orange. People walk through the doors, obnoxious little hats on their heads, sunglasses whose lenses are pink, green, and silver. I watch them as to not watch David, who is distracting me and making me forget which juice goes in what drink.

"Why are you here...you're supposed to be on tour," I say when I'm finished. What I really want to ask is: *Why are you here specifically? And how did you find me?*

"This was our last stop," he says quietly. "I decided to stick around, maybe have a Hendrick's and tonic?"

And divorce me, I want to add. The concert was weeks ago. I wonder just how long he's been sticking around, what he's waiting for? Penny has noticed our exchange and angles her stool toward him. She's nosy, she listens to all the bar gossip and then relays it to me. I smile uneasily at her. An already awkward situation and then you throw Penny in the mix. God, what a day it was already. Everyone would know by the end of the day that my husband came in to divorce me.

"Need some more juice and gin, Penny?" I ask.

She pushes her glass toward me, never removing her eyes from David.

"Do I know you?" I hear her ask him.

Someone waves me over at the end of the bar and I leave David and Penny to it.

"Don't forget my fucking drink," Penny calls after me in her singsong voice.

"Mine too," David echoes.

I eye him while I make his drink, just little glances to prove to myself that he's really there, but he catches me each time and smiles in turn. They're not divorce smiles, which confuses me more. They're just…genuine. I have no reason to distrust him, yet I still do.

You're the one who can't be trusted, I remind myself. *This guy only says what he's feeling. You tell lies about what you're feeling and then you run away.*

"It sort of feels like old times," I say as I slide the glass toward him. To his right, Penny nods.

"Old times, huh? You know, the first time I saw you in that bar it was as if someone plugged me into an electrical socket. Everything in my head lit up. I could have written ten songs, answered the age-long question about the meaning of love, and asked you to marry me on the spot."

"You did ask me to marry you on the spot," I point out.

"See."

"And you have written songs apparently making me the butt of the joke. So tell me, David Lisey, what's the meaning of love? Enlighten me."

For a moment I think he's not going to answer me. He stares down into his drink thoughtfully and when he looks up, his eyes are soft, sincere.

"I've thought a lot about that, actually. It's when you can't get someone out. They crawl inside you and they just live there for the rest of your life."

When he says that it feels like a jolt of electricity passes through me. There's familiarity, but I haven't thought about it that hard. Like I've been waiting for someone to tell me what I'm feeling.

"Like a parasite," I say. "Draining you of…well—everything. Not pleasant."

"Who says love is pleasant?"

He's right, of course. That's why people create art—because love crawls inside them and they need a way to get it out.

"I suppose it's not. It's mostly just painful."

"You two are giving me a headache," Penny says. She's wearing her big, dark sunglasses and I can't see her eyes, but her mouth is turned down in a frown.

"Maybe you shouldn't eavesdrop then, Penny," I suggest.

She sticks her tongue out at me. Very mature. I like to imagine what Penny was like when she was my age. There's still some of the wildness left in her eyes.

"Tell us how we're wrong, Pen," David says.

She turns to him and smiles, and I can see that she's thoroughly smitten. Who isn't once they meet David? I had to watch girls younger, prettier, and firmer than me throw themselves at him on a daily basis.

"You young people treat love like it's an accessory, not a matter of life and death. You're amused by it, in love with the idea of it. You make all of your songs and books about it, but don't know how to live it out. Love is not part of something else. It's the only thing."

Her words catch David off guard. He looks like he's been slapped.

I lean my elbows on the bar and stare at him. "Are you writing a song?" I ask. I know that face he's making, and I can't keep the smile off my lips.

"Hush," he says, still staring at Penny. "Tell me more," he says to her. "You're my new muse."

"Who was it before?"

He points a finger at me.

Penny glances at me and raises her eyebrows. "Fresh meat. Nothing I have is that firm."

I laugh, but I feel like I shouldn't. Nothing about this situation is funny, it's really quite uncomfortable, my husband who I ran out on, showing up at my work.

"Don't worry, Penny, I broke his heart. Have at him. He's done with me."

"Am I?"

I stare at him, too uncomfortable to know what to do. I want to ask him where he's stashed the divorce papers, but Penny turns to look at me, her drink cradled in her bony, wrinkled hand. She has a ring on every finger and she's wearing hot pink nail varnish. That's the thing about Penny: she's crackly and age-spotted, her voice is raspy and dry, and she smells of Chanel and mothballs, but there's something devastatingly elegant about her.

"American boy comes all this way for—"

"His band played a show here," I say, cutting her off. "That's why he's here."

Penny looks at David very seriously and asks, "Why are you here?"

David doesn't look at Penny when he answers her. He looks at me.

"I'm here for Yara," he says. "I came to find her."

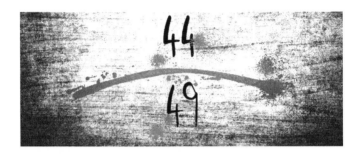

AT SOME POINT DURING my shift, I let Ben, my fellow bartender, know I need to run to the loo.

"Hurry," he says. "That bloody lot from the law firm just came in. You know how they love the mixed drinks."

I wink at him and hurry round the corner, glancing once more at David before I go. He's in deep conversation with Penny and I can't help but smile. Most people would dismiss Penny as eccentric and weird, but not David. He loves eccentric and weird. When I reach the toilets, I have to wait in line. I wash my hands and hurry out, ready for Ben to give me a mouthful for taking so long. When I round the corner Ben is fine, laughing with a guest, and David is nowhere to be seen.

"What happened to the guy who was sitting there?" I ask Ben.

He's juicing grapefruit and he doesn't look up at me.

"Paid his tab and left in a hurry," he says.

"Oh," I say casually. "Did he say anything before he left?"

I try to keep my voice nonchalant, but there is an urgency inside of me. I want to run out into the street and call his name. He can't just come in like that and then leave without saying goodbye. I need to know what he wants to do. I can't be kept suspended like this.

"No. Just handed me twenty quid and left."

I don't know if I feel confusion or disappointment more, but what had I expected? Maybe he just needed to see how he felt one last time. I suppose he could have even been walking by when he saw me inside, Trafalgar was a popular place for tourists to be wandering around. But he'd said, *"I'm here for Yara,"* like that had been his plan all along.

When I go back around to check on Penny, she hands me a scrap of paper. There's a strange expression on her usually impassive face. I breathe a sigh of relief. He's written me something, I think. A note, or a telephone number maybe. I unfold the tiny strip of paper and blink down at it, confused. Two numbers are written inside in red ink and nothing else.

"Did he say what this meant?" I ask her, holding it up.

She shrugs. He'd written 49. I recognize his handwriting right away, scratchy and slanted. 49? Was it a room number? A date? Should it have triggered a memory of something from our past? I shake my head, tears pooling in my eyes. I turn away before Penny can see me and tuck the slip of paper into my shirt pocket.

I take a cab home that night. I can't bear the thought of standing in the Tube squashed against all those people when I feel like I'm about to cry. The piece of paper David left with Penny sits open on my lap, the number 49 staring up at me like an accusation. I don't remember. If he's trying to trigger something from our past, I've forgotten. I search the internet for the meaning of the number. The San Francisco 49ers, a ski resort in Washington state, the DC comic episode 49 where Batgirl makes an appearance.

None of it means anything to me. When the cabbie leans back to tell me we've arrived, I'm thoroughly confused and already planning on buying another bottle of wine to carry me through the night. I hand him his money and walk a block to the corner shop. I could e-mail David, ask him what his note meant, but I'm too prideful. He obviously thought it would mean something to me. David was the aware one in our relationship. He knew the wine I liked to drink, and he knew my favorite color. When the time came for him to choose a wedding cake flavor and our honeymoon, he did so without pause—because he knew me.

I choose a bottle of white this time. White wine makes me loopy. I've been known to strip off all my clothes and try to run outside naked after drinking too much white wine, but I'm desperate to feel something, even if it's something that makes me behave badly. I carry my bottle up to my flat and search the cupboards for something to eat. I've not been shopping for food since before Ethan and I saw the flat. Everything else has been boxed up for the move. I'm too depressed to leave, so I text Posey and ask her to come over and bring food. I expect her to swear at me, tell me to go to hell like she normally does, but instead she texts back: *Be right there. Want a curry?*

I send her a thumbs up and finish off my bottle. By the time Posey arrives, two brown paper bags cradled in her arms, I'm drunk off my ass and singing Britney Spears circa 2001 at the top of my lungs.

"God," she says. "I don't even know who you are anymore. You were always more of a Mandy Moore girl."

I launch into a shrill rendition of "Candy" while I unpack the bags she set on the counter.

"So why are you drunk at six o'clock in the evening?" she says. Her voice is light and teasing, but I know she wants her question answered truthfully.

"David," I say, opening the plastic tub of rice. "He came into the restaurant."

She doesn't look surprised. "Of course he did," she says. "And what did he say? Does he need you to be a muse for him again?"

I stop in my spooning of curry to look at her.

"I don't know why he came," I say. "He just left while I was in the loo without saying goodbye."

"Figures." She licks the dishing spoon clean and I make a disgusted face. "Artists are dramatic that way."

I reluctantly tell her about the slip of paper he left with the number 49 written on it. I figured she'd make fun of me for not remembering what it meant, but she looks thoughtful instead.

"It's not an anniversary date then?"

I shake my head. "No. And I've ruled out apartment numbers, bus numbers, inside jokes, and songs."

"Maybe that's it then. He's writing a new song and giving you ample warning."

I shake my head. "I don't think that's it. There's something I'm missing."

"So why not just e-mail the guy and ask?"

"I feel stupid, I guess. I feel as if I'm supposed to know."

Posey shakes her head. "Your inability to communicate is going to fuck up your life for good, you know that? And where's that wanker boyfriend of yours? You walk out on him too?"

"Ethan found out I met with David and won't talk to me."

Posey closes her eyes like my drama is overwhelming her. "I suppose you haven't contacted him either to talk things over."

"He's the one mad at me!"

"Oh my God, Yara! You're such a narcissist. You met with another man—one you used to be in love with—and didn't tell Ethan about it. How do you expect him to feel? That's not how a partnership works. I'm not going to tell you what to do, but now seems like the time to apologize to him if you'd like to salvage that relationship."

"That's the thing. I don't know if I want to. Maybe it just ran its course."

Posey looks dumbfounded. She sets her fork down and just sits there staring at me.

"All right," I say. "I'm a narcissist and a coward. But, there isn't really a cure and I'm not always sure what to do. Can we take into consideration that there's a good chance I'm going to fuck things up with Ethan anyway, so maybe it's better if I just walk away now."

"Are you behaving this way because David's back in the picture?"

"No. And he's not back in the picture. He's just reminded me of how awful I am."

She drums her fingers on the counter as she considers my words. "But not everything needs to be focused on how awful you already are. That's what makes you a narcissist. Even in the middle of hurting other people you're focused on yourself."

"You're right," I admit. "What do I do?"

"Stop overanalyzing yourself, first off. You spend enough time thinking about yourself, and even after you obsessively overthink everything you do, somehow everyone else lands up being the bully."

"Do you think that's why all of my relationships fail?"

"See, you're doing it again."

I sit up straighter. "Okay. Sorry. I'm going to practice *not* thinking about myself. I'll call Ethan and apologize for my thoughtlessness."

"Good," says Posey. "The first step was admitting you're a narcissist. Now you need to change the way you think of things."

"Yes," I say, determined. "And I'm not allowed to think of myself, right?"

"Well, think more about how your behavior affects others, you know? Don't be so focused on your feelings that they're all you see."

By the time Posey leaves I'm a new woman. I won't even look at myself in the mirror. I call Ethan and when he doesn't answer, I send him an e-mail begging for his forgiveness.

He e-mails me back and says we can meet for lunch the following week. We make arrangements and I stumble to bed still half drunk.

45
LEICESTER SQUARE

THE FOLLOWING DAY I leave work, and instead of taking the Tube, I decide to walk to clear my head. Usually when it's time to clear my head, I pack up my things and move to a new city…a new continent. New cities give new perspective. You leave all the old stuff behind, the stuff that was corroded with memories, and you start again. New starts are unlimited. Don't like your friends? Go find new ones nine thousand miles away. It's easy when you're a bartender to just up and leave. Bartenders are needed, if you are good that is even better. Things aren't so bad if you keep moving.

I'd told myself I was going to stop running. I'd become accustomed to it and I didn't like the power it held over me. I read this book while I lived in Seattle, the author was local and that's why I picked it up. It was mostly shit—the characters drove me nuts—except there was this one line that struck a chord: Live barefoot and fucking fight. I decide to do that here in London. It is my home and I am going to stay.

There's a server at work we call Howie, even though his name is Stephen. We call him that because he looks like Howie Mandel and is as equally afraid of germs as the original Howie Mandel. I see Howie on the opposite side of the street. He waves at me and I pretend not to notice. He waves harder so I turn my head to the left. To avoid a conversation I don't want to have, I abruptly change my mind about crossing the street and wander in the opposite direction. I have no clue where I'm going except that I need to keep walking.

In Leicester Square I stop and sit on the wall to smoke a cigarette. A little brick wall for weary tourists. A musician is playing a guitar and singing "Stand By Me" as an Orion truck beeps incessantly nearby. In between verses he plays the kazoo. He looks like an unkempt Michael Bublé and he knows it too. Middle-aged female tourists giggle like schoolgirls as they stop to watch him. One drops twenty quid into his guitar case and then scurries away. He reminds me of David in the early days. I don't know what David is like onstage nowadays. I've avoided looking as to not cause myself injury. I imagine his presence has improved, much like his sound.

I can't stop smoking. I haven't smoked since I moved back, but I left work and went right to an off license for vodka and cigarettes. I feel as if I'm unraveling. I imagine myself as a spool of yarn rolling down the street. I roll until a bus squashes me. It's a lovely thought. I'm being dramatic, I know that. I blow the last of my smoke through my nose like a French girl and stand up to leave. The Michael Bublé lookalike smiles at me. I tell him to fuck off with my eyes. I hate musicians. They have no boundaries between their lyrics and real life. They think everything is supposed to be good enough to sing about. Maybe that's why I left David the way I did. I didn't want to be his temporary shiny thing.

I don't want to go home. I don't know why. I get on the Tube and ride it all the way to South Harrow and back again.

I can't stand it. I wish he'd just hand me the paperwork and disappear again. Marry that fucking bitch and be done with me for good. That's not true. I'm hurting and I don't know how to deal. It sucks.

I take my vodka home and get drunk on the floor in between the boxes. I don't even like vodka, but there was a sale and I like sales the same way druggies like drugs. I don't need or like half the things I buy. When I wake up I'm in my bed and I have no recollection of how I got there. I immediately think Ethan came over at some point in the night and put me to bed. I rush from my room despite the sharp pain in my head and the sick feeling I get in my stomach, but Ethan is nowhere. I put myself to bed. My phone is dead, but even after it's charged I see that no one has texted or called. I deserve it. I'm awful. I am the type of person that drives other people away.

I stare at the pink concrete of the bar and wait. David doesn't come back, not after one week or two. Not even after my lunch date with Ethan, who is cold but hears me out. I think something terrible has happened to David. I Google his name expecting to see headlines like: Lead Singer Dies in Terrible Accident. But, there's no such headline. There are, however, dozens of articles about him. I decide to save reading them for later. First, I have to find out if he's alive. It takes me a while, but I find a recent article online, a tabloid that has photographed David in New York. David was in New York, not London, about to deliver divorce papers. Maybe he never had them, I think. Maybe that's where he is now—having them drawn up. I suppose there are a lot of complications involved. He has a lot of money now. I don't want a thing from him, but his lawyers don't know that. They're trying to find a loophole, get him out of giving me anything. In the picture he's with

Petra. The photo is grainy but I can see that she's wearing a light blue coat over a black dress that goes mid-calf. They are walking arm-in-arm and her head is down, but I know her profile, her lips. I spent enough time thinking about the way they were all put together, why they had to be so perfect. Her coat is blowing out around her like they're walking fast, perhaps trying to get away from the paparazzi. I bet Petra the skank loves that, having paparazzi follow her around and snap pictures. David looks exactly the same as the last time I saw him. He's wearing a white V-neck T-shirt and a grey beanie that covers his hair. He looks like a beautiful, greasy hipster. There's a tattoo I hadn't noticed when he came to see me, on his forearm. It makes me feel sick to look at them together; her so beautiful and doll-like, him so sexy. He doesn't give a fuck, that's the best thing about him.

"Hey David," I say to the photo. "You have terrible taste in women."

Petra smirks at me. I slam my phone face down on the counter and walk away.

46

SAME OLD YARA

ETHAN AND I HAVE many talks over the next few weeks, during which time he seems to forgive me. He tells me that the offer to move in with him is still open on two conditions: I have to let go of David, and he wants me to get divorced. One of those things I can do, and one of those things I cannot. On the day before I'm supposed to move in with Ethan, I buy a train ticket and move to France instead. Divorce is easy, anyone can get divorced— the letting go part is next to impossible. Hearts are wild, uncontrollable things, you can't just instruct them. I imagine he'll burn my things when they arrive with the movers, but there's nothing I'm that attached to anyway. Not even Ethan. That's a hard ugly truth. It's sad how much of an asshole I am, but there it is. I thought that after David I could be more open to love, but as it turns out, I'm lost in him.

I have a friend in Paris. Well, friend is a stretch. We roomed together in college and barely spoke the first year, but then decided we liked each other enough to do it again the next. She once told me that if I ever ended up in France I could crash at her place for a while. I've never been to France. My determination was for America, so when I step off the train at Gare Du Nord, my eyes are as wide as my mouth. I have the sense that I've arrived somewhere familiar. The buildings tower, old and important. They're snobbier than London's mismatched buildings. Much of London was destroyed during the war, rebuilt in a different way. The Parisian buildings are not showing off, they're too gothic to care. I want to be like them. I walk with my head bent back so I can see everything closest to the sky. I walk into people, they swear at me in French, but I don't give a fuck; I'm a Parisian building now. Paris is going to change my life. I stop for a bite to eat at a cafe and check my e-mails. There's one from Posey.

Where the fuck are you? she writes.

Ethan is a bloody mess. You're a real arsehole, you know that?

I am. I know that. I've never let it get in my way.

I didn't want to hurt Ethan. I just panicked at the last minute, per usual. I send Posey an e-mail telling her I'm fine, not mentioning anything about Ethan or where I am. It's none of her business anyway, she just wants a reason to chew me out. I write Ethan a letter, handwritten on the pages of a notebook I bought at the station. I'd intended to write it on the train, but I spent the whole trip crying and staring out the window. I tell him that I thought I had changed, that I was ready to stay in one place, with one man and grow with someone. I tell him that I'm a coward and a fool, and that he deserves more than some broken runaway. I tell him that my life would have been better with him, in our little flat, but that in my heart I really didn't believe I deserved that type of life, so I kept running from it. It's not an excuse, I tell him. It just is. I ask for his forgiveness and sign the letter *Yara*—no love, no sincerely—just Yara. That's all I am, isn't it? Yara without love. I decide that I'm a sociopath.

I arrive at Celine's little flat late in the afternoon. She's at work, but she's left the key with her neighbor. I'm to knock on the door and ask for Pierre. Pierre is an older man, he silently hands me a key and closes the door in my face. Celine warned me that the French aren't initially warm—they make you work for it. I respect that. I didn't feel like talking to people anyway. I'm in love with her flat as soon as I walk in. She's decorated everything with only black and white. There's no other color, I search for it. I welcome this monochrome existence.

My first task is to find work. So I set up my computer and search for jobs. I don't want to be a bartender anymore. There is a family looking for an English-speaking nanny for their son. They want him to learn the language. I have no experience with taking care of children, but I send them my resume anyway, and say I've spent two years in America and can speak with a southern drawl as well. It's a joke, but the woman, the mother, e-mails me right away and asks if we can meet the following Monday. Her name is Celeste. I picture her as being tall, and blonde, and…well…celestial. Her son is Lucifer, I think. They can't find anyone else to take care of him so they're desperate. Then I wonder if Celine's monochrome flat is making me feel these extremes of good and bad, heaven and hell. I will fall in the latter in my mind, always.

Celine comes home around nine p.m. I've heard this is normal for the French who work long hours, then sit at cafes and drink wine until they have to work again. She is different than she was in college, which is no surprise, yet I am still surprised. In college she was mousy, she wore beiges, which melted into her beige skin. Now her hair is cut into a sleek bob, and she wears makeup and elegant clothes. I hug her, which we also never did in college.

"It's so wonderful to see you," she says in her perfectly accented English. "Are you comfortable? Can I get you anything?"

I need so many things: a new personality perhaps, a lot of perspective, a time machine, a mother—but I shake my head and take the wine she offers.

"I eat wine for dinner," she says. "You'll feed yourself, yes?"

"Yes."

I love it here already.

47

THE GYPSY'S CUP

ON A SUNNY MORNING four months after I move to Paris, I'm just leaving a cafe that I frequent every Thursday morning. I have a bag of croissants and a black coffee in my hand, and my plan is to take them to the park before I have to work. A few stolen moments of peace and nature before a four-year-old uses me as a human jungle gym. On Thursdays Henry has his Spanish and maths lessons with a snotty tutor who always looks like he's been sniffing sour cheese. I think he's too young, but his mother is raising a prime minister, as she tells me. Far be it from me to curb young ambition.

I've just pushed through the door of the cafe and stepped out onto the sidewalk when I look up and there he is. A jolt runs through me and I stop abruptly. I see his face everywhere nowadays. Last week I stepped off the train and he was right there on the back of a bench, smiling at me. There are posters of him all over the city and in store windows. But right now, he's standing on the sidewalk looking at me. I see someone, a woman, turn her head to look at him as she passes. Something crosses her face and she nudges her friend. They shake their heads like it couldn't possibly be *the* David Lisey. He's still just David, my David. Petra's David, I correct myself. I threw off love like it was a blanket in the middle of summer. Irritating, stifling.

I say his name as someone bumps into the back of me. I stumble forward. For a moment I think David is going to step forward to catch me, but he stops himself. I'm fine anyway, just a little jostle. He's wearing a beanie—that does something to my heart.

"Hello, Yara."

I think that's what he always says when he shows up like this. *Hello, Yara. Just another day of running into you.*

"What are you doing here?" I look around like I'm expecting someone else. Maybe Petra. What would I do if I saw Petra? Shady ass cow. I'd slam her damn face into the sidewalk.

"You know why I'm here," he says softly.

I nod. The business of divorce. Yes. Solemn, but necessary.

"Did you bring the paperwork?" I ask, trying to keep my voice steady.

"No."

I stare at him, confused. *The fuck?*

We stay like that for a few minutes, just staring and being confused. I think he's playing games with me, just showing up like this every few months with no explanation. People walk around us, but neither one of us moves.

Finally he says. "Would you like to get a drink?"

"It's nine o'clock in the morning." And then I add, "I have to work."

"Later," he says. "When you're done." The shade on his jaw is dark. He hasn't shaved in at least a week. He looks like the first time I saw him, when he pulled the splinter from my finger.

"Okay."

"Where?" he asks.

"I know a place." I rattle off an address and I know he'll remember it. He's like that. You only have to say something once.

"Is Petra here?" I ask.

He shakes his head. "She's…in Los Angeles."

What was that on his face? Regret? I don't know him well enough anymore. He has new expressions. I wonder if Petra knows we're still married? If he's sneaking off to get this sorted out without her knowledge.

"Does she know about…?"

"Yes," he says quickly.

"Okay," I say, relieved. "Okay."

"I have to get to work," I say.

He doesn't move as I walk past him. His eyes are soft as they watch me and then he slips on his sunglasses. I turn around just as I pass him and he turns too. We're just inches apart and I can see myself reflected in the blue/green of his lenses. I look scared, a deep line etched between my eyebrows. And I am scared about why he came all this way when he could have just slipped the papers in the post. There are better ways to divorce someone than showing up every few months out of the blue. And how does he find me? That is the fucking question of the hour, isn't it? I'll have to remember to ask, won't I?

"David," I say softly, as I cross the street. "David is here, in Paris."

It's been a long time since I allowed myself to say his name freely without the pain attached.

A few blocks down the street there is a gypsy woman standing with her back to a wall. She's holding a baby against her chest and her fingernails are black like she's been digging in the dirt. She stares at me through hooded eyes as I pass her. The baby is no more than a few weeks old and it wails in that thin way new babies do. Celine has told me not to give them money, but I can't help it. I pull the spare euros from the bottom of my bag and walk them over to her. She doesn't take her eyes from my face as I drop them into the paper coffee cup at her feet. I am kneeling in front of her, trying to ignore the smell of incense and body odor when I see that she has written numbers on the cup, scribbled in blue pen. I stare at the numbers, a tingling sensation sliding up my back like an invisible hand. 49. Why has this number shown up again on the same day David did? Is it a sign? A strange coincidence. I point to the number and ask, "Qu'est-ce que cela signifie?

What does that mean?

She gives me a strange look and I realize I probably should have asked: *What does this mean?*

"This number means something to you?" she asks in a strange accent.

I stand up so that we're on eye level. The baby has stopped crying. It's latched onto her breast and is making noises as it eats.

"Yes," I say. I'm not sure how much to tell her.

"Then I write it for you," she nods, "this morning."

I stare at the cup and try not to cry. Was the universe trying to send me a message? God? I don't believe in God. David used to tell me that not believing in God was a defense mechanism against human suffering. *It's easier to say nothing exists than to say something exists and He just lets us suffer.*

I wonder if this woman, who is reduced to begging for money with her infant clutched in her arms, believes in God? I don't know how to ask her, so I stare into her eyes and try to understand. The baby falls off her breast asleep; the smooth skin of its cheek has a line of milk where it ran out of its mouth. I try not to look at her puckered nipple, but it's right there on display.

"I have to go," I say, as if she cares. I turn and walk away.

"This number," she calls after me, "be careful of it." I wonder if her warning would be different had I not given her four of my euros. Would she have told me the number meant nothing? Would she have cursed me with it? Maybe I am already cursed.

I am already walking away. I lift a hand to indicate I heard her. I would, I would be careful. But that number is like splattering fat. It rises up every now and again to sting me.

48
EMPTY-HANDED

AFTER WORK I RUSH HOME to change my clothes. It wasn't until I was feeding Henry his lunch that I realized I'd been wearing my uniform when I saw David, a white polo shirt and tan chinos. What had David said once about people who wear polo shirts and chinos? I smile at the memory. He called them spa people.

"The poor serve the rich in polo shirts and chinos."

Henry asks for more fruit, and as I cut into the melon, I laugh at the irony. He'd had a job once, he'd told me, at a country club the summer he turned sixteen, collecting golf balls at the driving range.

"What do you think they made me wear, Yara?" he'd said.

I'd laughed when he described how high he wore his pants. How the older ladies, the wives, made comments about his backside. I am doing just what he said, too: serving the upper class, raising their young son while they are off getting rich.

Henry asks me why I look like I want to cry when I'm leaving.

"I'll just miss you so much when I'm gone," I say. He puts his little sticky hand on top of mine and says, "Je t'adore."

I sniffle on the train and all the way home. Child-tending is softer than bartending. For instance, they drink milk to comfort themselves, not liquor. And when they are upset with you, they too yell and call names, but they get over it faster—never holding a grudge longer than it takes for their tears to dry.

Rifling through my belongings, I find nothing to wear. I hadn't brought much with me during my last exodus. Just a few pairs of jeans and some summer tops. Celine once told me to help myself to her wardrobe. She'd always wanted a sister, she said. I imagine that's why she's yet to evict me from her tiny flat, though I am starting to feel hungry for my own space. She said her flat was haunted and I believe her. Things we've thrown away are always showing up again in closets or on dressers.

"Didn't you throw this away last night?" she'd asked, holding up a plastic tub of butter. I nodded. She'd found it in her wardrobe among her shoes. *"What type of ghost collects tubs of butter?"* She'd frowned, stepping on the paddle of the rubbish bin. I didn't know. I am haunted by the living.

I step into her room. It's chilly, the windows open, and her flimsy gauze curtains flapping about. I close them quickly and open her wardrobe, smiling glibly. All monochrome. I've never seen her in color. I choose a black shirt and jacket to pair with my black pants, and write her a little note telling her what I've taken. I don't feel myself when I step onto the street. I've been living in khaki and white, a single limp braid hanging down my back. Tonight I look stylish and French in my black pants and tailored jacket. My hair hangs in ripples down my back from the braid and I even put on mascara and lipstick. I used to think that loving someone split you in two: the person you were when you were alone, and the person you were as part of a team. I held things back from him thinking he'd not want me as I was, and as a result, I always felt trapped beneath my own skin, never fully able to be myself. I am myself now, and I don't care who sees that. The walk to the cafe is fifteen minutes. I'm already ten minutes late.

When I step into the café, I spot him right away. He's waiting for me at a tiny table, a French saying is painted on the wall over his head: *Au fait.* It means to be conversant with familiar things. *How appropriate*, I think as I make my way toward him. When I reach the table, he stands up like a proper gentleman and gives me a tight-lipped smile. He's all business and I'm all nerves. We both make a point of being covert lookers; under the guise of lowly hung eyelids and quick glances we study one another. His skin is the color of butterscotch. Only the wealthy are tan, I think. The rest of us work too much to lie underneath the sun. We both sink into our seats, relieved that the greeting is over—that's the hard part, the awkwardness of saying hello.

"Did you bring them?" I ask.

My hands are folded on the table to keep from shaking. If you looked closely you would see the tremor.

"Bring what?"

"The papers. Aren't you here to have me sign papers? And how did you find me anyway?"

"I hired a private detective," he says. "He's quite used to finding you at this point."

I make a face. "That's how you knew I'd be at the cafe," I say, nodding. "Why don't you just e-mail and ask?"

"Would you answer?"

I tap, tap, tap my finger on the tabletop, then abruptly fold them again.

"No, I suppose not."

He lifts his eyebrows in response.

I am hungry for him to tell me something. Something about his life, or even about Petra. If he imparts even a little detail it will mean he cares, that I am worthy of knowing things. I almost laugh at myself. I gave all of David up. I have no right to ask anything about his life. I am emotionally homeless, pandering for his attention.

"Why are you here?" he asks.

He gestures outside and it takes a moment to understand that he means Paris, not this particular restaurant.

I look around anyway, at the tiny white plates on the tables, and then outside at two women with cigarettes scissored between their fingers. They are gaunt, bare of makeup. In Paris, the women accept their bare faces and like them that way. I'm learning, but I love makeup.

"Same reason I'm ever anywhere," I say.

"Did you have a boyfriend you were going to move in with…Evan…?"

"Ethan." I shrug. "Why don't you tell me something about yourself since you seem to know so much about me," I say.

I want one of those cigarettes that the gaunt, barefaced girls are holding. David offers me his water like he knows I'm struggling. I take it gratefully and sip.

"Me?" he says, surprised. "What do you want to know about me?"

I thrill at the offer even though it isn't really an offer. There only seems to be one question important enough to ask. One I ask myself almost every day.

"Are you happy?" I figure his answer will answer all of my other questions.

"What does it mean to be happy?" he asks.

A question to answer a question. He's good at that.

A server appears with a bottle of Burgundy and two glasses. She's one of the gaunt girls I saw smoking outside. She isn't wearing a bra. I check to see if David has noticed, but his eyes are on me. I have a flashback of our last meeting in London and how that had gone south fast.

"Every time you order a bottle of wine we fight," I say.

He gives me an annoyed look as he fills my glass.

"We fight because we have things to fight about, it has nothing to do with the wine."

I shrug like I don't care, but I do care. I'm superstitious about some things.

"Are you going to marry Petra?" It feels like a relief to get the words out, but I also feel exhausted after I say them. He stares at me like my question is absurd.

"Are you going to answer any of my questions?" I ask, irritated.

David finishes his glass of wine. He reaches for my untouched glass and pulls it toward him.

"Where are the papers?" I ask. "This is the third time you've found me to deliver divorce papers, and yet somehow you disappear with them every time." I slam my fist on the table and the glasses wobble. David stares at me, not at all moved by my display, and suddenly I know.

"Oh my God," I say. I point a finger at him, just one jab in his direction. "You're doing this to torture me."

I stand up. I feel like such a fool. He's not looking at me now; he's staring at my wineglass, which confirms my theory. I act on impulse, lunging toward him, reaching around his left side and patting him down. I search for the papers that I already know are not there. The bastard came empty-handed…again. I'm so caught up in what I'm doing that when I look up I realize he's inches from my face, just staring at me. His hands are in the air, palms out like he's offering a surrender. We glare at each other.

"Full cavity search too?" he asks, glibly.

He's not smiling and neither am I. We're so close that I can smell the wine on his breath, see that his eyes are too bloodshot to indicate that he just started drinking when I arrived. He's drunk, he's been drunk. I wonder how often he spends his days like this, or if it's just me who brings it on. I straighten up, staring right into his miserable eyes, then I turn on my heel and walk out. I hear him call my name but I don't stop. I walk and walk until I don't know where I am, and I realize I'm crying, tears dripping down my chin and onto Celine's silk shirt, mingling with the mascara. I left her jacket at the restaurant, which makes me cry harder. I'm such a failure. I deserve it, whatever torture he sees fit to punish me with, I deserve every second of it.

49

BATH

HE COMES TO CELINE'S FLAT later that night. I hear the knock but I don't move. When she opens the door she speaks in French. I hear David reply in English. He asks to speak to Yara. My face is half submerged in bathwater. I blow bubbles out of my nose. Celine knocks on the bathroom door a moment later, her voice unsure.

"Yara," she says. "Your David is here."

I roll my eyes and hope he heard that. If someone has owned you once, can you ever be free?

"I'm in the bath," I tell her.

"He says he urgently needs to speak with you." Her voice is rising. She doesn't like to be in the middle of conflict.

"All right," I say, slowly. "He's welcome to come in here if he wants to speak to me, but I just got in and he's not ruining my bath like he's already ruined my day," I shout this so he can hear.

A minute later the little brass doorknob turns and David steps in. He keeps his eyes lowered as he closes the door behind him and sits on the lid of the toilet. His view is of the towel rack. On it one white towel hangs perfectly straight, sporting a black monogrammed C. Celine has an addiction to monograming things.

"The bath is filled with bubbles," I say. "You can look at me."

He swivels and then his eyes narrow.

I lied.

I shrug. "What is it that you want?" My words are clipped. I bend a knee, bring it out of the water, and he looks away, back at the towel.

"I've forgotten," he says. "I came here for something but now I've forgotten why."

I smile.

"Divorce," I say. "You came because you want a divorce."

"Do I?"

I reach for the glass of gin I carried in here with me and take a sip.

"Yes, so that you can marry that tattooed whore." I try not to sound bitter when I say it.

He looks at me again, but this time I've turned away. I'm running water between my fingers.

"Don't call her that," he says.

It's weak, his defense of the whore. Noted.

"I'll call her whatever the fuck I want. She's the whore my husband's been sleeping with." I say it slowly, deliberately. Let the words sink in.

He laughs and I look over. It's a nice sound. All these little meetups we've been having and he's never laughed until now. He's looking at me again.

"Since when am I your husband?" he says.

I arch my back so he can see my tits.

"Since you said 'for better or for worse.' This is worse."

"Is that right?"

"That's right," I mimic.

I stand up and reach for the towel that's sitting on the sink next to him. I let the water run down my body while he tries not to look.

"We're married," I tell him. "You can look." I'm being cruel, but I don't care. Cruel and the truth are the same thing.

He looks over slowly, like there is a tether to the back of his neck and he has to pull against it. His long eyelashes flutter and his lips part. It's been a few years since he's seen me without a fabric skin. There are a few changes, not many.

"And how many men has my wife slept with since she's been married?"

This time I laugh. "We're just two cheaters, aren't we?"

I step out of the bath and onto the mat, toweling myself off. David watches me, but there's not lust on his face. Just sadness.

I can hear Celine moving around the kitchen. She's trying to hear what's going on, worrying that we'll soil her white towels. I wrap the towel around myself and step around him to open the door, letting the steam run out. He stands up to follow me.

"Wait here," I say, and he sits back down.

My things are still in my suitcase after all this time. I pull it from underneath the sofa and take out underwear and clothes. I get dressed in the living room where Celine gives me a wide-eyed look, like—what the fuck is going on—and then I go get him.

"I'll be back in a bit," I tell her. "Have to sort things out with my cheating husband."

Her brow creases as she frowns.

We walk without direction, down this street and that. The buildings loom over us as people move past their windows, feeding their families and winding down for the night. As always, I wish to know what they're doing, what they're saying to each other. Is there a right and wrong way to be human? David walks close to me, but we don't touch. I want him to reach out and grab my hand like he used to. I want that so badly. When a couple of drunk guys amble down the narrow street, he moves between me and them, a human barrier. I get a lump in my throat remembering what it's like to feel protected. I've never felt like I needed protecting, it was just the fact that someone wanted to do it. For a long time there's just the consistent stride of two people not knowing how to start, then I ask the questions I've been waiting to ask.

"Did you and Petra have something when we were together?"

"No. Never. She came to a show about a year after you left and we…"

"Fucked."

"Connected," he corrects me.

"All right then," I say, licking my lips. "Tell me about her."

He stops abruptly and looks around. A light breeze lifts his hair.

"I'll need a drink to do that. Or many."

I point to a cafe across the street. "Drink away."

He looks at my finger, my arm, my face, then turns his body to study the bar I'm pointing to like he's in a trance.

"That place?" he asks.

I shrug. "It's as good as any."

It's a lie, of course. Anyone can see that it's grungy. The windows are filmed over with scum and the crowd standing outside has a drug mafia look to them. He nods like he doesn't care, and I feel disappointed. I wanted him to be disgusted, maybe refuse to step foot into the place, then he'd give me reason not to like him, a real stuck-up asshole. I follow him across the street and through the door. The people standing outside don't even look at us. The inside smells of bleach and beer, a day at the pool. I scrunch up my nose as David leads us to a booth. The benches are a deep red leather, split in some places. I slide over the cracks, and to my surprise, David slides in next to me.

"What are you doing?" I ask.

"Shielding you."

"From what?" I already know what but I want to hear him say it.

"Sex slavery, harassment, the mafia…"

I laugh and he smiles at me, it's genuine right down to his eyes.

Our shoulders are touching, so are our thighs. I lean my elbows on the table as the bartender comes to take our drink order. Beer for both of us. We hold the glasses between our palms and stare at the empty seats in front of us.

"Petra is complicated. She loves me and has given me a lot of room to be myself."

"Who is yourself?"

"I guess I don't really know anymore. I'm half wrapped up in grief, half wrapped up in music. She mostly gets that."

"But she loves you, she stays." There's a catch in my voice, but I'm just stating the obvious, the truth.

"Yeah," he says. "She knows I'm here, but she didn't want me to come."

I nod. "I wouldn't have either." We take a sip of our beer to kill the awkwardness.

"Why did you come?" I ask.

"I wanted to look at you."

"And so you have. You've looked at me in England, and you've looked at me in France. Why do you need to look anymore? Give me the goddamn papers and let me sign them!"

"I haven't made up my mind," he said.

"About what, David? *What?*"

He looks startled. I see the bartender peep out from behind a wall and then quickly retreat. I quiet my voice, but it's still angry.

"You thought you'd come here and hate me? You thought you'd feel relieved that I walked out and you can pretend it was all for the best? Or did you think you'd take one look and know that you're no longer in love with me? So tell me, David. Do you feel those things, or is it still me you'll write songs for?"

This time he is silent.

"I came because I love you," he says. "Still, after all these years."

50

THE OCEAN

"HOW CAN YOU STILL LOVE me after what I did?" I ask him.

His chin is dipped down to his chest and he seems to be in deep thought after having confessed that to me.

"I never loved you for what you did or didn't do," he says. "That's not what love is."

I don't quite know what he means and he doesn't explain further. My hands are trembling around my beer, which has warmed to room temperature, but I can't seem to let it go. It's a sad day when beer becomes your anchor.

"I never went looking for love," he says. "I didn't know what I was missing. I had women who I thought I loved, who I spent time with, who I made love to. It all felt good until you came along. Then those encounters didn't feel good anymore. It's like living by a lake your whole life and then being taken to the ocean."

I stare at him, not sure how to process what he's saying. It's a compliment no doubt, coming from the husband I abandoned six weeks after our wedding.

"But then the ocean shipwrecked you," I say. He is an artist and I am a dose of reality.

"All that beauty and power turned against me," he agrees.

It feels better to speak in metaphor, easier. It's saying the truth without actually saying the truth. You could only speak to an artist this way. No one else would get it.

"Do you hate the ocean now?"

He shakes his head. "I just don't believe in it anymore. It's not something that's wonderful and beautiful like I thought it was. It's dangerous. I won't go in past my knees."

"Maybe it's better just to look at the ocean," I suggest. "Maybe none of us should go in."

He turns to look at me then. "But I can't stop thinking about the ocean. It got in my head. The roar it makes—both peaceful and angry. The way its mood changes every day. The way it washes some things away and drags some things to your feet. It gives and it takes away. It cleanses and kills. It's a fury, but also the most beautiful thing I've ever seen. I can't look at a lake the same way again. Lakes are shallow, lakes are predictable, lakes dry up."

I bite my lip and turn my head away to stare out the window. My heart is racing in the way hearts race when they're afraid. I want to ask him if Petra the whore is a lake or an ocean, but I don't have the balls.

"So what will you do?" I'm asking about the divorce, his marriage to Petra, the papers he never seems to produce, but that's not what David Lisey hears. He's the type of person who hears selectively. That's what makes him a good songwriter, I guess. He listens for the things he wants to hear and then makes beauty out of them.

"I'll write a song," he says.

That makes me angry. I'm on the wrong side of the booth. I can't shove my way past him. I can't climb over his lap. I'm trapped. I realize he sat next to me this way on purpose, to keep me there when I tried to run. He's learning me.

"That's why you keep finding me," I say. "Because I'm your goddamn muse."

I push my weight against him so he knows I want out. I'm rageful; my eyes are burning with righteous tears.

"Maybe you shouldn't marry a girl who doesn't inspire you in the same way." I'm looking for something mean to say, something to make him hurt, and I find it.

"I didn't," he says simply. "I married you."

"Yes, and now you're here asking for a divorce."

"I've never asked for a divorce," he says.

My mouth is open to shoot out more words. I close it to think. Had I been the one to surmise that? Had he ever said the word *divorce*?

"You told me that you're engaged to Petra," I say.

His face falls. I wonder at the sudden darkness.

"I am."

"Ugh!" I make a noise. I sound like a woman giving birth. I drop my head into my hands and wish to God that I hadn't sat on this side of the booth. Trapped like an idiot, trapped like a fool. And in this dingy bar where no one would help me even if I screamed. But, I'm not trapped, am I? I look up, suddenly hopeful. I've always been the one in power just because I cared less—or let's be honest—pretended to.

"Move, David," I force those two words out, hard and steady. "I'm done here."

"No, you're not," he says. "And I'm not either."

"Oh please," I say it just as harsh as I intended to. "My mother lives somewhere in England. She neglected me for half my life and hasn't made a move to find me in over eight years. That's unfinished business. I'm just some girl you married on impulse. It was a blow to your pride that I left, not your heart." I shove at him so that he slides an inch in the right direction. "You shacked up with the girl who caused me insecurity in our relationship." I shove at him again. "I may be a runner, I may be a coward, but I'm an honest whatever I am. I didn't try to pull one over on you. You knew exactly what you were getting into with me." He's on the edge of the booth now. One more shove and I'll be free. "You're with Petra to hurt me. Don't even deny it."

I push at him with my whole body and then he's on his feet and so am I. I head for the door, stumbling past men holding drinks like they're props. What the fuck is this place? I bump into someone, knocking his drink onto his shirt. He's a thick guy, neck like a bull. When his vodka spills, it makes an arc in slow motion and lands on his very expensive looking silk tie. I've never seen a man with thicker wrists, seriously.

"Bitch," he says the word like he says it a lot. He's the type of man who calls women bitch like it's their name.

"Say it again," I say. "And I'll cut your fucking tongue out."

I say it in English but he understands me. His eyes become two hard, amused things. I mean it. If he calls me a bitch again I'll claw at him until I'm dead. I don't care a thing about what bad people can do to me. I care about what good people can do. David swoops in. I don't know where he comes from, or how quickly he moved, but he's there between me and Hercules, telling him I'm drunk.

Hercules looks at me over David's shoulder like he's evaluating whether or not to believe the story. I don't look drunk. I'm not swaying or bleary-eyed and I don't want to pretend to be. I return his gaze, not faltering for one second. I'm not scared of him and I want him to know it.

"Get that bitch out of here," he says to David.

And then I'm loose like a rock out of a slingshot. I launch myself at him, aiming for his face. David grabs me before my hands can make contact, and I am left clawing at the air. The men around start to laugh. I am just a girl thwarted, pulled aside by men stronger than me. As soon as his grip loosens I move quick as a bird. I have a promise to deliver. I reach Hercules and punch him in the nose. I have so much anger invested in that punch that his meaty head snaps backward and blood sprays. Next thing I know it's David who is getting hit. Right in the jaw for protecting me. I watch fists rain down on him as he tries to steady himself. He hits too, first Hercules, and then a bystander. My body clenches in worry. They'll kill him—these are the type of men who will kill him. My phone is in my pocket. I pull it out and dial the police.

What have I done? What have I done? What have I done?

My hand is throbbing from the contact with Hercules' nose. There is blood on my knuckles and my clothes. Someone grabs my hair and yanks me backward as I see David go down onto his knees and then his side. I scream, but my scream is drowned out by everyone else's noise. Someone is holding me back. I kick at them until they release me and then I run for David, throwing my body over his. For a few minutes I sustain the blows. Kicks to my back and legs. My abdomen is crushed against his body, so they hurt what they can. And then there is the sound of police sirens and the men scatter. We are taken to the hospital separately. With David there is a sense of urgency. I get a flash of his face as they carry him into the ambulance and I can't make out his features amidst the blood.

What have I done? What have I done?

51

NEWSWORTHY

DAVID HAS A CONCUSSION, a broken nose, a broken rib, and severe swelling to his face. The media catches the story the day after it all goes down and the street in front of the hospital becomes the type of place where the paparazzi and the news break bread together. Celine and I sit side by side on her sofa, our knees pulled up to our chests, and watch the news in silence. My ribs are sore, and I have a raging headache, but it's nothing compared to the injuries David sustained to protect me. When the news story ends, we open our computers and read what they have to say online. There are suspects. Police are in the process of questioning people as to their whereabouts. A source reports that when David Lisey's fiancée, Petra Dilator, walked into his hospital room, she burst into tears and insisted that the man in the bed was not him. I can still see his bloody face in my mind. I sustained bruises to my body that can mostly be hidden by clothes. The ones to my mind are more severe. My hardness insisting that we all have demons that need to be conquered, cannot sleep, cannot eat. I replay what happened over and over in my mind, hating myself so fiercely I can't look at myself in the mirror. Three days later I'm so sick with worry that Celine tells me to go to the hospital to see him.

"They won't let me in," I say. "That place is a media circus."

She types media circus into her phone and nods when she reads the definition. "You're still his wife," she says. "They'll have to let you in."

I stand up as soon as the words are out of her mouth. That's right. I am his wife. I have just as much right to be there as Petra, maybe more if I can justify things the right way in my mind. I march for the door, grabbing my bag. I'd text David to warn him I'm coming but I don't have his phone number. What a shitty wife I am.

When I arrive at the hospital, I have to fight my way through the throng of people gathered outside. A few reporters look at me curiously, but I ignore them and walk for the doors.

"Purpose," Celine told me before I left. *"Look like you have purpose. Don't falter…"*

"But what if he doesn't want to see me?" I asked.

She rolled her eyes and brushed me off.

But, it was there—that worry of rejection. That he'd turn me away. It's funny that I'm the one who's been turning him away for years, yet here I am sick with worry over it happening to me. We are such hypocrites, us humans. I sign in at the desk and present my ID to a girl who can't be older than nineteen. Her hair is pulled up in a tight bun, and when I tell her who I'm here to see, she blinks rapidly.

"You're not on the list," she says to me in French.

She doesn't look at me—she looks at the computer screen in front of her. I want to peer round and see who is on the list.

"Call his room," I say. "I'm his wife."

She looks unsure, but picks up the phone. She speaks in rapid French that I can't follow. I wish I'd brought Celine along to help with this sort of thing. When she hangs up she holds a finger up.

Be quiet, we don't understand each other, help is coming.

My mouth is open to speak, but I quickly shut it. Sometimes you just need to wait. A few minutes of awkward standing around go by and then an official looking man in a suit walks up and stands next to the girl. They're ganging up on me, I realize. I lift my chin. When he speaks, his accent is American, but there's something else too, like maybe he spent time everywhere like I did and picked up a little of this and that.

"I'm here to escort you from the premises," he says.

Not what I was expecting. I thought they'd ask me to produce a marriage license, or perhaps call up to David's room to get clearance. Instead they are getting me the fuck out of here.

"On whose order?" I ask. "David's or Petra's?"

"Mr. Lisey's doctor and his fiancée have discussed the matter and have made a decision for his well-being. They both agree that he needs rest at this time."

I nod. Of course. A rush of uncertainty hits me. It was wrong of me to come here. I had no right. I smile at the receptionist who is looking at the floor, and the muscle who looks like he's ready to tackle me to the floor, and I walk out. I can't blame Petra. Once upon a time I had been the one trying to keep her out of his line of vision. I thought that if he saw too much of her he'd realize I wasn't enough.

I watch them for a while, deciding which one I like most. Four women and three men. Two of the women look like the type of career bitches who are willing to trample the weak underfoot just to have a better view. I dismiss them right away. The older guy with silver hair is out because he keeps looking at his reflection in a small mirror he keeps in his pocket. That leaves two women and two men. I choose the mousier of the women. In the five minutes I've been watching, she's spilled coffee on her skirt and tripped over her own feet which resulted in a scrape to her ankle. She hasn't even done anything about it, just let the blood drip into her shoe. The other reporters sniggered when they saw her fall. Typical human nature but it still irks me. She's having a shit day, sort of like me. Perhaps even a shit life. She deserves a break.

I unbutton my blouse as I walk, just to get the tedious part out of the way. I like to get things done quickly, unless it's sex, then I like to take my time. The story circulating the news was that David Lisey had been with an undisclosed woman when he was attacked. When I reach her, I pull off my shirt and stand in front of her in nothing but my black bra. She looks around alarmed, but then her face changes into something else. I turn so she can see the bruises on my back; they've already started yellowing.

"My name is Yara," I say. "I am the woman David Lisey was in the bar with." I pause as she watches me, her eyes growing larger as she decides if she believes me or not. I smile bitterly. "I am also his wife."

In ten minutes the reporter, whose name is Lunya Louse, has me powdered and miked, standing in front of a heavy camera, which is balanced on a man's shoulder. She's eaten tuna for lunch. I can smell it on her breath. Lunya tells me to loosen up so I do, shaking my shoulders free of the tension. She hands me a tube of lipstick and tells me to put some on.

"The camera washes you out," she says.

I realize Lunya isn't as helpless as she looks. The red lipstick is a nice touch for an estranged wife. Adds that extra—where's she been whoring around all these years—drama. I have to show her a photo of David and me on our wedding day. She holds my phone between her short stubby fingers and peers at the photo for a full minute before she hands it back.

"Until we can verify record of the marriage, I'll have to say you're claiming to be his wife."

I nod. That is fine by me.

In the picture, which after all these years I still have saved in my phone, David has his arm around my waist, smiling toward the camera. His smile is so genuine it's infectious. I see the corners of Lunya's mouth turn upward and I don't know if she's smiling because she just fell into a juicy story or because David looks so happy. I suppose it could be a combination of both.

My side of the photo is a different story. I'm holding one side of my dress up, smiling close-lipped, a huge bouquet of red roses behind us. You can almost see the fear in my eyes. The picture itself brings on a great deal of pain. I don't look at it often, but with each new cell phone I've had through the years, I always make sure it is there.

Lunya is briefing me, her English perfectly accented. She will ask me three questions in French, and I am to answer them in English. They will dub the video later. The other reporters have taken notice and are walking over, their eyes narrowed in anticipation. They stop and consult each other as Lunya ignores them. She will break this story. It's a big one. A beloved and well-known musician has an estranged wife no one knows about, that's media gold. Strangely enough my heart is not racing, I'm comforted by the fact that I'm not lying. This is my story to tell, my truth. I am relaying it as it happened. I am David Lisey's legal wife and soon the whole world will know.

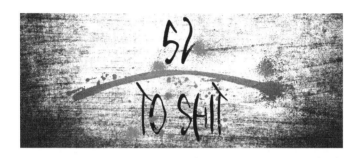

MAKE A PLAN, WATCH IT GO TO SHIT—something my mother used to say after her third beer. She'd be glossy-eyed by then, her cupid bow lips slashed angrily with the coral lipstick she wore every day. It was probably wrong to imprint a child with this sort of pessimism, but my mother thought warnings and wisdom went hand-in-hand. I had some warning at least. I didn't expect the world to open up for me. I was prepared to make a plan and watch everything go to shit. I think about those kids a lot—the ones who had two parents and three non-microwaved meals a day. What was it like for them when things went to shit? Were they expecting it? Did it hurt more because it was so foreign? With a truth teller for a mother life can't blindside you.

My plan goes to shit faster than I expect. As it turns out, revenge is best taken after much planning and consideration. Impulse on the heels of anger is wrought with the type of issues a sane and private person would want to avoid. After Lunya Louse's short but efficient interview, I am ushered into a black Range Rover wearing red lipstick and driven home to Celine's flat. The driver, a man Lunya referred to as Gerard, did not speak a lick of English, and I had to type the address into my phone and hold it out to him in order to get home. In our confusion over language and phones, we did not see the white van following behind us, though I'm assuming Lunya did. What does it matter to her? She has her story and they can chase her source all they want.

A nasty throb has started behind my eyes, a headache to rule all headaches. I open the picture of David and me on our wedding day and stare at it until my appetite for memories has been sated. What have I done? I'm not sure, but it's too late to change anything now. I step out of the Range Rover after thanking Gerard and make my way up the stairs, wondering how I am going to explain all of this to Celine. She told me to go, to talk to David, not aim at ruining his life. I stare at my feet, shamed. What is it about me that sends me over, over, over the edge? I can't blame my mother, or my father, or my loneliness. Cheap tricks. Sure, I carry around your average bitterness, but it doesn't stop me, I'm not drowning in it. Outing David to the whole world was brought on by something else.

Celine greets me when I walk through the door. I fall into her arms, a rag doll. She shushes me when I start to cry and settles me on the couch before bringing me a plate of olives and cheese. I pick at the food while she pours two generous portions of wine and carries them over in her small, white hands. Everything looks too big for Celine's small hands.

"Yara," she says. "Tell me what has occurred."

What has occurred.

I want to repeat her phrasing but she gets flustered when I do.

"Turn on the news," I say.

"Oh, no," she says. "What have—?"

I shake my head indicating that I don't want to say more. The story runs on the six o'clock news. Celine and I have drunk most of the bottle and are spread out on the sofa like a couple of college girls. I jar when I see my face appear on the screen, the blonde hair and red lipstick. I look like a whore, not a wife.

"Oh my, Yara," she says. *Oh my, indeed.*

My roommate listens raptly as Lunya Louse asks me about my marriage to singer/songwriter David Lisey.

"Yara Phillips, who claims they were together in a bar on Rue Bezout the night David Lisey was attacked, is also claiming to be his estranged wife…"

Celine glances at me then back at the TV. "You certainly know how to cause a stir," she says. "I sent you to the hospital to talk to David, not the entire country." She waves her hand outside the window. "World," she corrects herself.

"Yes, well, they wouldn't let me see him and I got a little carried away."

She raises her eyebrows but doesn't say more.

The phone begins to ring and we stare at each other.

"Do we answer it?" I ask.

Celine stands up and walks over to the dated house phone on her wall. She answers in her usually chirpy way and I hear her speak in rapid French before hanging up. She comes back with a new bottle of wine.

"Someone just called you a whore," she says. "In French. It sounds much better to call someone a whore in French."

"More elegant," I agree. "Do you think it was the lipstick?"

Celine sits back down, and her eyes are bright and angry. "I think it's the jealousy."

Petra is on the screen now, images of her flash and change so we can get every angle of her beauty. Petra walking into a restaurant in downtown LA holding David's hand, Petra at lunch with David's mother, Petra sitting on David's lap at an awards show. The public is curious about her, they love her: the silent and supportive fiancée to America's newest sweetheart. She's grown her hair out, added some tattoos. She wears the right clothes and paints the right makeup, looks devastatingly classy. Jealousy, such a complicated word. I don't want to be her, I don't want to look like her, but I want it to be easy to love him—like it is for her. What is it exactly that I'm admitting to myself?

David was mine. He could have left me. He could have annulled the marriage. He never gave me divorce papers. *Oh my God.* He hadn't been trying to torment me; he'd come to find me. Once, twice, three times. I start rocking on the sofa, head buried between my knees. Celine wordlessly strokes my back. She knew…who else knew…Posey? Ann…? Was I the only one?

"Celine," I say, sitting up. "You're the most peaceful person I've ever known. Peaceful," I reiterate. "As in filled with peace."

Celine waves me off. "You're drunk, Yara."

"No, no—let me finish," I insist. I'm holding up a single finger. I tuck my hand away behind my back, embarrassed. I can taste the wine on my tongue, coating the inside of my mouth. I am drunk, but that's when you're most honest.

"You and your monochrome," I say. "I came here to think. Oh God. I came to you for peace."

It sounds so stupid, but it's true. When I went home to England after Seattle, Posey was my voice of reason. She was willing to tell me when I was being stupid, immature, narcissistic. I had these friends spread about the planet and each of them brought something so unique to my life.

"I have to go," I say. "I've had time to think and now I have to go."

"Go where?" Celine's lips and teeth are stained from the wine.

I grab her face between my hands. "London." I have to go back.

I DID A BAD THING and now I have to wait and see if he'll forgive me. Cat and mouse, cat and mouse. I do the responsible thing and instead of just running like I normally do, I turn in my two weeks' notice to Henry's family. Henry weeps when I leave work the next day.

"Not yet, little love," I tell him. "Two more weeks!"

He nods, tears streaming down his face.

"Mama will find someone even more fun than me!" I shoot his mother a warning look and she shrugs, knowing her Henry will be stuck with someone not even a little bit fun.

"I can interview them," I offer before I leave. "I don't trust him with just anyone."

Henry's mum agrees to put an advert out in the morning and I feel better about that. At least I can find him someone who will play with him; otherwise, the poor kid will never have a childhood.

On my walk to Celine's flat I check the news on my phone. David has left Paris and returned to the States with Petra. There is a picture of him, his arm in a sling and his face still bruised as he walks through the airport with her on his healthy arm. I can't read his face because his head is down. He has yet to make a statement about his estranged wife, though the strong support Petra is showing him is what's really making headlines. They love her more, if that is even possible, for standing by her man.

I stare at the picture of her, hair hanging loose, long slender legs. So he chose not to contact me and went home instead. I know this time he won't be delivering phantom divorce papers himself. They'll come from a fancy attorney's office in New York or someplace like that. How many houses does he have now? Where are they? Did Petra buy the furniture and choose the art? Did they cook and laugh together? Make love over spilled M&M's on the floor? Did he sing Michael Bolton to her? My heart hurts. I'd not entertained thoughts about their life together until now. I'd not wanted to replace myself with her. But there it was, their romance all over my thoughts.

I think of the way he kissed me, pulled back, smiled a little, and then kissed me some more. I think of the way he was always feeling me up, no matter where we were. I think of the way he always knew what I was thinking and called me out on it. Now it is all Petra's; every second of David belongs to Petra. I hate her, and I hate him, and I hate myself.

At the end of my two weeks, I kiss Henry goodbye and sob all the way to the train station. This doesn't happen when you are a bartender. You don't get attached this way. His little chubby hands hadn't wanted to let me go, they'd held onto mine until his mother had to pull him away and take him for an ice cream. I found him a good nanny, a kind woman who never had children of her own and delighted in hearing him laugh. They'd be friends for a long time.

Celine was at work when I left for the train, we'd said our goodbyes the night before, but I left her a long letter that I'd written in bed after she went to sleep. She'd taken me at my worst and I'd never forget that. She was my family now. I told her so, along with a lot of other things I'd never said to a friend before.

The next day I catch the train back to London not really knowing why or what I am going to do. I just know that I need to go back. Faith. I am having faith. In what I don't know.

I crash at Posey's house when I get back to London. She's vacationing in Mauritius with her family for the week and left the key with a neighbor. The whole transaction reminds me of when I arrived in France at Celine's just months earlier. My life is a cycle of hello/goodbye and it's starting to feel empty. Her flat feels empty and void of life without her. I wander from room to room, studying things I've seen a thousand times before, until I get the courage to leave. I'm afraid to face London, as silly as that sounds. I'm also afraid to run into Ethan or someone else I know.

I pull a beanie over my hair and step into the street, not really knowing which way to go. I'm wearing a dress, something new for me, but I think dresses are who I am now. I don't want to dress tough anymore—I *am* tough. My faithful New York boots push me forward through the tourists, and school children, past Tower Bridge and then across. I walk and walk the streets of the city I love so much, weaving this way and that until I don't really know how long I've been walking. I get hungry at some point and pull out my phone to find a restaurant. The app on my phone says twelve restaurants are in my vicinity. I scroll through looking at their star ratings until something catches my eye. Wow. I want to laugh. Someone stole our idea. A restaurant called IOU is just a few blocks away. I decide to go check it out. When I arrive there's a wait out the door. I ask if I can sit at the bar and the hostess waves me through. I push through a dozen people cramming up the entrance and head for the bar, which is to the left. It's a nice setup. The booths are cream colored and the tables are gold. There are giant pots of pale pink peonies everywhere. The atmosphere is soft and feminine. *Soft.* I stop dead in my tracks and look around suspiciously. No. That would be crazy. I laugh at myself until I see the wall to the left of the bar; mottled pink the color of the peonies, there's a neon sign that takes up most of the wall.

Come back to me. Come back. Come.

I turn toward the bar and slide into a seat. The bartender is tall and lanky. He has matching sleeve tattoos on both arms, wild roses and skulls.

"Gin and tonic," I say. "Please."

He nods and sets about making my drink even though he's backed up.

"Hey, who owns this place?" I ask.

"Lead singer of that band," his accent is cockney, "Lazarus Come Forth. That's why all these people are here, we're busy every night."

He hands me my drink and I down it.

"Whoa girl, that's not a shot," he says.

I slam my glass on the counter. "Another," I say. And then I turn to look at the neon wall.

Come back to me. Come back. Come.

"How long has this place been here?" My eyes are watering from how fast I threw back my drink. I hold the back of my hand against my mouth, not taking my eyes from the wall.

"Six months."

Six months, six months, six months. I just missed it when I left to Paris.

"There's one in Seattle too," he says. "And Miami, New York, New Orleans, Chicago, and LA."

All the places I've lived. I feel lightheaded. I drink my second drink and then leave twenty quid on the bar and walk out.

Come back to me. Come back. Come.

I call Posey as soon as I get back to the flat.

"Yara," she says as soon as she answers. "Well, well, well. The prodigal son returns."

"I have to leave again," I blurt.

She's quiet.

"Posey…are you there?"

"Yeah…yeah," she stumbles. I hear her say something to someone on her side and then she's back.

"Yara, did David contact you?"

"Not since the news things, no. Why?"

"Yara, he came to see me. After you left."

I drop the phone on the bed and have to scramble to retrieve it from the rumpled sheets.

"What the fuck are you talking about, Posey?"

She sighs. "Did you find the restaurant?"

"Yes," I say. "But what does that have to do with you seeing him?"

"Nothing," she says, quickly. "He did a Tour de Friends, Yara."

"What does that mean?" I snap.

"Look, this is between you and David, but he came round after you left. He wanted to know you. The parts that he didn't. Your London life, I suppose."

"Why didn't you tell me?" My tone is angry.

I walk into the kitchen with the phone still pressed against my ear and pull a bottle of Burley's from the liquor cabinet.

"Fuck you, Yara," Posey said. "You disappear every few years and I don't hear from you. You don't call and you don't answer e-mails. I didn't know you married the guy, thanks for telling me, by the way."

My anger dissipates. She's right. It's my fault. I've been doing this to everyone in my life for years. Posey was the only one who consistently forgave and accepted me for who I was.

"I'm sorry, Posey," I say. "You're right. I'm so sorry."

I hear her switch the phone to her other ear. "You're going to Seattle, aren't you?"

"Yeah," I say. "I have to go find him."

"Do you need me to come?" she asks.

And I know she would if I asked her to. She'd hop on a plane and come all the way to Seattle with me.

"No, you're my London life." I laugh. "I'm not ready to cross my worlds."

"Okay," she says. "Text me when you get there, yeah?"

"Yeah."

When I hang up I go straight to the computer to book a flight. I have my savings, but they wouldn't get me far. If this didn't work I may be stranded in America without a work visa and no money to get back. I book a one-way ticket and close my eyes.

Please God, who I don't believe in. Don't let it be too late.

I write an e-mail to Ann, my old friend and neighbor. I tell her I'm going to be in town and ask if I can stay with her. I know she'll say yes. Ann is a sixty-year-old agoraphobic. She never leaves her apartment—hasn't in years. She'll be glad for the company, and she is my last friend stop. Posey set me straight. Celine cleared my head and brought me peace. Now I need Ann's wisdom. She'll know what to do next.

54

FERDINAND

I SLEEP ON ANN'S PULLOUT, just long enough to conquer my jet lag, and then I stumble into the shower. Ann makes me scrambled eggs and toast, and we sit down at her little table to eat while I tell her everything.

"Runaway bride," she says, shaking her head. "What's the plan for today then?"

"I'm going to see if I can track him down," I tell her.

I look over her shoulder and out the window and my stomach does a little flip. I love it here. I missed it.

"Good, that's a good plan." She winks at me and stands up to clear our dishes.

David doesn't live in his old condo behind Pike Place Market. A man answers the door and tells me that he rents it.

"I send my checks to an agency," he says. "I don't know anything about a David Lisey."

I go to The Crocodile next.

"Man, if I had a dollar for every time some girl showed up here and asked for David Lisey," the bartender says. He's wearing a 49ers hat. Does that mean something or does it not count if it's a sports team? He wipes circles on the bar and shakes his head at me. "No, he don't come in here no more, not now that they're big time."

I thank him and leave. I think about going to his mother's house, but I'm too afraid. She must hate me as much as he does.

"I don't know how to get in touch with him, Ann," I say when I'm back at her place. "He's a celebrity now, it's not like his information is public."

Ann waves off my comment like it's the dumbest thing she's ever heard.

"He has a best friend, right?"

"Yeah," I say. "He's in the bloody band too."

"Don't you still have his phone number?" she asks.

I think about it for a moment. I don't, but I do know where his mother used to live.

"You're a genius, Ann," I say, kissing her forehead before I run out the door.

When I knock on Ferdinand's mother's door, a plump lady answers wearing an apron with apple pie all over it.

"Hello, Mrs. Alehe?"

"Yes," she says, looking around. "You're not a reporter, are you?"

"No," I say. "I'm an old friend of your son. I was wondering if you could give this to your Ferdinand. Tell him that Yara came by."

"Yara," she repeats, suspiciously.

I smile.

"Yes, Yara Phillips. He'll know who I am."

"Did he knock you up?" she asks.

I try not to laugh. "No, Mrs. Alehe. I'm really just a friend."

I eye her crucifix as I hand her the paper and then walk back down the drive and to my waiting Uber. I know she'll call him right away, just to make sure I wasn't carrying her illegitimate grandchild.

Forty-five minutes later my phone rings. The number says Private.

"Yara?" I recognize his deep voice right away.

"Yes," I say. "It's me."

"Where are you?"

"I'm in Seattle. Can we meet somewhere...tonight maybe?"

There's a long pause on his end. "Yeah, sure. Where?"

I tell him to meet me at the brewery by David's house. And then I hang up. One step closer.

I meet Ferdinand at the taproom we all used to go to near David's old place. I'm thirty minutes late by the time the Uber pulls up to the door, typical Seattle traffic. Ferdinand is outside, smoking against the wall. He has the hood of his jacket pulled up around his face and I wonder if it's to keep people from recognizing him. Their lives have changed so much since I was last here. He has tattoos on his fingers that weren't there before, and he's wearing heavy silver rings on almost every finger.

"Hi," I said. I feel so awkward I stick both of my hands in my back pockets.

"Hi," he says back. "Want a beer?"

I nod, and he tosses his cigarette on the ground before turning around and walking into the taproom. He orders an IPA for himself and a Stella for me.

"You still like that shit?" he says, turning around to check.

I nod. We carry our beers to a table near the pretzel machine and sit down.

"So," he says.

"Congratulations. On everything," I say. "You guys really made it happen."

He nods slowly, his eyes drilling into me. Ferdinand is frightening as fuck. I try to remind myself that this was the guy who had a kitten screensaver on his computer.

"Yeah, I guess I should be thanking you," he says.

I flinch. So, it was going to be like that.

"You would have made it one way or the other. David is a talented songwriter."

He finishes off his beer and then looks at me. "So what do you want, Yara? Why are you back, or do I even need to ask that?"

"I need to find him. I tried to e-mail him, but he changed his e-mail, I guess."

"Yeah, after that little stunt you pulled in Paris I don't blame him."

My face rearranged itself. I could feel it happening.

"Or you don't blame Petra," I say, raising my eyebrows.

The corner of his mouth lifted in what I perceived was a smile. Wow. I made Ferdinand half smile.

"I need a smoke," he says.

I stand up to go outside with him. The traffic is thick, rush hour. I kick at his last cigarette butt with my boot as I wait for him to light up. Eventually I can't take it anymore.

"Ferdinand, tell me where he is."

I put both hands on my hips like I can intimidate a six foot four bull of a man. He blows smoke out of his mouth and for a moment his face is lost behind the cloud.

"Your mother named you after Ferdinand the bull, didn't she?"

His eyebrows jump at the sudden change of subject, but it just occurred to me that she must have and I felt the need to ask.

"Yes," he said.

"Because you were huge or preemie?"

"Preemie," he says, frowning.

I nod. "What a prediction." Then I drop my hands to my sides letting my shoulders droop. That's how I really feel: droopy.

"I'm sorry I never got to know you before," I said. "I had—have issues." I sit down on the wall outside David's old building and stare up at the sky. It's getting ready to rain, I'm going to get drenched.

Ferdinand sits down next to me, sighing deeply.

"I never liked you," he says.

I look up at him. "You knew I'd hurt him."

"Yeah," he says. "David sees the best, I see the truth. And you had that look of panic in your eyes the whole time you were with him."

I nod. That was true. "I love him very much," I say. "I just wasn't good at love back then."

"Why not?"

I look at the street, a couple is crossing a few feet away—they remind me of David and me back in the day.

"I didn't have anyone show me until David and then it scared me off. When you're unhealthy, healthy things are frightening."

"Are you healthy?" He looks at me and I resist the urge to look away.

"No," I tell him. "But, I'm getting there. I know what I need to do."

"Find David," he says.

"That's part of it, yes. We're still married, for God's sake. Something has to be done one way or another."

He stares at me long and hard. "All right," he says finally. "I'll give you his address. But, you have to promise me something."

I nod, vigorously.

"No more games," he says.

I cross my heart. Ferdinand shakes his head as he texts me David's address.

"I can't believe I'm doing this," he mumbles.

"Thank you, Ferdinand," I say as I stand up. "Thank you, thank you, thank you."

I start to run toward 1st Street, but he calls after me. "Yara! That address is for a houseboat." I hold up my hand to show him I've heard him and I keep running.

I run to Ann's flat—apartment—and fling open the door. She's sitting by the window watching the traffic as she does every day at this time.

"Ann, I got it. I got his address. Now help me decide what to wear."

She turns to face me, a small smile on her lips. "How do you know he'll be there?" she asks.

I stop on my way to the bathroom and frown. I guess I don't. I'll wait outside if I have to.

"What if that hussy shows up with him, that Peeta?"

"Petra," I correct her, staring into my suitcase. "I don't know. I'll have to cross that bridge when I come to it."

"There will be a fight," Ann decides. "A catfight."

"Sure," I shrug, pulling out a dress I brought just for this occasion. "Let's see if she's scrappy."

Ann claps her hands and then returns to her spot. I glance back at her. She's been in this apartment for thirteen years, she told me so when we first met and she invited me in for tea. Thirteen years of never leaving this one small place. I close the bathroom door and rip out my hairband, letting my hair fall free. I have one shot. I'm going to use all my weapons.

55
HOUSEBOAT

WHEN THE UBER PULLS UP to David's houseboat, I am trembling.

"Bloody hell," I say as I climb out of the car.

He used to say he wanted to buy a houseboat one day, but people say things like that all the time. I tell people that I want to live in a tree house, for fuck's sake, that doesn't mean I'll live in a tree house. There are dozens of them, their front yards a long, narrow dock, their backyards the blue/green expanse of Lake Union.

I look at the address on my phone, the one Ferdinand texted to me and I trace it to a grey houseboat with white shutters. It's not very large or extravagant. Pink bougainvillea climb around the front door in a stunning arc. The door itself is bright yellow with a music note as a knocker. I step forward, off the dock and onto the walkway. Next to the welcome mat are two pairs of flip-flops sitting side by side: one a man's, one a woman's. It makes me sick to look at them, to know that neither of them is mine.

"Petra," I say, under my breath.

Dodgy bitch and her stupid flip-flops. I never thought about her in my rush to get here, that she'd actually be living with him—though it makes sense, doesn't it? I breathe deeply and step forward to knock on the door. I knock hard, three times, and then I step back, preparing myself for whatever is about to happen.

I see someone move across the rectangular windows that frame the door, a flash of white. I steel myself as I hear the bolt slide open. Silver hair, lavender lips.

"Petra," I say.

She looks startled. Of course—I'm supposed to be in France. She grips the door with one hand and stares at me.

"Where's my husband?"

"Fuck you, Yara."

She's about to close the door in my face, but I stick my foot in the gap so she can't close it. She's flustered as I try to peer past her into the house. Most of the lights are off, but I can hear the sound of a TV. If David were here surely he'd have come to the door.

"Where is he?"

"If you don't go I'll call the police," she says.

I laugh. "What will you tell them? That David's wife is harassing his whore?"

Red is not a good color on Petra—it clashes with her makeup. I watch as her face turns an ugly beet color and panic rises in her eyes.

"You're crazy," she says. "You won't give him a divorce and now you're stalking him."

"He's never asked me for a divorce, Petra."

She blinks at me, unsure. I can see the uncertainty on her face.

"You left him," she says.

"Yes, I did."

"You never deserved him," she adds.

I shove the door and it hits her in the chest. She's pushed back a few inches and then she flings the door open, her mouth puckered and angry.

I laugh. I meant to antagonize her and it works because she takes a step toward me.

"I may not deserve him, but he chose me. I always knew what you were up to," I say. "All of your questions and underhanded insults. You think you have him? You silly little girl. I feel sorry for you because you've never had him. You don't even know what it's like to have him."

Her faces flushes and then she slaps me. My head snaps back, my cheek on fire. I don't retaliate because I've made her hurt. It's what I wanted and it will last longer than the sting of her hand.

"Goodbye, Petra. Pack your shit and get the fuck out of my husband's house."

And then I walk away. The wind has picked up and my dress blows around my ankles. I lift my arms above my head as I walk and let the Seattle wind lick my skin. It's cold and I am alive. Finally, I am alive.

I know she's afraid. I can feel her fear on my back. She only had him because I didn't. I walk until she can't see me and then I double over and cry so hard my stomach hurts.

I left him. The person who is so afraid of being left. I hurt him the way others had hurt me. What did that make me? I didn't know what he'd say or do when he saw me, if I were David I'd never take me back. Never. I broke his trust.

I don't call an Uber. I walk, and I know what I have to do. I don't know where he is. But, he made it so I could find him. He gave me an IOU.

56

DON'T LIE TO ME

THERE IS A HARDWARE STORE on 4th Avenue. I stop to peer into the window, giving myself a minute to decide if this is what I really want to do. The next twenty minutes go by quickly. I press the call button on the wall and one of the guys who works there comes over to open a case for me. I make my selection without speaking. If I speak I will cry, and if I cry I will not stop crying. So it goes, so it goes.

It wasn't even gradual, the change in me. It came suddenly, clarity...maturity. *Grow up, Yara,* I told myself. And so I did. I put away the childish things and I grew up.

I follow him to the register and he asks me if there's anything else I need. I shake my head and pull the dollars from my wallet, green and crisp. They're foreign to me again, all the male faces. I've been gone a long time.

When I leave I carry my bag up streets so steep my thighs burn, past men and women who hold cardboard signs asking for help, past Westlake Center, and across the 405. I feel the mist as the clouds open and rain gently rests on my head. It's a soft caress, a reminder of where I am, and for that reason I don't call a car. I need to think, burn off all this emotion. He did big things, and I've done big things, but surely this is the biggest thing, changing.

I flew across the world to show David that I'm not over him. That I'd never be. I had to snuff out my pride and fears to do that. And what he did with this grand act makes no difference anymore. This was for me first, then for him, then for us. I deserve love. Maybe not from this man who I'd abandoned and hurt so deeply, but from someone. It's a matter of being ready to accept love.

I follow the directions to Capitol Hill. A white brick building with three pink letters above its door: IOU. People stand outside waiting to be called on, some of them huddled underneath umbrellas, some of them not. They look hungry. I walk right past them and step into the restaurant, shivering from the change in temperature. The smell of garlic and butter floats past me as a server walks by holding a plate over her head to avoid collision. The restaurant is much the same as the one in London—same structure, same booths, same dress code for the servers and bartenders. The only difference is the Seattle skyline painted on the main wall of the dining room. I head straight to the bar, shaking my can of spray paint as I walk. The roll of the ball syncs with my steps, an unlikely instrument that plays along with Nirvana's "Where Did You Sleep Last Night." There is the wall: *Come back to me. Come back. Come.* Kurt sings—*My girl, my girl, don't liiie to me...*

I pull off the cap and toss it on the ground. Shaking, shaking. The roll of the ball inside of the can. My heart beats steady and fast.

I tag the wall, underneath the neon sign. There's enough room for my message.

I'm back. Find me.

The talk in the bar slows, dims. Over the music I hear someone say—"Oh my God, what is she doing?"

I walk over to the bar when I'm done. The bartender is panicked, looking around for a manager. I set my can of spray paint on the counter.

"Are you hiring?" I ask. I grin at him as he stares openmouthed from me to the wall. "Guess that's a no, then?"

No one tries to stop me and I walk out singing, "In the pines, in the pines, where the sun don't ever shine. I would shiver the whole night through…"

It only takes me the length of one song to deliver my message.

57

PINK CAMO

DAVID

"DAVID...?"

I shake my head, squeeze my eyes closed, and then hold them open. I had been dreaming when the phone woke me. I rub my eyes and look at the clock: 10:00 p.m. I must have passed out watching *Californication*. I mute the TV.

"Yeah," I say.

"David, sorry to bother you, but there was an incident tonight at the restaurant..."

The voice...I know his voice. What was his name? Dan...Mark...Greg! That's right, Greg, the manager of the Seattle IOU. I reach for the nearest glass and take a sip, expecting it to be water. Vodka. I flinch, but keep drinking. Half the bottle is gone, no wonder I passed out.

"What's up," I say. The fuck with the bright lights in this place? I stumble over to the light switch and turn them off.

"A girl came in, she wasn't a customer, as far as I know. One of my servers said they saw her walk in from outside. She…uh…she vandalized a wall in the bar."

"What?" I set the glass of vodka on my chest. My head is aching. A hangover.

"I wasn't there," he said quickly. "She had a can of spray paint…"

God. "Okay…" I wish he'd just spit it out. I look around for my bottle of Tylenol. The room is trashed. I knock things off the narrow table and find it underneath a pile of clothes.

"She spray-painted the wall in the bar. Under the sign…"

"What does it say?" I rip off the lid with my teeth and pour the last three pills in my mouth. Greg hesitates. I can hear him moving things around and I wish he'd just spit it the fuck out so I can go back to sleep. I lie down on the bed, pulling a pillow over my face.

"I'm back. Find me…"

I sit up, the pillow rolling onto the floor.

"What?"

"I'm back. Find me," he repeats.

I'm already up, looking for my jeans in the pile of clothes on the floor.

"Don't touch it. I'm on my way."

When I arrive it's past midnight and most of the staff has left for the night.

"We need to stay open till two," I tell Greg as I walk in. "We're not fucking Cinderella."

I walk through the main dining room and toward the bar with him trailing behind me. The first thing I see is the can of spray paint, which is sitting on the bar top where I presume she left it. I pick it up to read the label: Pink Camo. Then I look at the wall.

She doesn't have a career in graffiti art—that's for sure. The words are slanted like she did it in a hurry. *I'm back* is larger than the *Find me*.

"She color coordinated," I say.

Greg rushes forward. "What? I wanted to call you first. Before the police."

"No need to call the police," I say, not taking my eyes from the wall.

"We have security cameras," he says. "We can…"

"Show me," I interrupt him.

He leads me through the kitchen and to a small office in the rear of the building. I sit in the only chair and swivel back and forth as he fidgets with the computer. She was here. *Here.* In this building.

"There," he says, finally.

I stare at the image on the computer screen; it's grainy, devoid of color. I watch with my eyes narrowed as a woman walks across the restaurant, shaking a can of spray paint as she goes. Her gait is sure…determined, but even so, I can see the sexy sashay of her hips. She doesn't hesitate before she tosses the cap onto the floor and vandalizes my bar. I laugh, and Greg looks at me like I've lost my mind.

"Sir—" he says.

"Don't call me that. Did anyone see where she went after she left?"

"No. We were…in shock. She had to be on drugs or something."

I laugh again.

"Okay," I say, standing up. "Okay."

"Okay what, Si—David?"

"Leave it," I say. "Just as it is."

"But…"

"Leave it," I say, firmly. "It's exactly how it should be."

When I leave the restaurant, my headache has disappeared and I feel wired. Yara doesn't wait to act, and for this reason, I know she must have just arrived in Seattle. How long? A day...two days? Where is she staying? Her e-mail, the one I used before, doesn't work anymore. I tried to send her an e-mail after the stunt she pulled in Paris, and then realized she must have deleted the account because of the reporters. I have something I have to do tomorrow night. Somewhere I have to be. Once that is done I can find her.

58

ALMOST

I REALIZE HE MAY be angry with me. The restaurant was there long before the stunt I pulled in Paris. There is a chance that what I did changed the way he felt. If someone did that to me I'd…

Come back to me. Come back. Come.

I try not to think about David being angry. That was beside the point, wasn't it? I came here to make a stand, to bring some kind of closure to my life so that I can move on to the next chapter. I can go back to the houseboat and wait there until I see him, but I'm afraid of the potential rejection.

I'm lying prostrate on Ann's living room floor when I get a text from Posey.

He has a benefit concert tomorrow in Portland.

I sit up abruptly.

How do you know? I text back.

The internet is a wonderful thing, Yara. You should learn how to use it.

"Ann…?" I call out. "I have to go to Portland."

Ann comes out of the bedroom where she's been watching one of her shows.

"For David?" she asks.

"Yes. What does my horoscope say?"

It's a joke between Ann and me. She makes up horoscopes for me. Ann's horoscopes mostly say things like: You're detached and emotionally stunted. Let love into your life when it comes knocking!

Ann frowns. "An opportunity will come to make big changes. Take the trip. You don't have a driver's license, so be resourceful."

"Shit," I say. "Do you have a driver's license?" I sit up suddenly. "Come on, Ann, I can't rent a car without a driver's license."

"Can you even drive?" she asks, propping her hands on her hips.

"Yes. Well…er—it's been a few years for sure. And I've never driven on the left side of a car. Should be a piece of cake, right?"

She shakes her head. "Take a cab."

"To Portland, Ann? Don't be daft. That'll cost a fortune."

"The train," she says. "Don't you do that sort of thing in London? I watched *The Girl on the Train.*"

"Right," I say, heading for the computer. "I'm a bloody idiot."

"Yes," Ann says, watching me from the doorway.

I'm looking at train schedules on Ann's computer, biting my nails down to the quick when my phone rings. I find it sort of alarming whenever my phone rings. So few people have my number, especially since I change it so often. I expect it to be either Posey or Celine since I'm already with Ann, but when I look at the screen it's a number I don't recognize. I answer it despite my better judgment.

"Yara Phillips?"

"Yes," I say.

The voice on the other end of the phone is hollow like she's calling from far away. I press the phone closer to my ear so I can hear her better and plug my other ear, even though it's not noisy in the apartment.

"Who is this?" I ask. Her accent is from home.

"I'm calling from Manchester Regional Hospital..." My head jerks back involuntarily. It is never good news when a hospital calls you—never, ever, ever.

"Your mother, Grace Phillips, was airlifted here this morning. She had a massive stroke..."

My mother...?

"How did you...?" I shake my head. Not the time for that. "Is she all right?"

"I'm afraid not," she says. "A friend found her; unfortunately, we don't know how long she was like that. She's in critical condition. We've stabilized her, but...you might want to come in to say your goodbyes."

"All right then," I say. I hang up and I'm chilled all over. I sit down.

"Why are you shivering?" Ann asks.

She closes the window and drapes a throw over my shoulders. I'm shaking from the shock, but I don't tell Ann that. The only one who knows about my relationship with my mother is David.

"Here," I say to Ann, handing her the throw. "Our plans have been thwarted. My horoscope was wrong this time." She watches me sadly as I go to retrieve my passport from my bag.

"But, you just got here," she says.

"I know, but I have to go. It's complicated."

"Isn't everything?" Ann sighs.

"Word."

Instead of booking a train ticket to Portland, I book a plane ticket home. Some things are not meant to be. Perhaps I need to take the hint that the universe is sending me. I came to find David for closure, and instead, my mother found me. So off I go.

I hug Ann goodbye and take the skyrail to the airport.

My mother has brown hair, blonde at the roots. Her hands are those of a gardener's, tan from the sun, with black dirt underneath her fingernails. As I sit next to her, holding her hand, I rub my thumb back and forth over her skin like David used to do to comfort me. I don't know if she can hear me, but I tell her where I've been and what I've done over the years. I tell her about the song of David. I tell her that I forgive her. I tell her what I've learned. She dies forty-nine hours after I arrive, at 7:49 in the evening. I do not cry when they take her body away, nor when the kind nurse puts her arm around my shoulders. I cry when I see David getting out of a cab as I am leaving the hospital to go back to my hotel. I don't have to question why he's here. I know he came for me. When he walks toward me, I can barely hold myself up I'm crying so hard.

He grabs me before I hit the ground and he holds me up.

Two mornings later we pick up her things from the hospital: the clothes and jewelry she was wearing when they found her, and her house keys, which a nurse tells me her neighbor dropped off.

I tell him that she died forty-nine hours after I got there and he raises his eyebrows. We're sitting across the table from each other in a little coffee shop. Neither of us has eaten much in days and we decide to split a sandwich.

"I still have it," I say, pulling the piece of paper from my purse. I slide it across the table and he picks it up.

He starts to laugh.

"What, David? What does it mean?"

"The lady at the bar," he says. "—She told me to write something random on the paper and leave."

"What?" I say, shocked. "Penny?"

He nods. "She said that if you give a random object to a person who is searching for something they would create their own meaning around it, and that meaning would reflect the deepest desire of their heart. It was a way for the person to find their way back to you. Even if it took a lifetime. There was no way I could have said anything to make you realize it was me you were looking for your whole life. You had to realize that on your own."

"Let me get this straight," I say, frowning. "Penny told you to leave me a random something—something that had absolutely no meaning—to torment me?"

He nods.

"Why the number forty-nine? You could have left me a toothpick or a...shoelace."

David shakes his head. His hair is under a beanie even though it's warm outside. He wears hats to disguise himself, though it's hard to miss him. Even as we sit in our little corner table people turn to look.

"It was the first thing that popped in my head," he admits.

"It did torment me," I say in wonder. "I would lay awake at night turning the possibilities over and over in my head. A scrap of paper with the number 49 written on it. She's a bloody genius, that Penny."

"It's always the eccentric ones who have the most wisdom," he tells me.

I roll a piece of napkin between my fingers. "I don't know how my mother had my phone number," I say. "I change it so often..."

"I gave it to her."

"How did you have it?"

He sips his coffee and studies me over the rim. "Posey."

I nod. "She never used it..."

"I think she would have eventually. She was working up the nerve. When I gave it to her I wrote it on a notepad she had on her fridge, so it was right there—your name and number." I nod. This was all so hard to talk about.

There's something I want to ask him that I've been putting off.

"Did Petra tell you that I went to your houseboat?"

"Yeah," he says. I wait for him to say more but he just stares at me. Fine, I'll play.

"Um, where is she now?"

He leans back in his chair and puts his hands behind his head as he stares up the ceiling. "She's still there. We ended things shortly after we got back from Paris. She's staying there until her new place is ready. I moved into the Four Seasons."

"Nice view," I say. "Did you end things because of what I did?"

He repositions himself so that his elbows are resting on the table and he's leaning toward me. "Are you talking about that one time you went on live television and announced to the world that I was yours? Yeah, that caused some problems between us. Especially when I watched it and she caught me smiling."

I put a hand over my face, shaking my head. "That's just awful. I was being vindictive, acting on impulse, per usual."

"Well, I enjoyed it," he admits. "I waited for years for a sign that you loved me, and there it was. Go big or go home, right, English?"

His laugh warms me. I squirm in my seat as tiny cliché butterflies fly around in my belly.

"Yara, I'm just a man, you know? I lost hope and Petra…"

"It's all right," I say quickly. "Let's worry about today, not yesterday or tomorrow. We'll leave tomorrow to worry about itself, yeah?"

"Yeah," he smiles.

We eat our sandwich in silence and then he says, "There's something I have to tell you that's unrelated to us."

I set down my mug of coffee and look at him warily.

"When I was looking for you I Googled your name. That's how I found your mother. I came to see her, but she knew less about you than I did."

I press my lips together. Posey had already told me, but it was still unsettling to hear it from him. He'd spoken to her before she died and I had not.

"But how did searching for me on the internet lead you to my mother?" I ask him.

"Have you ever Googled yourself, Yara?"

I shake my head.

He smiles. "I didn't think so."

My hands are fisted on the tabletop, knuckles white. He reaches out a finger and touches each of my knuckles with his fingertip until I stop squeezing and relax my hands.

"I found a website," he tells me, looking into my eyes. He hesitates for a moment. "The website was called Dear Yara."

I blink at him, confused.

"There were letters, written to you. Dozens of them. The posts dated back three years. They were written by your mother."

There are cliché things one can say about moments like these, things I would never think to say out loud, but in this moment I feel them all.

"She was trying to find you. As a last resort, she started a website and wrote letters to you on it."

He waits for me to say something, but I have nothing. I stare at my hands, my mind blank.

"Yara, your mother was trying to find you. I thought you would want to know."

"What was she like?" I ask.

"Soft-spoken...contrite. When she spoke about you, she cried..."

"What did she want from me?" I can't look at him. I look at my coffee instead.

"Forgiveness. To know you."

I shake my head. I'm trembling.

"English..." he says, softly...pleadingly. He reaches for me and touches my cheek with only his fingertips, running them to my lips then chin, his tanned fingers against my pale skin.

"I told her that I forgive her," I say. "Before she died."

"That's good. You don't forgive because they deserve it. Most of the time they don't. You forgive to keep your heart soft. To move forward without bitterness. Forgiveness is for you."

"What the fuck?" I say. "Why are my eyes burning?" I shake my head and David laughs at me.

"Tears are this thing," he says. "Saltwater eyes." Something on his face changes. I know that look.

"Oh my God," I say. "You're writing a song about it."

"Shit," he says. "Yeah..."

"Saltwater eyes," I mouth while I watch his face. For a moment I forget my mother and the pressure on my heart, and I try to be in his head, listening to the song he's writing.

His eyes are closed. I reach out and touch his hand.

"David," I plead. "Tell me some of the words..."

His eyes open suddenly and I regret my request. Soft eyes on fire. It's a combination I'd rather not stare directly into.

"She won't let go," he says softly. "She's been here before. Folded, worn, drowning in the saltwater. Someone grab her before she's gone. All she wants is forgiveness, all she wants is to forgive. She's gone. In the saltwater. It's in her eyes. She's died alone without you by her side. Somebody grab her. She's gone."

I let go of his hand.

"I have to go," I say.

I don't look at him. I don't want him to know that I'm on the verge of tears. He doesn't try to stop me. He knows what I need and in this moment it's aloneness. I walk back to the hotel, stopping at the off license for a bottle of wine. I wander around the lobby until I find a small business center near the vending machines. There are five computers set up in upholstered grey cubicles; two of them are occupied by men wearing seriously large headphones. I choose the cubicle furthest away from them and settle into the stiff-backed chair.

I type my name into the search bar just as David said, and wait. I have no nails left to bite, my fingers are swollen and tender. The site is third down on the list. I click on it and then press my fingers to my eyes. Do I really want to do this? No. But I am curious and I need it more than I want it. If someone wanted to apologize, it was only fair to hear them out. I screw the cap off my wine bottle and take a swig.

Dear Yara,

I live in a small house in Manchester. You'd hate the color, beige. But the front door is bright blue, a cobalt. It looks like a home,

a home that I never provided you with. There is more than Frosted Flakes in the pantry, and there are pictures on the walls. I'm not very good with art, but I've hung things that I think you'd like. There is a jacaranda tree out front, and I think of you every time I look at it. I keep my curtains open, even at night when people can see into my living room—just so I can always see it. That tree is you. It sounds so stupid, doesn't it? It doesn't matter. That tree is you, Yara. My lost daughter. Do you remember how you loved jacaranda trees? How you always wanted to run through the blossoms when they fell to the street. All of that purple.

I work for a Catholic primary school. I am the headmaster's secretary. I see all of those little faces every day and I think of your little face—all of that white blonde hair. You would look at me like I wasn't a terrible mother, like you were waiting for me to look back at you. I never did. It hurts me so terribly. What can I say, Yara, except that I was a selfish, depraved woman and I didn't know how to be a mother to you. I had another baby. You were about seven years old and I don't know if you understood what was happening. It was a boy. A couple from Ireland adopted him. I held him once before they took him, and I remember thinking how much he looked like you. Only he had black hair, Yara. So much of it. He found me about a year ago, showed up on my doorstep with a handful of daisies. His name is Ewen and he lives in London. I often wonder if the two of you pass each other on the street. That is if you still live in London. I hired someone to find you with no luck. I don't know where you are, but I can feel you. I was wrong, my love. I don't expect you to forgive me, but I pray you will. I pray one day you will come find me so I can look into your eyes and ask you to forgive me.

Your mother,

Grace

I close out the internet window and turn off the monitor. I can see my reflection in the dark screen. My lips and teeth are stained purple from the wine. My heart is stained with hurt. If you love me, why'd you leave me? It's the question that nags at me even though I know the answer. I suppose it's a sad song that a lot of women could relate to. I wasn't the first woman in history to have a lonely childhood, and certainly my childhood wasn't the worst. She didn't leave me physically, she left me emotionally. I did the opposite to David, fleeing across the sea to get away from what he made me feel. In the case of both my mother and me, it boiled down to our insecurities. That we couldn't be enough. And instead of staying to fight, we shriveled up, defeated.

I have to forgive her so that I can forgive myself. Sometimes people just get stuck and they need a David Lisey to break them out of their stuckness. My mother never had a David Lisey; so many women don't. And that is the saddest thing of all. I pick up my phone and dial his number.

"David," I say when he answers. "Will you come? I need you."

"I'll be right there," he says.

He drives me to my mother's house. I know which one it is before he pulls the car against the curb, just the way she described it. We sit outside in the car for a long time; me with my arms wrapped around my knees, staring at the little single story with the jacaranda tree outside. Her window boxes are filled to the brim with flowers. I inherited her love of plants but not her skill with them.

"Finished looking for today?" David asks.

I look at the clock. Twenty minutes have passed since we pulled up.

"Yes," I say.

He drives me back to my hotel.

"How did you know I just wanted to look?" I ask later when we're lying in bed. My head is on his chest and he's been holding me like this for the last hour without moving a muscle.

"I know."

"Yes but—"

"I know," he says, firmly. "And I'm sick of you not knowing that I know."

"Fine," I say. "I know that you know."

"You don't."

I lift my head to look at him. He's frowning. I suppose we have a lot to say to each other.

"Okay," I say, "let's talk about things."

"Now's not the time. We'll have this conversation when you're done grieving," he says.

I sit up. "We've been grieving each other for years. Now's the time."

"No. You think you can handle this right now, you always think you can handle everything. And then you know what happens? Tomorrow morning I wake up and you're gone. Off to serve caipirinhas on a beach in Brazil."

He stands up and walks toward the bathroom, closing the door behind him.

"Can we at least have sex?" I call after him.

He opens the door. "No." And then he shuts it again.

I fall back against the pillows smiling.

For the next week we do the same thing every day. We have breakfast in the hotel room and then David drives me to my mother's house where we sit outside for exactly twenty minutes before I ask to leave. We spend the rest of the day walking. Very few words are spoken, and I know he's giving me quiet for my thoughts. On the morning of the eighth day I decide that enough is bloody enough. I want to have a conversation.

"I have caused you so much hurt, for years," I say. "Please forgive me for leaving. I don't know how to be what you need and I'm afraid you won't let me try."

"I'm here, Yara. I don't need anything from you," David says. "You put those expectations on yourself. I've loved you for five years and out of those five years we've had maybe six months of uninterrupted happiness. The rest has been me loving you from a distance. I can and will keep doing that if you don't give me a choice. I am committed to loving you. I'm just a simple man who fell in love with a complex woman."

I laugh, I can't help myself. "You're not even a little bit simple," I say.

"When it comes to love I am."

I lean back in my chair, pressing the heels of my hands to my eye sockets.

"How?" I ask, straightening up. "Tell me how and maybe I can be that too."

"You can't," he says. "For years I wanted what my parents and siblings had. The spouse, the house, the stability, the kids, and the plastic tires rolling over asphalt. The pure love, you know? But love has made me unstable for five years. I've written my best music in this unstable state."

We both laugh even though it's not funny.

"We don't always get what we think we want. Actually, we very rarely do." He smiles.

That was true. That was so true.

"I got you. And you are the opposite of stability, yes?"

"Yes," I agree.

I don't know where he's going with this. I'm nervous.

"If I can't have you I don't want nobody, baby," he sings and I laugh. "I don't want a divorce," he says. "And there's no one else for me. I've had so many years to think about this, Yara. To deal with all of it."

He smiles absently and runs a hand over his face. He's tired. I've made him so tired. I want to be the peace in his life, not the conflict.

"I can't promise perfection, David, but I won't be like I was, and I won't do what I did. I won't run again."

"Even to your old age and grey hairs I am he, I am he who will sustain you. I have loved you and I will carry you; I will sustain you and I will rescue you," he says.

I sling my arms around his neck and he bends down till our noses are touching.

"I'm your style, English," he says, kissing the corner of my mouth and then my lips. His kiss lingers for too long and I hit him on the chest with my fist.

"Oh my God, David. Now's not the time to write a bloody song!"

He laughs against my mouth and then we're both laughing, holding onto each other so we don't fall.

Later that day, I open the car door, walk up the narrow sidewalk, and slip the key into the lock of my mother's house. That's where I stop, my hands frozen on the doorknob, panicking. I don't know how long I'm there, but suddenly David is behind me. He stands so close, my back is pressed against his chest. I lean into him, my eyes wide and unfocused. The blue of the door blurs in front of me. David reaches around my shoulder and puts his hand over mine where it rests on the doorknob. I turn it and step inside.

ACKNOWLEDGMENTS

Ellie who worked tirelessly to create the cover I imagined. And who broke her own rules to prove friendship.

Lori Sabin, best friend and best eyes. Thank you for always putting everything aside to clean up my manuscripts. Erica Russikoff for proof reading, your attention to detail is amazing. Jaime, Tasara and Kirsty. Ally Hyne, for your most excellent spreadsheet abilities. Jovana Shirley, Christine Estevez, Stephanie Alcala, the PLNs and the many bloggers who take beautiful photos and give heartfelt reviews, thank you so very much. Colleen Hoover, the best example of class, kindness and support in this industry.

Amy Holloway who I cannot live without. Your rare enthusiasm helped me finish this book. Also your wine.

Serena, my God. Where do I even start? Of all the great blessings that I have been given since the beginning of this journey, you are by far the greatest. I wanted to give you something special. So here is the book of my heart.

Kayla, thank you for your Cheeeto's and your wit, and your beauty. You were the perfect muse.

Joshua Ryan Norman, you're fucking dreamy you know that? Thank you for showing me what love looks like and for restoring my heart. I can't believe we got married. The fuck?

Abba. Most High. The Beginning and the End. Jehovah. The Lion and the Lamb. Elohim. Adonai. Yahweh. Yeshua. Yahweh Rapha. Yahweh Shammah. El Elyon. El Roi. Ancient of Days. Jehovah Jireh. I Am, that I Am, that I Am. Father, my Father.

I am

I am

I am

yours

www.tarrynfisher.com

www.facebook.com/authortarrynfisher

http://twitter.com/DarkMarkTarryn

http://instagram.com/tarrynfisher

45988881R00188

Made in the USA
Middletown, DE
19 July 2017